Happy spring, my friends!

In this installment of the Marble Cove series, Diane's first book comes out, and she is overwhelmed by nerves. Writing this has reminded me vividly of the day I sold my first book. I called everyone I knew; a shower of congratulatory cards, flowers, balloons, and cookies ensued. When the book was published, our local Friends of the Library held a signing much like Diane's signing in this story. I tried to recapture those memories as Diane enjoys her moment.

The piano scenes were easy to write, because I have known the sense of panic Beverly feels. And not even for myself. My daughter was the accompanist for her high school choir, and I used to get so nervous before her performances I felt nauseated. It bothered me far more than it ever did her!

In this story, April has arrived in Marble Cove. As spring arrives, so does "baby season" for those of us who work with animals. At both the wildlife center where I volunteer and in the kitten program I coordinate, we soon will be receiving dozens of orphaned babies in need of care. If you have a moment, spare a prayer for these little ones. Like Beverly, nerves sometimes pop up when I am performing some critical task, and a prayer for steady hands would be appreciated as well.

God's blessings on you and yours,
Anne Marie Rodgers

NEW HORIZONS

MIRACLES *of*
MARBLE COVE

NEW HORIZONS

ANNE MARIE RODGERS

Guideposts

New York

Miracles of Marble Cove is a trademark of Guideposts.

Published by Guideposts
110 William Street
New York, New York 10038
Guideposts.org

Acknowledgments

Every attempt has been made to credit the sources of copyrighted material used in this book. If any such acknowledgment has been inadvertently omitted or miscredited, receipt of such information would be appreciated.

"From the Guideposts Archive" originally appeared as "His Mysterious Ways" by Leonard E. LeSourd in *Guideposts* magazine. Copyright © 1982 by Guideposts. All rights reserved.

Cover and interior design by Müllerhaus
Cover photo by Jeremy Charles, www.jeremycharles.com (street scene) and Shutterstock.com (women and sky)
Typeset by Aptara

Printed and bound in the United States of America
10 9 8 7 6 5 4 3

───────────── DEDICATION ─────────────

In memory of Max (2001-2011) and
Blaise (1999-2011)

We wish you sunny spots and warm days, an
abundance of tasty bones, soft beds to snooze on,
and little angel children to snuggle you.
Take good care of our hearts until we meet again,
beloved friends.

During the writing of this story, my family bore the sorrow of losing two canine family members within two weeks. Our sweet old collie had been slowly failing for several months. But our mastiff, also a senior, had seemed quite hale and hearty for his age, and we were blindsided by his sudden decline. Special thanks to our friends at Centre Animal Hospital for their support, particularly Dr. Renee Calvert, Yvonne Kottwitz, and Dr. Jennifer Nunnery.

———————ACKNOWLEDGMENTS———————

Special thanks to Christopher Trider, Training Director of the Augusta Electrical JACT, International Brotherhood of Electrical Workers Local 1253, Fairfield, Maine, for his detailed answers to my questions about electricians' training apprenticeships and the differences that distinguish the various types of electrical work. Without Chris, Dan Bauer would have quite a difficult time figuring out all the ins and outs of becoming a journeyperson, and I would be even more clueless than I already was!

Special thanks and much love to my son-in-law Captain Robert A. Walters, US Army Air Ambulance Division, who keeps me straight on all things army.

CHAPTER ONE

Margaret Hoskins paused to admire Diane Spencer's flowers as she hurried up the pretty brick walkway to her neighbor's home on the last Saturday of March. Diane had been as busy as a squirrel hiding nuts last autumn, planting drifts of spring bulbs around her house and yard to hasten the departure of the first winter she would be spending as a resident of Marble Cove, Maine.

The green tips of daffodils were out of the ground, with a few early varieties daring to show their sunny faces despite the remnants of the last snowstorm still clinging to the area. Striking blue Glory of the Snow blossoms blanketed a bed at one side of the house. Diane must have planted several hundred of the tiny bulbs to produce such a show. Here and there around her borders, clumps of snow crocus in lavender, purple, yellow, and white had pushed their way through the snow to promise the arrival of warmer weather.

She was going to order some of the more unusual spring bulbs next fall, Margaret promised herself. Like Diane, she loved to putter around in her flower beds, but daffodils and tulips had been the bulk of her spring plantings to date. As she studied the contrast of the bright colors against the gray shingles of Diane's house, her painter's eye automatically sought the best angle for a sketch...there. In front of that holly bush. The glossy dark leaves and red berries stood out against the house, with the daffodils and crocuses ranged in front of them. For anyone truly in love with the season, it would be a feast for the eyes if she could capture it on canvas.

The door of Diane's house opened as Margaret stood lost in thought on the walkway.

"Come on in, Margaret," Shelley Bauer encouraged. "What are you doing?"

"Thinking about painting," Margaret answered her young neighbor. She dragged her mind away from her mental images and entered the house, letting Shelley close the door behind her. "Am I the last one to arrive?"

"You are." Shelley moved back into the living room and resumed her seat on the couch. She wore a rose-colored sweater layered over a turtleneck with navy corduroys, indicating that Margaret's dream of spring was still just that—a dream.

"Yay, you're here. Now we can get started." Diane Spencer rubbed her hands together gleefully, her blue eyes sparkling. Like Shelley, Diane wore corduroys, although hers were a nut-brown and were paired with a butter-yellow sweatshirt, across which was printed, "It takes PROSe to write novels." After years of working as a journalist, the tall, slim woman had written a novel that was about to be published any day.

Diane had been the driving force behind the formation of the four women's circle of friendship nearly a year ago. "I can't wait to see the results of your search for old maps of Marble Cove. We've got to figure out where that treasure is."

"If there's any treasure at all," Margaret cautioned. She tapped a large envelope she carried. "I did find another old map, but it really doesn't match with the one from Jeremiah Thorpe's letter. On this map, Marble Cove is in the spot where it is today."

Beverly held up the folder she carried. "Here you go. I took the digital photo we snapped of Jeremiah's map and used a program that enhanced the images. I think it came out pretty well."

Diane snatched the thin file and plopped down on the couch beside Beverly, who had just taken a seat. Since Beverly had begun working from home, she'd had more flexible hours, which had allowed her to spend more time with the others than she had when she lived in Augusta and only came to the coast on the weekends to visit her father. It was nice to have her around more. It would be even nicer after she left her job at the State House and launched her consulting business full time, a transition she was planning to make just before Easter.

As usual, Beverly looked like she'd stepped off the cover of a magazine, clad in a pair of herringbone-patterned wool pants and a button-down shirt visible beneath a soft blue angora cardigan sweater. A silk scarf was looped around her neck in a casually elegant style, and she wore one of the popular charm bead bracelets in blues that matched the sweater.

Surveying the map Diane had extracted from the folder, Shelley frowned. "This still doesn't look familiar at all. Are we sure it's even Marble Cove? Or Maine, for that matter?"

Margaret leaned across the coffee table and laid a second map beside the one in question. "This is a topographical map of the Marble Cove area from maybe fifty years to a century later. Look at the coastline." She pointed, tracing the spot where land met water with her index finger. "They match almost exactly. It's got to be Marble Cove."

Beverly and Diane stared at the map, while Shelley craned her neck to see over Diane's shoulder, pointing at the edge of the coastline. "But Marble Cove is over here. This town is . . ." She stopped and thought for a moment. "This town is in the salt marsh out past the lighthouse."

"There must be some mistake," Beverly said.

Diane nodded. "That land is way too low and wet for buildings."

"Maybe it isn't really Marble Cove," Shelley said. "Maybe this is just an amazing coincidence that the coastlines look the same. I mean, wouldn't it look really different a century later, with erosion and all that?"

"Not necessarily," Diane said. "The beaches might have changed shape, but the bedrock bluffs along a lot of that area wouldn't have eroded much." She stared down at the map. "No, I think it really is our coast. Although I don't know what to say about the placement of the town."

Margaret had been standing back, watching her friends puzzle over the original map. "You're right," she said to Diane. Stepping forward, she tapped a finger on the lower corner of the paper. She had found a barely visible handwritten note in the bottom corner. Although some of the ink was extremely faded, the words could still be made out.

"Marble Cove, 15 October," Beverly read.

"And look, there's a number behind it." Shelley leaned forward to squint at the map at the same moment Diane did, and the two bumped heads.

"Ow!" Diane straightened, laughing as she held a hand to her head.

"Sorry!" Shelley rubbed the spot on her own head where they'd collided as she continued to peruse the map. "I can't make out the rest. It's too faded. But it must be the first numeral of the year, don't you think?"

Beverly nodded. "Probably. But even if it's Marble Cove, it's still in the wrong place. And look, the streets are laid out differently, and they don't seem to have the same names. It's hard to tell, but this looks like Pine Street, maybe Maple Street—"

"Someone was stuck on native trees," Margaret said with a smile. "But there's also First and Second Avenues."

"Well, it can't be our Marble Cove," Shelley said, "since the street names don't match."

"Perhaps it isn't exactly ours, but it's located just to the south of the current town, so I suspect there's some reason for it." Diane gave a happy sigh. "Another mystery. I love mysteries."

"And she-e-e-e's *off*!" Margaret clapped her hands sharply, sounding like the commentator at a horse race.

Beverly laughed. "I knew that when I showed this to you three, Diane wouldn't be able to leave it alone until we figured out why there are discrepancies."

Shelley giggled, and Diane made a face at Beverly. "Inquiring minds . . ."

"Want to know!" Shelley, Beverly, and Margaret chorused.

In the flurry of laughter that followed the moment, Diane offered her friends some tea and cookies. As Diane went to the kitchen and returned with a tray of treats, Shelley asked Margaret what Allan and Adelaide had been up to.

"Oh, the usual," Margaret replied. "Allan is busy with his woodworking and Adelaide's going to be taking another life skills class down at the community center."

"That's wonderful," Beverly said.

"What, exactly, will she be learning?" Shelley asked.

"Financial tasks mainly. We've realized since you began paying her for babysitting that she can take on more financial responsibility. So this is actually an advanced class where they'll be teaching more complex things about money that we've never taught her, like how to set up and handle savings and checking accounts, how to cash checks, how to budget."

Diane was eyeing her friend speculatively. "Skills she'll need when you're not able to care for her someday." It wasn't a question.

"Yes," Margaret admitted. "Allan and I aren't spring chickens, and Adelaide is probably going to outlive us." She tried to keep her voice level and pragmatic. "We want to prepare her for that eventuality without scaring her."

There was a moment of silence.

Then Shelley said, "I think you're wise to be thinking of the future."

Diane's usually merry countenance was still and somber. "I agree. Who knows what the future holds?"

Beverly merely nodded.

A pang of compassion shot through Margaret. Diane and Beverly both knew what it was like to have one's future change in an instant. Each of them had lost her husband unexpectedly far too young. Quietly, she said, "Yes, we realize that there are a lot of things Adelaide isn't prepared to do on her own. I hope this class will be a start."

There was a long moment of silence.

Then Diane broke the mood. "My, aren't we somber all of a sudden? Let's look at these maps again. There's got to be a reason why the town appears in two different locations."

CHAPTER TWO

"Who art with them, forever One, eternally confessed." ... Beverly smiled as the music from the last hymn of the service faded and Reverend Silas Locke ended the service with a benediction. As the organist began a stirring postlude, Beverly and her father rose to make their way out of the sanctuary. Jewel-toned light washed over them where the spring sunshine shone through the elaborate depictions of biblical scenes in the stained glass of the many large windows.

"Beverly!" A woman in one of the choir's signature white robes with crimson stoles approached, stylish spectator pumps peeking from beneath the robe. "May I speak to you for a moment?"

"Certainly." Beverly recognized Maddie Bancroft, Old First's energetic choir director, although she hadn't realized Maddie knew *her.*

The tall, slender woman extended a hand. "We haven't been formally introduced. I'm Maddie Bancroft. I believe we have a mutual friend in Shelley Bauer."

"Yes." Beverly accepted the firm handshake, inclining her head. "Shelley's my neighbor as well as a close friend. And this is my father, Harold Wheeland."

Maddie's hair was expertly cut in a contemporary style, her makeup emphasized her wide blue eyes in an understated, natural way, and the powder-blue skirt suit beneath the robe Maddie had unzipped looked to be an expensive slubbed silk weave. Add that to the oversize personality and the efficient energy she radiated, and it was no wonder Shelley sometimes felt intimidated by this woman.

"It's nice to meet both of you." Maddie smiled, flashing perfect white teeth and dimples in each cheek. "I see the congregation every Sunday from the choir loft, but I don't often have the opportunity to talk with everyone."

Beverly smiled politely. "I imagine preparing the worship music takes up a lot of your time."

Maddie nodded. "Very true. And that's what I had hoped to talk to you about."

"Me?" Beverly couldn't hide her surprise.

"Yes." Maddie smiled. "Our friend Shelley tells me that you play the piano."

"I do." Beverly nodded cautiously. *Where is this going?*

"She says you're quite good. Do you accompany?"

"Only briefly, in high school."

"Oh, good! If you played that long, I bet you're quite good. I have a favor to ask." Before Beverly could protest, Maddie rushed on. "I need an accompanist. Our regular piano accompanist, Linda Hayford, slipped and fell on the ice last week, and she injured her wrist. She expects to be able to play again during Holy Week, so I only need to find someone to help out for the first few weeks of April, beginning this Wednesday."

"I'm so sorry to hear about her misfortune, and I'm glad she wasn't badly hurt." Maddie hadn't actually asked a question, so Beverly pretended she didn't understand what the choir director was angling at. "If I think of anyone who might be able to pitch in, I'll certainly send them your way."

Maddie looked nonplussed for a moment, but after blinking a time or two, she regrouped. "Oh, you misunderstood. I'd like *you* to be our accompanist, Beverly."

"I couldn't possibly." *There. A firm refusal should take care of it.* "My skills are very rusty and really only fit for my ears."

"But—"

"I appreciate the offer," Beverly said. "But I haven't accompanied in years, and even then I wasn't that good. I'm simply not the right person for this job."

"Oh, I think you are. Most of it isn't difficult music," Maddie assured her. "And it's only for a few weeks, in front of a couple dozen choir members. I'm confident you could handle it, Beverly. Shelley speaks so highly of your pl—"

"No, really, Maddie, I couldn't," Beverly said, breaking into Maddie's animated speech. "I haven't played seriously for years. In fact, I only sat down and noodled around a few times a year until Christmas, when I began playing more frequently again."

"Those skills come back fast," Maddie said. "Good ol' muscle memory is an awesome thing. I'm sure you could do this, Beverly."

"No," Beverly said positively. "I couldn't. I'm sorry, Maddie, but I'm not nearly good enough to try to accompany a choir."

There was a tense moment of silence as Maddie raised her eyebrows, and Beverly braced herself to refuse yet again. But then Maddie smiled. "All right," she said. "Let's leave it like this: you think about it and I'll ask again in a few days. Honestly, Beverly, it won't be that difficult. And you'd be among friends."

And before Beverly could tell her that a few days wasn't going to change her mind, Maddie had given her a wave and whirled away—no doubt to corral some other unsuspecting soul into a job.

*   *   *

"Hey, Mama, your shoe is untied."

Shelley Bauer smiled, rolling her eyes at her husband Dan as their four-year-old played what had to be his fiftieth April Fools' joke of the day. Ever since Aiden had been tricked first thing that morning by a little friend at Sunday school, he'd been testing his own credibility quotient. Some of his jokes made more sense than others; fortunately, this was one to which Shelley could respond. Obediently, she looked down at her shoe.

"April Fools!"

"Oh, Aiden." She swooped down on her son, dragging him to her and blowing noisy kisses against his neck until he screamed and wriggled away. "You got me, didn't you?"

"I did. I got you, Mama. An' I got Meemaw, and I got Pappy, an' I got—"

"And you've got to get your pajamas on, buddy," Dan interrupted.

"But I'm not done playing with my Legos." Aiden's tone was completely reasonable.

Dan shrugged apologetically. "Sorry, buddy. If I could stop time, I would. But you know what happens at eight o'clock, right?"

Aiden gave a mighty sigh. "Bath time, an' a story an' then bed."

Shelley chuckled. "Right. Would you like to play with your soap crayons in the bath?"

Aiden brightened. "Yeah!" The soap crayons weren't an every-evening event.

"All right." Shelley pointed toward the stairs. "Go get undressed, and I'll be up to start the bathwater." As Aiden clattered up the stairs, she crossed the living room to where Dan sat in his easy chair with their daughter Emma. She blinked like a little owl, and Shelley leaned down and kissed the toddler. "Night-night, sweetheart. Daddy will read your story and put you to bed."

Dan rose from his chair, shifting the toddler to one shoulder, where she curled up and turned her face into his neck. "After the kids are in bed, I'd like to talk to you, honey. I've been researching what it would take to become an electrician, and I want to tell you about it."

Shelley's eyes lit up. "All right."

"I really think I would enjoy the work. And electricians make good money."

"It would be nice to have steady work that made you happy and paid the bills," she told him.

She knew Dan fretted about not being able to provide for his family as he thought he should. He had been seeking a new career path for over a year, and then he had been laid off at the docks in February, forcing them to cut expenses everywhere they could. Shelley's baking business had become a reality in part because of their need for income; without that incentive, she might never have gathered the courage to pursue it.

Anxious to hear what Dan had to say, she hurried Aiden through his bath and bedtime rituals with as much haste as possible—which was to say, not much.

Finally, Aiden was in bed, and they had finished reading the very last page of *Sylvester and the Magic Pebble*. She passed Dan in the hallway as he entered Aiden's room for a good-night kiss. "Would you like a piece of cheesecake?" she asked him quietly. Heaven forbid Aiden hear her question. He'd be out of bed and downstairs in a flash.

"I'd love one!" Dan paused to hug her. He'd been eyeing the marbled white chocolate raspberry cheesecake ever since he'd caught her making it that morning. He probably would have eaten some earlier, except that she'd forbidden him because the cheesecake needed to set for at least eight hours before being garnished with raspberry sauce and curls of white chocolate.

Dan entered the kitchen just as she slid the first creamy slice of cheesecake onto a plate.

"That looks fabulous," he said with an exaggerated moan of delight.

"I hope it tastes as good as it looks. The recipe was highly recommended by a number of people online. Of course, I added a couple of personal touches."

Dan picked up his plate and a fork and made for his seat at the table. Before Shelley could even seat herself, he had taken his first bite. Closing his eyes, he said, "You, my dear wife, have outdone yourself with this. Is it for some special occasion?"

She nodded. "I'm providing the cheesecake for a wedding. The cake is going to have a raspberry filling and red raspberry decor, and they wanted another type of sweet to go along with it."

"They're going to love this," her husband predicted.

"I hope so. The couple is stopping by tomorrow over their lunch break for a taste test."

Dan smiled, taking another bite and closing his eyes as he savored the flavor. "They aren't going to know what hit them."

"Thanks." It was always helpful to have another person's opinion when she tried something new, though she knew

Dan was perhaps a little biased. She regarded him across the table. "So you've been considering electrical work. What have you learned?"

"This is really exciting," Dan told her. "There is an apprenticeship program offered by the electricians' union. I would actually earn a salary while I'm learning, and it would go up as my skill level increases."

She tilted her head as she considered his words. "It would be indoor work too. I know how rough it can be in the winter months to have to work outside."

He nodded. "It would sure beat working on the docks on a frigid winter morning. I'm definitely ready for a trade that keeps me indoors. And this is something I find interesting and challenging. It's a growing market too."

"It is?"

"That's what the training director said when we talked on the phone. The starting salary isn't great, of course, because I'd basically be doing an apprenticeship, but even from day one, I'll get paid half salary. That's a big attraction for me. I haven't felt as if I could start at a trade school. I mean, what would we live on?"

Shelley nodded glumly. Their budget already was so tight it squeaked, and Shelley's baking earnings could not yet cover all their expenses.

"I think this may be our answer." Dan put his hand over hers and squeezed. "Starting salary at half pay is in the twelve- to fourteen-dollar-an-hour range. And I would get benefits right from the very beginning."

"It sounds too good to be true." Shelley didn't mean to be skeptical, but really...why would someone with absolutely no skills be able to get benefits by going to school? "What would you have to do? Sign your life away?"

Dan laughed. "No. It's a three- to five-year program, depending on what I choose to do, and I'll be a journeyman apprentice working under a master electrician. I'll have school too, part of the time."

"And they pay you for this?"

"They do. And as I learn more, I get paid more." He grinned. "I know how you feel. I couldn't believe it when I first learned about it either."

"So what will you be qualified to do?" She took a bite of her own cheesecake, absently noting that it tasted absolutely marvelous. This was definitely a keeper recipe.

"I'll have a couple of choices. I'm not sure yet which one to specialize in."

"What are you considering?"

"I think I'd like to be an inside wireman. As an inside electrical worker, I can get both commercial and residential experience. So with a little luck, I wouldn't have long periods of unemployment."

Shelley shuddered. "Good." Her baking business was growing by leaps and bounds, but after the roller coaster the economy had been on for the past several years, she was afraid to count on its success. They were just scraping by now and she didn't think her business could support them for much longer.

"I'm excited about this, Shell. I think I will enjoy this type of work and it would be great to have a steady income." Dan paused and looked down at the cheesecake on his plate. "Wow, this is really, *really* good! You've outdone yourself with this recipe."

"Thank you." He liked almost everything she baked, but she could tell he was extremely impressed by this one. "Since Tami left, it feels more important than ever for me to give customers a top-quality product. This is delicious, and the raspberry sauce and white chocolate curls give it a striking presentation."

The young woman who had talked Shelley into letting her be Shelley's assistant earlier in the spring had recently returned to culinary school in New York City. Her flair for presentation and willingness to try new and exciting things had impressed upon Shelley the importance of both in her business planning.

Dan chuckled. "It did look nice, now that you mention it. I guess I was so focused on the fantastic taste that how it looked was the last thing on my mind!"

CHAPTER THREE

H i, Margaret." Diane came through the door of the Shearwater Gallery shortly before closing time Monday afternoon.

"Hello." Margaret paused, holding the paintbrush she'd been using to scumble an area of her current painting that would depict the sea. Scumbling was a technique in which she overlaid the first layer of paint with a semitransparent glaze that would soften the harsh edges of the colors, giving them a more natural look as one shade blended into the next. "What are you up to?"

"Inviting you to come over tomorrow evening and celebrate with me."

"Celebrate what? Your book?"

"Yes. My advance copies came today!"

"Oh, Diane! I can't believe you didn't bring one along to show me."

"You have to wait until tomorrow night. I invited Beverly and Shelley too, so everyone can ooh and aah at the same time." She chuckled, but then she shivered and wrapped her arms around herself. "Oh, this is nerve-wracking!"

"You mean the fact that your book is finally coming out?"

"Yes." Diane heaved a sigh. "I'm making myself crazy. Can you talk me down off my ledge?"

Margaret chuckled, resuming her work. "And which ledge might that be?"

"The 'first book' ledge. Tomorrow I have a photographer coming to take some head shots and candids of me for my Web site. Every time I think I've figured out what to wear, I find something wrong with it."

"Oh, you'll probably figure it out at the last minute. That's what I usually do when I have a fashion dilemma." Margaret glanced at the clock on one wall of the gallery. "I'm quitting for the day. Will you wait and walk home with me?"

"Great." Diane paced around the gallery while Margaret closed her acrylics and gathered the brushes she'd used that day. She carried them to the deep sink in the storage room behind the desk and began to wash them, listening to Diane's restless footsteps.

"Why are you so nervous about some photographs?" Margaret called.

Diane came to the doorway. "It's not just the photos, although I do want them to look nice, and I don't photograph particularly well, so this guy has his work cut out for him. It's the launch. What if no one comes to my signing? What if people don't like the book?"

"You've gotten a couple of good reviews already," Margaret pointed out.

"Yes." Diane paused and smiled. "I have. But the bookstore has gone to a great deal of trouble to make this local author event memorable. What if I'm a dud when I do the reading from my book?"

Margaret had to laugh. "You couldn't be a dud if you tried," she informed her vivacious friend. "Your reading is going to be great. Have you chosen a selection?"

Diane nodded.

"And afterward, you're going to shake lots of congratulatory hands, autograph lots of books, and have some of Shelley's excellent red velvet cupcakes that I happen to know the bookstore has ordered."

Diane's eyebrows rose. "You want to be my publicist? Sounds like you've got everything organized already."

"I've just been listening," Margaret demurred. "It's going to go wonderfully, Diane, and you're going to be a big hit."

She finished cleaning the brushes, shaped them, and set them to dry. Then she took care of the details of closing the shop, locking the register, and dead-bolting the back door. It might be April, but it was still awfully chilly, and she was glad she'd worn her down-filled parka and boots. Winding a scarf around her neck, she ushered Diane out onto the street and flicked off the lights before locking up for the evening and joining her friend.

"Thanks for the pep talk," Diane said, linking her arm through Margaret's. "It's ridiculous to be so nervous, I know."

"Maybe, but you're always going to feel that way when a new one of your babies leaves the nest. I still get butterflies whenever I show a new group of paintings."

"Oh, great," Diane moaned. "You mean I'm going to feel like this over and over again?"

"Well, maybe not quite like this," Margaret amended. "You only have your first reading, signing, or showing once."

They quickly came abreast of the Crow's Nest, the adorable little bookstore that was sponsoring Diane's reading. Until recently, it had been scheduled to be held there, but Beth Levesque, the bookstore manager, had feared the small shop wouldn't hold the crowd they expected, so they had decided to hold the reading at the library instead.

"Look," Margaret said, pointing to the display the bookstore had created to publicize the event.

The cover of Diane's book had been enlarged and accompanied a large photo of her above a neatly printed sign announcing, "Local author!" and the date and information about the reading.

Diane pressed a hand to her stomach. "*Oooh*, I have butterflies. I can hardly believe this has finally happened."

Margaret smiled. "You've been published for years. But I guess writing an entire book feels different from writing nonfiction articles."

"Very different," Diane agreed.

Margaret opened her mouth to say something else, but as a book cover in an adjacent display caught her eye, the words caught in her throat. "Oh my goodness," she breathed. "Would you look at that!" She stepped closer to the window, peering through the glass at the book jacket.

The cover illustration was one of her paintings.

Margaret blinked and looked again. Surely she was mistaken. She was certain she hadn't given anyone permission to use her work in such a manner. She painted works of art, not cover illustrations.

"What's wrong?" Diane asked. They both had paused and were looking at the window display.

Margaret shrugged, instinctively minimizing her disquiet. It felt extremely personal and not a little silly to be worrying about a book cover. After all, she had a contract. "Nothing," she answered her friend. "I just remembered something I forgot to do before I left."

"Do you want to go back?"

"No, no, I'll just get to it tomorrow." Dear Diane. She meant it too. Her neighbor would go back to the gallery with Margaret if she asked.

Margaret sneaked another look at the book jacket. She wished she could get closer, but the bookstore was closed for the evening. It was still pre–tourist season, and most of the local businesses weren't keeping extended hours yet. It really looked like her painting; she could recall the way she had agonized about the exact shades to use for the sky. Tomorrow she would have to take a closer look.

Unaware of her friend's anxiety, Diane chattered about the reading at the library, the minitour the publisher had planned for the following month, her children, her plans for her summer garden, and more. It was a distinct relief when the two women reached their neighboring homes. Margaret's front walk came first, and she made an effort to smile as she turned to say good-bye.

"See you tomorrow, I'm sure. Thanks for walking home with me."

"You're welcome." Diane flashed her familiar smile before striding down the sidewalk to her own home. "See you tomorrow."

Margaret entered her home with a disproportionate sense of relief. "Allan?" She called his name the moment she stepped through the door.

"In the kitchen," he called.

"Hi, Mom. Welcome home!" Adelaide came to the top of the stairs; in her arms she held a striped tabby cat. "Lizzy says welcome home too."

Margaret laughed. "Thanks, Lizzy." As her daughter turned back toward her bedroom, Margaret made for the kitchen.

Allan was at the stove busily stirring something in a skillet. Margaret could smell the delicious aroma of an herb bread he'd made before in the air. "What's for dinner?" she asked.

Allan turned and smiled at her. "Sweet potato fries and baked salmon with green bean casserole."

Margaret tried to smile. "Sounds fine to me!" But her face clouded as she recalled the rude shock she'd received a short while ago. "Honey, something odd happened today."

"Oh?" Allan cocked his head, eyebrows rising. He smoothed a hand back over his scalp, taming his hair in a habitual gesture even though his smooth scalp belied the necessity.

"Diane and I were looking in the bookstore window on the way home..." She went on to tell him of the painting and its suspicious likeness on the book cover. "I need to look at it more closely, but I'm positive it's my work."

Allan frowned. "Did you give permission for your work to be used on book covers?"

Margaret shook her head emphatically. "At least, not to my knowledge. I certainly don't remember doing so."

"Maybe it isn't yours," Allan offered. "Not that I think you wouldn't recognize your own work, but after all, there are a lot of seascapes. Perhaps this one just resembles yours a great deal."

Margaret cast him a narrow-eyed glance.

"On the other hand," he said with a diplomatic smile, "it's hard to imagine that you *wouldn't* be able to discern your own work."

"It's my work," she said flatly. "I'm certain of it. I didn't get close enough to verify it, and I'll have to go in when the store is open, but I know my own painting when I see it. And I remember that one a bit better than some others because the day I painted it was the day I drove up to Belfast to Moose Point and saw a moose, remember?"

Allan nodded. "Scared you half to death, as I recall."

"It would have scared you too," Margaret retorted. "It was practically looking over my shoulder! I was so focused on my work I tuned out everything—you know how I get."

Allan grinned. "I do indeed." He nodded. "And I am 100 percent certain that you would recognize your work from that day."

"Thanks." She sighed. "I guess I'll go in tomorrow and take a closer look, just to be sure."

"Buy a copy of the book," Alan suggested. "We can check the copyright information on the cover art and take some photos."

"Good idea."

"I know." As she snorted, he grinned at her and turned back to the oven. "Would you like to call Adelaide? This fish will be done soon."

★ ★ ★

Beverly's mobile phone rang just as she pulled into her driveway after work on Monday. It had been a long day, since she'd driven to Augusta and back, and she was tired. "Hello?"

"Hello, Beverly, it's Maddie Bancroft. I know you said you didn't think you were interested in accompanying the choir, but I'm hoping you've reconsidered."

Beverly made a face at the mobile unit. "Not really. I don't—"

"Please, Beverly? It's only three little rehearsals. I am just desperate. No one plays the piano anymore, and Shelley said she thought you could do it."

Remind me to thank Shelley the next time I see her. Beverly shook her head and then realized Maddie couldn't see her. "I don't think so, Maddie. I really meant it when I said I haven't played very much at all in years."

"But you said you'd started playing regularly this year. If you're playing anyway, couldn't you practice with the choir music?"

Honestly, the woman was a steamroller. Beverly hesitated.

"Please?" Maddie asked again. "You'd be a lifesaver. *My* lifesaver."

"All right." It was clear Maddie was prepared to beg and plead until Beverly changed her mind.

"Oh, that's wonderful! Thank you, Beverly." Maddie sounded truly relieved, as if she'd genuinely feared she wouldn't find anyone to help. "You'll never know how deeply I appreciate this. Really, if there's ever anything I can do, don't hesitate to call."

Beverly couldn't imagine that she'd ever be desperate enough to pick up the phone and call Maddie Bancroft, but she forced herself to laugh a little. "I'll keep that in mind." Then she said, "I'll need to get the music from you."

"Yes. The first rehearsal I'll need you for is this Wednesday, so I'll give you a call tomorrow and arrange to get it to you."

They concluded the conversation after Beverly listened to Maddie gush again about how grateful she was.

The moment she cut the connection, Beverly let out a moan and laid her forehead against the steering wheel, momentarily contemplating hitting herself in the head a couple of times. "What have I done?"

Slowly she climbed from the car, hitching her purse strap over her shoulder and grabbing her laptop with her right hand, then slamming shut the car door with the left.

What had she been thinking, to say *yes* to Maddie? She wasn't up to this. Even if she had played every single day between Christmas and today, that didn't make up for years without playing. Her stomach felt queasy just thinking of it.

She'd had the same feeling in high school when she'd played in annual recitals and a talent competition for a scholarship pageant. Her stomach had twisted and rolled, her hands grew clammy, and her fingers shook. And that was when she was only responsible for herself. If she made a mistake while accompanying, it would affect the entire choir. She swallowed, nausea rising. *How on earth are you going to get through this?*

She fumbled in her handbag for her phone. She had to call Maddie back and tell her she couldn't do it, that she'd made a mistake. But even as she prepared to punch the button that would bring up Maddie's number for a return phone call, she hesitated.

You'd be a lifesaver. My lifesaver... You'll never know how deeply I appreciate this.

Maddie had sounded deeply appreciative. In fact, Beverly thought her relief had had a touch of desperation in it. She tried to imagine herself calling Maddie back and rescinding her agreement to accompany the choir.

She couldn't.

Maddie had the reputation of being a superwoman. In fact, Shelley and her friends had a name for the frightening efficiency the choir director displayed: *MBS. Maddie Bancroft Syndrome.* With four young children at home, no one should be as organized as Maddie appeared to be. The woman seemed to be linked to half the volunteer organizations in town, and she probably was the chairwoman of several of those.

Beverly certainly wasn't that capable, but she was dealing successfully with a full-time job while getting another business off the ground. And at the end of the month, she would officially assume the job of a self-employed businesswoman.

That thought brought on a whole new wave of anxiety. Sometimes she thought she must be crazy, giving up an established career with great benefits. She enjoyed her job, and she liked most of her coworkers at the State House, truly she did. As a consultant, she'd see people sometimes, but there was no denying that a certain amount of her preparation and work would be solo.

Although not just yet. Over the next few weeks, she had several projects she had to whip into decent enough shape that they could be handed off to new leadership. She had more meetings scheduled than she had hours in the workday, it seemed on occasion.

Well, there were no more meetings she had to make today. She hurried up the steps and into her house, where she set aside her briefcase and handbag.

The sight of the piano caused her stomach to clench, and she immediately forgot about her career concerns. She gritted her teeth, riding out the nerves. If Maddie could do everything she did, Beverly surely should be able to manage three little choir rehearsals.

Even if she did have to take antinausea medication to get through them.

"Hello, Father," she called as she hung up her coat.

"Hello. I didn't hear you come in." He was in his den, ensconced in his leather chair while he perused a book.

"What are you reading?" she asked.

He held up the book so that she could see the front cover. It was the biography of a World War II pilot, a recent best seller that Beverly had thought looked interesting. Her father shared some of his reading with her and asked about her day. Just as Beverly stood and said, "I'm going to start dinner," her cell phone rang. "Excuse me, Father." She stepped into the hallway and checked the readout on her phone as she headed for the kitchen. It was Jeff.

"Hi, Beverly."

"Hello, Jeff. How are you?" Pleasure warmed her voice. Jeff Mackenzie was a photographer from Portland with whom Beverly had developed a bit of a romance. The memory of the kiss he'd given her beneath the mistletoe on Christmas evening still had the power to make her blush.

"I've been busy. And I've missed you." Jeff's voice was warm and intimate.

She sank into a kitchen chair. "I've missed you too." She'd seen him earlier in March, but for the past couple of weeks, they'd both been too busy to do more than speak on the phone for a few minutes.

They caught up, chatting of general things for a few minutes, and then Jeff said, "Beverly, I have to go to San

Francisco for a conference in July. I'd like you to come along with me."

Beverly's mouth fell open. She was glad he couldn't see her face. "You ... want me to ...?"

"Go to San Francisco with me," Jeff repeated. He chuckled. "You sound stunned. I hope that's a good thing."

Beverly didn't say anything; she didn't know *what* to say.

"I'd book you your own private room, of course." The amusement faded from his voice as he registered her lack of reaction. "Beverly?"

"Sorry," she managed. "Could you give me the dates and some time to think about it?"

"Of course." He rattled off the trip dates. "There wouldn't be anything inappropriate, I promise you. I'm speaking at a small conference, and a number of my colleagues from the West Coast will be there." He hesitated. "I'd like them to meet you."

"I see." It was a feeble response at best, and she knew she had disappointed Jeff with her lack of enthusiasm. But he'd caught her completely off guard, and she felt ridiculously spooked.

She had been enjoying their budding romance. Jeff, apparently, considered them far more than friends. *It's only some other photographers, Beverly,* she scolded herself. *It's not like he asked you to come home with him and meet his family.* Beverly had met Jeff's grandfather, Edward Maker, but not his mother.

Still, it felt very much as if the trip would elevate their relationship to a whole new level, and she simply wasn't sure if she was ready for things to advance so quickly.

She cleared her throat, aware of his silence. "Thank you for the invitation," she said, as sincerely as she could given her state of disquiet. "I'll let you know as soon as possible."

That seemed to conclude the conversation and, moments later, she ended the call with the tap of a finger.

"Oh my goodness," she said out loud. "What am I going to do now?"

CHAPTER FOUR

Shelley was exhausted. Rising early enough to get her standing orders largely completed before the children awoke meant that she turned into a pumpkin at a disgracefully early hour in the evening.

She set down her mechanical pencil with a sharp click. *There.* She had spent the last hour going over their budget, rearranging, cutting, eyeing a number of cooking ingredients she wanted to add to their grocery list and reluctantly discarding most of them because they were too costly.

"Honey, I need to talk to you about this IBEW thing," Dan said, barreling into the kitchen.

Shelley suppressed a sigh, plastering a smile on her face and nodding. "I remember." Dan had made a telephone call to the training director at the Augusta chapter of the International Brotherhood of Electrical Workers. He'd been very excited when he got off the phone, but Emma and Aiden were both acting up because they were hungry, so he'd said it could wait until the kids were in bed. "What did you learn?"

Dan consulted a notebook in which he'd been keeping all his notes on an electrician's career path. "I've decided I definitely want to be an inside wireman, with emphasis on commercial projects. In terms of getting steady work, that's probably my best option. The director, Jeb Raines, says he already has someone lined up for me to apprentice with. All I have to do is go talk with him—Mr. Raines—first, and then go meet this guy who would teach me, and if everything works out, I could start pretty soon."

"That's great!" Shelley felt a stirring of excitement. It would be so nice not to be so cash-strapped all the time, she thought, glancing at the grocery list.

"Mr. Raines can see me two weeks from Wednesday in the afternoon, and then I'd go visit the master electrician I'd work for the following day. I want you to come with me. We could stay overnight in Augusta and grab some dinner, have ourselves a little overnight getaway. What do you say?"

Shelley's shoulders sagged. "Dan, we can't do that. How on earth could we afford it?" She gestured brusquely at the grocery list. "I'm trying to figure out how to buy groceries, and you're talking about getting dinner and a hotel. Do you hear yourself?"

Dan looked completely taken aback. "Besides," she said, "we can't afford a babysitter for such a long time, and I can't really take off. Who would fill my baking orders? I don't have a helper anymore, remember?"

"I know." Dan wouldn't meet her eyes, and she could see that she'd hurt his feelings.

"You can stay with Hal and Lilah. They'll be delighted to have you stay overnight. Hal's always complaining that he never sees you." She tried to infuse her voice with enthusiasm. Hal was Dan's brother who lived in Augusta.

Dan nodded. "Yeah." He closed his notebook and turned away.

"I'm sorry," Shelley said, realizing she should be more supportive. Trying to imagine herself in Dan's place, she winced. "I didn't mean to react so negatively. I know this is a really exciting opportunity for you."

"For us," Dan corrected.

"For us," she echoed. "It's just that I really can't take time away right now. Going alone won't be so bad, will it?"

Dan simply shrugged, not even looking back as he walked around the corner into the living room.

Shelley hung her head. She hadn't handled that very well. But honestly, where did he imagine they would get the money for an overnight trip? Good heavens.

★　★　★

Margaret and Allan were getting ready for bed. While Margaret washed her face and brushed her teeth, Allan stood in the middle of the bedroom with a small laser pen. As he directed the tiny red light over the floor and along the baseboards, one of Adelaide's cats streaked after it, determined to catch the elusive little "creature." He was moving so fast he was little more than a black-and-white blur.

Allan laughed out loud. He stopped and turned toward Margaret, holding up the little penlight. "Greatest toy ever invented. I can exercise the cat without working up a sweat."

Margaret smiled, but she was still thinking about the book cover she'd seen earlier. "Do you think that book cover really is my painting?" She shook her head. "It's hard for me to imagine that Matt Beauregard would do something so...so shady behind my back." Matt was the CEO of Lighting the Way Greeting Card Company, who had purchased the rights to reproduce some of her paintings on greeting cards. And more recently, he contracted the rights to use the images on merchandise.

Allan's amusement faded. "It is hard to imagine. How sure are you that it's your work on that cover?"

"One hundred percent." Margaret's tone was flat. "I'm trying not to make a big deal of it until I see that cover up close and personal tomorrow, but I'm positive it was made from my painting, and the only way that could happen would be if Matt let it happen. I'm not going to sleep a wink tonight until I see it."

"Have you looked online?" Allan asked. "It's probably up on some Web sites. You could get another look at it tonight."

"Great idea! Why didn't I think of that?" Margaret hurried from the bedroom, returning a few moments later with their laptop computer cradled in her arms.

She crawled into bed and propped herself up against the pillows, setting the computer in her lap and turning it on. Allan brushed his teeth and then turned off the bathroom light. He propped up several pillows beside Margaret and joined her.

The moment the machine booted up, Margaret opened an e-bookstore's home page. Then she froze. "I can't remember the name of the book!"

"Hmm. That's a problem." Allan smoothed a hand over his hair, which had thinned considerably since they'd married more than four decades ago. "How about the author's name?"

Margaret's forehead wrinkled. "Give me a moment, give me a moment...ah! The book is called *Heartbeat on the Horizon*. Isn't that unusual?"

"I wonder why they chose your painting to grace the cover," Allan said. "Maybe it's just—oh. *Wow.*"

Margaret had searched for the book while he was speaking. As the cover flashed into prominence on the screen, Allan said, "I'm not an artist, but that sure looks like your moose painting to me."

Margaret nodded. "I know." She was thrilled to have her suspicion validated, but the ramifications of the find were disturbing. As soon as she confirmed that it really was a print of her work, she would have to call the CEO of the greeting card company to whom she had sold the rights to some of her art. "Matt doesn't have unlimited rights to my work. I know that's not in my contract." She looked at Allan. "Remember when we discussed the rights to my images back in February? He can use them on merchandise—mugs, magnets, and such—but there was nothing in that clause about book cover illustrations."

"I can't imagine that he would try to cheat you."

"No, I can't either. He's such a nice man. But don't you think it's odd that he wouldn't mention something like this?"

Allan sighed as he pulled his pillow from behind him and punched it a couple of times. Then he laid it in its customary spot and slid down beneath the covers with a yawn. "You need to get a look at that book cover tomorrow. If it really is yours, which I agree it is, then we'll figure out what to do next."

Margaret powered off the computer and set it on her bedside table. "No carts before horses, is that what you're telling me?" She rearranged her own pillow and turned out the light before slipping into her spot with a yawn of her own. "I'm not going to leap to conclusions, but I *am* going to find out what's going on if it is indeed my work. And I just know it is."

CHAPTER FIVE

On Tuesday morning, Beverly walked to Old First. The weather had suddenly thawed and become unseasonably warm for early April in Maine, and she soon stripped off her thick sweater and tied it around her shoulders.

Maybe walking hadn't been such a good idea. It wasn't far, but it was so balmy. She was afraid she was going to be hot and sweaty when she arrived, something she'd never even considered when she'd dressed for the day in trim khaki pants belted at the waist, with a burgundy long-sleeved knit top and matching sweater. On her feet were a classy pair of burgundy Cole Haan "moccasins" that were very similar to the penny loafers her mother had worn when she was small. The shoes were one of her guiltiest pleasures. They were far too costly, but she justified the price because she often kept and wore them for as long as a decade. She generally bought conservative styles that never went out of fashion.

Gracious, she thought, *I'm going to be able to run in shorts today!* Unless the weather was totally unsuitable, Beverly tried to fit in a several-mile run most days. It had been a little more challenging this past winter in Marble Cove, where there weren't nearly as many cleared streets and sidewalks as there typically were in Augusta.

She arrived at the church early, as she'd hoped. Ducking into the ladies' room, she gave her head a shake, and her perfectly cut hair fell into its customary sleek style that brushed her shoulders. She got a compact out of the large burgundy shoulder bag she'd carried, erased the slight shine on her nose, and checked her appearance. Then she headed to the church office to let them know she was there to use the piano in the choir's rehearsal room.

The piano in the sanctuary was an ancient concert-size Mason & Hamlin grand in a deep brown stain that still showed the wood grain through its crackled finish. She had never played it, but she'd heard it and approved of its powerful bass and bright treble notes. In the choir room was a smaller piano, a gleaming ebony Yamaha studio upright of more recent vintage, positioned on an angle facing the podium from which the choir director worked. She hung her sweater on the coatrack at the back of the room, then walked up to the piano and took a seat on the bench. She'd brought a few pieces of practice music to warm up with, in case Maddie wanted to hear her play, so after running through scales and warm-ups, she chose a Schubert sonata in B-flat major. It was one of her favorite pieces of music ever written, and she let herself sink deep into the lush beauty of the piece from the Romantic era. She knew it so well that she didn't really need the music in front of her, and she closed her eyes as she soaked in the sound reverberating around the room.

When the last note of the sonata drifted away, a solitary clapping began. Beverly's eyes snapped open.

"Very, *very* nice, Beverly." Maddie Bancroft walked around still clapping. "Shelley told me you were good, but I had no idea you were *this* good."

Maddie wore charcoal slacks with a light blue twinset, stylish flats, and discreet jewelry. Much the same as herself, Beverly realized, silently amused.

"Thank you," she said in response to the praise. "I'm just 'getting my fingers back.'"

"For which I am unbelievably grateful," Maddie said, smiling. "God's timing is amazing, isn't it? When Jesus said, 'Ask and ye shall receive,' I'm certain He wasn't speaking of accompanists, but I admit I've been praying hard ever since poor Linda fell." She shook her head. "And here you are."

"Here I am," Beverly agreed, rising.

But Maddie motioned her to sit down again. "I've had an unscheduled change of plans," the choir director said. "I'm so sorry to run you down here, but my son fell and hit his head at the park with the homeschool co-op. I need to pick him up immediately. The mom in charge is a little worried about a concussion."

"Oh heavens," Beverly said. "Go. This isn't important."

"Oh, but it is!" Maddie handed over a folder of music. "I'll just give you this and let you take it home to look over. I was going to tell you to let me know if anything seemed too complex, but after hearing you play, I'm not concerned one little bit."

Beverly glanced at her watch, realizing that time had flown, and she had work to do too—a great deal of governmental work in her home office, which still wasn't organized to her satisfaction. And there were things she needed to do for her own business too. She was determined to get it off the ground as fast as possible; it would be all too easy to fritter away her days with other pursuits while working at home. "I'll look over it and let you know," she assured the choir director. "And rehearsal is tomorrow night?"

"Wednesdays at seven," Maddie confirmed as she turned to go. "Most folks get here a little early to socialize, but we start singing promptly at seven."

Beverly just bet they did, given Maddie's reputation for perfection. "All right. I'll see you then," she said. This time, she didn't even put the cardigan on, just tied it around her shoulders and left the church.

She walked briskly along Main Street, but just before the turn onto Newport Avenue, she heard a male voice calling her name. Since she'd begun going to church, she'd met a number of people, but she didn't recognize the voice. Turning, she shaded her eyes from the sun.

"Hi, Beverly. I thought that was you." A tall, rangy man walked toward her, and she recognized Dennis Calder.

"Hello, Dennis. How are you?"

"I'm great. How about you?" His grin was quick and charming.

"I'm fine," she said, smiling. Dennis was nice, but he seemed determined to impress her, when she much preferred a man who was just himself when they interacted. Like Jeff, she realized.

"Coffee?" he asked. Reaching her side, he crooked an elbow.

"Oh, I don't—"

"Aw, come on. Ten minutes. We'll make it quick. I want to catch up." Before she could finish her refusal, Dennis reached for her hand and placed it in the crook of his elbow, holding it there with his other hand over hers. "We'll just go down to the Cove."

Beverly was a little taken aback by the easy way Dennis made assumptions about what she wanted. But they'd been friends—acquaintances, really—for a long time, so she let him lead her down the street to the Cove.

They could smell the eatery before they arrived. The aromatic waft of coffee caught Beverly's nose, and she inhaled deeply. "That smells wonderful."

"Addictive." Dennis held the door, and the wonderful aroma drew them in. He steered her to a seat at one of the well-worn wooden tables. "What would you like?"

Beverly gave him her order and watched as he threaded his way to the counter. His long legs were covered by dark denim and he wore practical work boots. Beneath a flannel shirt, he wore a thermal layer, but he wore no jacket. Plainly, he'd gotten the memo about the weather.

As she waited, he teased Brenna at the counter, making her giggle.

Flirt. But there was no rancor in the observation. Dennis was outgoing and friendly to everyone he met.

He returned to the table in a few minutes, setting down her ceramic mug and his own before pausing to hand her a spoon and a napkin. There were creamers and sugars in a container on the table, and for a moment, she was occupied with doctoring her coffee to her satisfaction. When she glanced up, Dennis had settled back in his chair and was watching her.

Flustered, she asked, "What?"

He chuckled. "You're so elegant. You even make getting a cup of coffee look genteel."

She waved a hand in dismissal. "You're awfully fanciful this morning."

He shrugged. "I'm having coffee with a beautiful woman. I'm allowed."

She laughed. "Flatterer." But his undisguised interest made her uncomfortable. *Time to change the subject,* she told herself. "You look like you're dressed to visit job sites today. Do you stay busy through the winter?"

"I try to. It's difficult to survey when there's four feet of snow on the ground though. I have several things in the works right now."

A thought occurred to Beverly. "Dennis, have you ever seen old maps of Marble Cove?"

He thought for a moment. "Occasionally. Why?"

"I just wondered." She suddenly realized maybe she shouldn't be sharing information about the map they'd found without checking first with Diane and the others, so she quickly tried to change the subject. "How's your grandfather?"

Her companion chuckled. "As cantankerous as ever. If I don't visit, I hear about how neglected he is. So I go see him, and he complains that he can't get anything done with me underfoot."

Beverly laughed. "'Underfoot'? That makes you sound like you're five."

"His words exactly." His eyes crinkled at the corners when he grinned. "So tell me why you're asking about old maps of the town."

"I—" Beverly shook her head. "Just curious."

He tipped his chair back and regarded her with a gleam in his eye. "You're a terrible liar."

She felt her cheeks growing red. "I *am* curious."

"But it's not just casual curiosity, is it?"

She sighed. She should have remembered that Dennis was like a dog with a bone when he wanted to unearth a secret.

"Tell me about this map. How old are you talking?" His chair made a solid *thunk* on the old pine floorboards as he let it down on all fours and leaned forward, elbows on the table.

She made a helpless gesture, annoyed at herself for introducing the topic. "As old as you've ever seen."

His eyebrows shot up. "Now you've got me interested. I think the oldest ones I've ever seen are from around the time the town was incorporated. That would have been around 1800, plus or minus a few years."

Beverly nodded. "Did the town look much the way it does now?"

Dennis nodded. "A lot smaller, of course. There were only a few streets named on the first map, plus the roads leading into and out of town. It was tiny."

"But everything was in the same place it is today?"

Dennis looked at her strangely. "Once streets are laid, they generally don't get up and walk away."

Beverly laughed. "I know. It's just that I saw a map not long ago that said it was of Marble Cove, but it was a different street layout with different names."

"That's easy to explain," Dennis told her. "Do you know how many municipalities in this country are named the same as something else in another state? There are fifty different towns named Greenville alone."

"Really? How do you know that?" She deliberately changed the subject. She had no intention of telling him about the exact match of the coastlines with the second map Margaret had found.

He grinned. "Trivia sticks in my mind."

"Such as?" He seemed to have taken the bait.

"Okay, here's some lighthouse trivia: the oldest lighthouse in the US that is still in service is Sandy Hook in New Jersey. It was built in 1764."

"Wow." She thought of the story of Jeremiah Thorpe being so grateful for being saved that he organized the building of their little light out on Orlean Point. If it was still in service, it would be about that old.

"The tallest lighthouse in the US is Cape Hatteras in North Carolina."

"How tall is it?"

"Two hundred and eight feet."

Beverly shook her head. "You're like a walking encyclopedia."

"Give me another category," he told her.

"Churches," she said, thinking of the fruitless search they'd conducted of Old First's cemetery in the quest to find the treasure.

"The oldest church in the continental United States is San Miguel Mission in Santa Fe. It was constructed in 1610."

"Snow," she said, thinking of the winter just past.

He hesitated for a moment, then grinned. "The world's tallest snowman was built in Bethel, Maine, in 1999. He was one hundred thirteen feet and seven inches tall, and took about five months to melt."

"Now that's trivia!" She laughed. "Do you have a photographic memory? I'd love to be able to remember things like that."

He shook his head. "No, but stuff sticks. Not everything. I can never remember where I laid my phone. I have to call my cell from the house phone to find it sometimes."

Beverly laughed. They chatted for a few more moments while they finished their coffee, and then she gathered her shoulder bag. "I must get going. I have work to do."

"Headed home?"

She nodded. "I've got quite a bit to do on a project I'm working on in Augusta. But my new business is taking a lot of time to set up too. I've been getting calls from potential clients, and I'm really not organized enough to be able to give them coherent information."

"Somehow, I suspect that's an exaggeration," he said, holding the door and motioning for her to precede him back onto the street. He took her hand before she could forestall him. "Beverly, I'd like to take you to dinner. You name the place and time."

She smiled. She'd enjoyed herself with him today. His cocky attitude didn't seem so abrasive now. Still, she sensed that if she gave him an inch, he'd take the proverbial mile. "Dennis, coffee was lovely, and I thank you for the pleasant break. But I can't accept a date. I'm seeing someone."

"Pleasant?" he grumbled, but there was a twinkle in his eye. "I must be doing something wrong if that's the best adjective you can find. I must be losing my touch." Then he heaved a sigh, the laughter fading from his face. "Thanks for having coffee with me. If you ever change your mind about a date, call me. Any time, all right?"

Beverly nodded, gently tugging her fingers from his grasp. "All right. You take care, Dennis."

"You too."

As she turned and hurried toward the intersection that would take her up Newport Avenue toward home, Beverly was aware of him looking after her. Was she making a mistake by dating Jeff exclusively? She had enjoyed that chat with Dennis. But if she went to dinner with him . . . no, he just didn't float her boat in the same way Jeff did. And part of her wasn't sure she was ready for any relationship at all.

She thought of Jeff's invitation to the conference in July. If she didn't intend to get serious with him, she really had no business accepting such an invitation.

She sighed. There should be a manual for dating the second time around. She'd forgotten anything she ever knew about the topic!

Rounding the corner, she caught sight of the lighthouse in the distance beyond Diane's home at the end of the street. Maybe, she thought, she should have asked Dennis more about the maps he said he'd seen. He was a contractor as well as a native of the little town. He probably had access to maps she would never be able to see.

Still, something had held her back. She just hadn't felt she should explain about the letters and the treasure. Knowing Dennis, he would try to take over the whole search. It was *their* project—Shelley's, Diane's, Margaret's, and hers—and she couldn't help feeling that they were meant to find the treasure to which those letters had referred.

CHAPTER SIX

Diane paused in front of Augie Jackson's home shortly after lunch on Tuesday afternoon. After her photo shoot, she had worked on her current manuscript briefly, but she hadn't been very productive. She couldn't stop thinking about those maps.

Finally she decided she might as well try to learn a little more about it. And who better to speak with than August Jackson? Augie was nearly ninety years old and had lived in Marble Cove for much of his life. A retired reporter, he knew a great deal about the town's history.

She had promptly called him and made an appointment to visit him that very afternoon.

Augie might have the greenest thumb of anyone she had ever met. If he touched it, it grew, as proven by the mad jumble of perennials that took over his small yard as soon as the weather warmed up. He never had to worry about mowing; every square inch was devoted to things that bloomed.

Even now, in early spring, Augie's yard was showing the first signs of the annual flower explosion. Daffodils turned their sunny trumpets to the sky, while crocuses and a host of lesser early-blooming bulbs were beginning to pop out of the ground at random intervals.

As someone who spent an inordinate amount of time attempting to envision the perfect landscaping for her own cottage, Diane found it hard to imagine that anyone could take such a laissez-faire attitude toward their garden plans. But it certainly seemed to work for Augie. His yard was a riot of color from the last snow to the first of the following autumn.

"Hey, Diane. You gonna stand there all day?" The elderly man had opened his front door and stood in the entrance, peering out at her through his tiny, black-rimmed glasses. He wore a stunningly clashing pair of yellow and aqua plaid pants and an apricot knit shirt that was edging toward orange. Over it, he had pulled a V-necked yellow cardigan sweater that he wore open. As usual, no one could fail to see him coming.

Diane flashed him a sparkling smile. "Hello, Lucy. Just admiring your flowers." Augie had written several cookbooks under the nom de plume Lucy Lamb.

Augie gave a bark of laughter at her jest. It ended with a deep, hoarse coughing spasm, and Diane winced, but Augie didn't appear to be bothered. "My flowers are lookin' pretty good. Some of them need to be divided this year. You like bulbs?"

As she started up the walk, Diane nodded vigorously. "Oh yes. I planted a lot last fall, but I'd be happy to purchase your extras."

Augie's expression darkened. "Purchase-smurchase. I'm just going to toss them out. You'll take them free. Now come on in here and tell me what you're up to. My curiosity's about killing me."

Diane followed her aged friend into his tiny cottage. Augie showed her to a seat in the living room and hurried to the kitchen for a plate of cookies.

The couch on which she sat was a dark blue and burgundy pattern. The little room also was crammed with a burgundy recliner, a large-screen television in an entertainment cabinet, end tables, and a coffee table, and bookcases overflowing with books on every conceivable topic. There was a small fireplace with a mirror over the mantel, and nearly every surface in the room was covered with books and newspapers. Diane spotted a half-finished crossword on the end table beside the recliner, along with a magnifying glass, which she noted with compassion.

She couldn't imagine what she'd do when or if the day came that she couldn't read. She suspected she'd be like Augie one day, using large-print publications, large font on her computer monitor and other devices, and a magnifying glass when those weren't available. But what happened when the eyes got too bad for those measures?

She didn't know, but she resolved to keep up with Augie a bit better in the coming year. She could read to him a few days a week if he needed her help. *And,* she thought, *if he isn't too proud to accept it.*

"What are you smiling at?" Augie demanded as he returned with a plate of cookies trembling in his hands.

"Just thinking silly thoughts," Diane responded. No way did she intend to tell Augie exactly what those thoughts had been.

"You want to bring in the drinks?" the old man asked. "My hands aren't so steady anymore. If I carry them, we're likely to have a trail of lemonade to clean off the floor."

She laughed as she rose and went to the kitchen for the lemonade. To her surprise, Augie's was in a mug. And it was hot.

When she returned, Augie had settled into his recliner.

"Why are you drinking hot lemonade?" she asked, making a face.

Augie thumped his chest. "Got a cold I can't get rid of, that's all. A little honey and lemon does wonders. Now what did you want to talk to me about?"

Diane set down a glass for each of them. Hers, she was amused to note, had a Tweety Bird painted on it, while his displayed Winnie the Pooh, Piglet, and Eeyore. "My friends and I need your opinion," she told him. "We found a map. I'd like to show it to you, because it's a little peculiar."

Augie's eyes already had lit with interest behind his spectacles. "Peculiar how?"

Diane had brought along a copy of the old map. "Look at it first before I say anything."

She handed Augie the map. The old man picked up his magnifying glass and perused the paper for long minutes. "Hmm," he said after a moment. "Ah."

Finally, Diane couldn't stand it any longer. "What do you think?"

Augie smoothed a finger over his luxurious white mustache, and Diane whimsically wondered what it would be like to have hair on your face but not on your head. Augie's pate was as smooth as the iridescent blue glass gazing ball that graced Fred and Cindy Little's front yard.

"Well," he said slowly. "I know I've never seen this before. And I see what you mean. It's more than a bit peculiar. It's downright mysterious. I wonder if there's another Marble Cove in an alternate reality, and somehow this map slipped through a time-space warp and ended up in the wrong reality."

Diane's eyebrows rose. "You should be writing fiction," she informed him. "That's quite a flight of imagination."

Augie grinned. "I know." He tapped a finger on the map. "But I sure don't have an explanation. If we go by this, Marble Cove should be down the coast a mile in the salt marsh. Really, other than the fact that it's labeled Marble Cove, there's very little that makes me think it really is our town."

Diane shook her head. "What if I told you we compared it to a topographical map and found that it corresponds almost exactly with the coastline as it would have been a couple hundred years ago?"

"Huh. Guess I'd have to say it's the same land. But why would this show a completely different town?"

Diane threw up her hands and slumped against the back of the couch. "I have no idea. I was hoping you would."

Augie opened his mouth to speak but began to cough again as he had at the door. It seemed to go on and on, and the old man was gasping for breath afterward.

Alarmed, Diane sat forward, but he held up a hand to forestall her. "I'm okay," he said. He reached for the lemonade and took several sips. "There. That's better."

"Maybe you should have a doctor check that cough. You could have bronchitis."

"Or I could have a cough I can't quite get rid of from my last cold," he retorted. "It's getting better, even if it doesn't sound like it."

"All right. You win." Sensing he hated to admit to a weakness, Diane returned to the topic of the map. "I don't know," she said. "Maybe the streets are mislabeled, and it just got transposed onto the wrong site by the person who drew it." It sounded feeble even as she said it.

"Don't think so," Augie said promptly. "Look. This town is different from ours. It wouldn't fit here without running into the ocean. The topography's too different. See where it's wider down there?"

Diane followed his finger. He was right. It couldn't be just a simple placement error, even if one ignored the street names. "So it's not just an error." She shook her head. "This is going to drive me crazy until I figure it out."

"I've got a couple of old volumes of Marble Cove history that aren't in the library," Augie told her. "I'll check through them for you and see if there's anything that might give us a clue."

"That would be great." Diane smiled at his use of the inclusive pronoun. Augie was going to be a wonderful resource to help her friends and her puzzle this out.

★   ★   ★

Beverly sat at her piano bench, fingers idle. She was too stunned to even look at the rest of the music Maddie Bancroft had given her.

Why, oh why hadn't she glanced through the folder when Maddie handed it to her? The woman flustered her, that's why. But if she had, she would have told Maddie right away that she couldn't possibly do this.

One of the pieces was the "Hallelujah Chorus" from Handel's *Messiah*. The "Hallelujah Chorus"! Was Maddie kidding? That piece required a tremendous amount of skill. Oh, Maddie probably assumed she could after hearing Beverly play, but the Schubert was one she'd played in a recital when she was seventeen, and she'd had it memorized. It came back to her far more easily than a less familiar piece.

The Handel wasn't completely foreign. Fortunately, she'd accompanied her high school choir one year when they'd done it. But regardless of how much she'd been playing since Christmas, she couldn't possibly play this tomorrow night.

To make it even worse, the piece had both piano and organ accompaniment. Would there be an organist there to whom she'd have to match her playing speed? This was a disaster.

Completely panicked, Beverly popped up from the piano bench and walked rapidly around the room. She went to the kitchen and got herself a glass of water, noticing that her hands were trembling slightly. What had she done to herself?

Calm down, Beverly, she told herself. *This is not the end of the world.*

No, but it might be the end of her reputation in Marble Cove if she totally botched this.

Only in a small, select group, she reminded herself. She was only the practice accompanist. If she messed it up too badly, she could always just play chords to help support the pitch. Maddie had said the regular piano accompanist would return in time for Easter Sunday. That was a comfort.

Returning to the parlor, Beverly carefully reseated herself on the piano bench, adjusting her position so the pedals were under her foot just so. The walnut-finished Baldwin upright was an old and familiar friend that her parents had purchased when her skill outgrew her first little Yamaha spinet. She took a deep breath, letting the familiarity soothe her for a moment, laid her fingers over the keys, and began to play.

Within a minute, she had mangled it so badly it was practically unrecognizable. At least in her ears. She stopped in the middle of a measure, close to tears. Forcing herself to go back to the beginning, she went through each measure, making sure she caught every eighth and sixteenth note that sneaky old Handel had inserted.

Then she remembered an old trick her piano teacher had taught her. She picked up her clockwork metronome and set it at a very slow tempo. It was more important to train your fingers to play the proper notes than it was to fumble your way through a normal tempo, the teacher had said. Each day, she had counseled, increase the tempo a bit until you were playing the piece at the proper speed.

Which was great advice, but the first rehearsal at which she had to play this piece was *tomorrow night*. As well as three others. Oh no. Remembering the other pieces, she snatched up the folder again, fearful of what she might find.

But thankfully, the rest of Maddie's selections were a piece of cake. And she had even played versions of two of them before.

She glanced at the time on her phone. She could spend the rest of the day and much of tomorrow playing Mr. Handel over and over, slowly notching up her speed. And maybe, with a lot of prayer and a dash of luck thrown in, she could manage not to make a total fool of herself tomorrow night.

Maybe. As panic fluttered in her stomach again, she bowed her head and began a fervent plea for help.

CHAPTER SEVEN

It had cooled down considerably since the pleasant warmth earlier in the day, but until all of her friends arrived, Diane still left her front door open with only the storm door to keep the chill at bay.

Shelley was the first to appear, carrying delectable-smelling chocolate chunk brownies.

"Oh," moaned Diane as she took her friend's coat. "There goes my diet. I have to fit into my clothes this coming weekend, you fiend."

Shelley giggled, her blue eyes dancing. "These are calorie-free."

"Uh-huh." Diane cast her a dark glance. "You are an evil temptress."

"And turning it into a great business," Shelley said proudly, bearing the brownies off to a place of honor on the coffee table.

Margaret arrived next. She handed Diane a platter heaped with glistening red strawberries. "On sale at the market," she said, thrusting the plate into Diane's hands as she shucked off her jacket and hung it in the front closet.

"It's a good thing. Strawberries are still hideously expensive." Diane set the forest-green glazed ceramic bowl next to the brownies. "My mouth is already watering," she said, surveying the goodies. "Who wants a drink? I have coffee, tea, water, or a cranberry spritzer."

"That sounds refreshing," Margaret said. "What's in it?"

"Lemon-lime soda, cranberry juice, orange juice, and unsweetened pineapple juice." Diane ticked off the ingredients on her fingers. "Over ice."

"Yum." Shelley grinned. "I vote for that too."

"I made plenty of it," Diane said. "Why don't I just bring a pitcher in here?"

The three friends settled around the coffee table. Diane had a low blaze going in the fireplace and soft jazz playing in the background.

Margaret tucked her shoeless feet up on the couch beneath her and sighed. "This is so relaxing. We should end every day like this."

Shelley laid her head against the back of her comfortable overstuffed chair. "If only we could." The three women chatted for a minute, and then Shelley lifted her head. "Is Beverly coming?"

Diane frowned from her seat in the other chair. "She said she was." She glanced at her watch. A scant moment later, Beverly appeared at the door. She didn't wait for Diane but let herself in, turning to close the heavier house door behind her.

"I'm sorry I'm late." She sounded breathless. She slipped out of her black wool peacoat and hung it on the doorknob of the closet, keeping the loosely woven black scarf with gleaming strands of midnight blue metallic yarn looped around her neck. Her slacks and fitted sweater were both black as well, and she looked as elegant as always.

Though perhaps a bit wild-eyed, Diane noted. "Are you all right?"

"Ha!" It was a short, sharp exclamation that edged toward hysteria.

Shelley sat up straight, clearly alarmed. "Did something happen to your father?"

"No, Father's fine." Beverly shook a finger at Shelley. "You and your big mouth."

"Me?" Shelley's eyes widened. "What did I do?"

"Maddie Bancroft asked me to play piano for the next few choir rehearsals," Beverly said grimly. "I wonder where she heard that I play."

Shelley flushed a deep red, slowly sinking down into her chair. "Oh, Beverly, I'm so sorry. It was just a passing comment. That woman makes me so nervous I just run on at the mouth. I never dreamed she'd try to entrap you."

Beverly let out a laugh. "I'll survive," she said. "I hope. One of the pieces she's got me playing is the 'Hallelujah Chorus.'"

Diane ran a few bars of the piece through her head, hearing the complex chorus she so loved. "Wow. I'm not musical, but I'm sure that's challenging."

"*Challenging* is a kind word for it," Beverly muttered. "I can't believe I agreed to torture myself like this."

Margaret poured a glass of the cranberry spritzer for her. "Here, have a drink and a brownie. Shelley's brownies make everything a little better."

Beverly sighed as she accepted both. "I'm sorry," she said to Diane. "I didn't mean to monopolize your celebration."

"It's all right. Sounds like quite an ordeal." Diane patted Beverly's knee as the slender woman plopped down on the couch beside Margaret with less grace than she normally displayed.

Rising, Diane went to a side table and picked up three identical packages wrapped in silver paper with gossamer-thin pale green and lavender ribbons tied expertly in a fluffy bow atop each one. She handed one to each woman, glancing at name tags on the bottoms as she did so.

"I hate to open this," Shelley cried. "It's so pretty!"

"But we can't wait to get our hands on what's inside." Beverly clearly made an attempt to set her own concerns aside, carefully untying her ribbon before gently loosening the tape on the paper.

Shelley, in contrast, ripped hers right and left and discarded the wrap with abandon, while Margaret pried the ribbon off one side and tore the paper with one long *r-r-rip*.

Diane laughed. "This is an experiment in unwrapping, watching you three."

"Oh, Diane, it's beautiful!" Shelley held her copy of Diane's book at arm's length. "I can't believe I know a real live author."

"As opposed to a deceased one?" Margaret chuckled, but her eyes were on her own copy.

"They're all personalized and autographed," Diane said. "I can't tell you three what a source of support you were when I was just starting this first book, and how much I appreciate the friendships we've developed."

Beverly looked up from her copy and smiled. "We're so proud of you," she said.

"So Friday evening, the fun begins," Shelley said. "Tell us all the details, please."

Diane smiled. "Well, I had an outdoor photo shoot today to get some pictures for my Web site. The photographer took some head shots of me, as well as some candids of Rocky and me walking along the beach and perched on a rock with the lighthouse in the background."

Shelley picked up her book and flipped it to the back cover, then looked inside, frowning. "Isn't your picture in here?"

"No. Just my bio. I guess I'll have to get famous before they bother with things like that."

Shelley laughed. "More famous, you mean. When I was in the bookstore the other day discussing the refreshments they're going to have for your reading on Friday night, a lady came in and asked about you. She'd seen the sign in the window. You should have heard Beth bragging about you, telling her all about how Marble Cove inspired you to write your first book."

Diane laughed. Beth Levesque, the manager of the Crow's Nest, could talk the ears off a cornstalk, and she seemed to know everything about everyone who lived in Marble Cove. It probably helped that her husband Ham delivered the mail to most of the town. "Anyway," she said, "as you know, Friday night is the reading Beth is hosting at the library. I'll be signing books and visiting with folks at the reception."

"For which I am providing cupcakes, a vegetable tray with three different dips, fruit, and a platter of cheese and crackers. I've been trying to decide what drinks to offer, and"—the young blonde paused to wave her glass at Diane— "I believe I've decided. If you'll share the recipe."

"Of course." Diane was flattered and surprised. The cranberry spritzer was something she'd served for many years, a delightful alternative to soda or lemonade at a party.

"So Friday night is your official appearance as an author," Margaret prompted. "I bet the whole town will turn out to celebrate."

"Well, I don't know about that," Diane said, "but I don't want to be an embarrassment."

Her friends were all starting to tell her how silly she was being when the doorbell rang. All four women looked up.

"You expecting someone?" Margaret asked Diane.

Diane shook her head. "No." She walked to the door that Beverly had closed and pulled it wide—and her mouth fell open in shock. Her son Justin stood on the porch! She scrambled to pull open the storm door and gave him a huge hug, despite the rucksack he had over one shoulder. "What are you doing here, honey? I thought you were at Fort Benning! I didn't know they gave you leave."

"Um, it's kind of complicated. I really messed up, Mom." Her son's deep voice above her head sounded tired and dull.

Then his body stiffened, and she realized he had seen her guests. "Oh man, I'm sorry. I didn't mean to interrupt your party." He drew back and sketched a wave in the direction of the living room. "Hello, ladies."

Her friends responded with a flurry of greetings.

As he turned back to her, Diane saw that he looked deeply unhappy. "I'll just go on to bed. Is it okay if I sleep in the guest room?"

"Of course. There are clean sheets on the bed, and you know where the fresh towels are, right?"

He nodded and summoned up what she assumed was a smile. "Great. Thanks, Mom. We can talk in the morning."

"Are you sure? Because I can—"

"Mom. It's okay." He bent and pressed a kiss to her cheek, and before she could respond, he was tromping down the hallway to the bedrooms.

Diane turned back to her friends, spreading her hands helplessly and shaking her head in bewilderment. "I have no idea what that's all about." She tried to summon the lighthearted mood of only moments ago, but worry for her son dampened her excitement.

He had just been home at Christmas, and he finally had been headed for Officer Candidate School after a long wait for a slot to open up.

Margaret rose from the couch, clutching her book to her chest. "Diane, thank you for the book. But I'm afraid I'll have to leave because I need to go read it right now."

Diane laughed. "You're welcome. But don't rush off. Justin says he's going straight to bed."

But Shelley rose as well. "I hate to run too, but I'd better. Lots to do before tomorrow's baking begins."

"And I should get home too," Beverly said. "Although I may have to sneak in because if Father sees my book, I can guarantee he's going to try to steal it! I've already promised to bring him down to the library Friday evening for your reading."

"Oh, that's lovely." Diane gave up the attempt to talk her friends into staying. The party atmosphere had stepped out the door when Justin stepped in. And truthfully, she was so worried that she would struggle to be good company.

Retrieving everyone's coats, she bade them farewell. Shelley insisted on leaving the brownies for Justin, and Margaret nearly tripped over the doorstep trying to read on her way out.

Beverly, the last to depart, gave Diane a warm hug. "I'll keep you in my prayers tonight." Obviously, she saw the worry Diane couldn't hide.

Diane cleaned up the small amount of mess her little gathering had made and went to her office, intending to put in a couple of hours of work before bedtime. It was barely eight o'clock in the evening.

Instead of writing, she pulled out her photo albums from her children's childhoods. She intended to give them to them some day. She got such pleasure out of looking through them occasionally even now that she was considering having copies made.

She had made sure she got a professional photo taken at least once a year with the two kids together as well as separately. In the first year after Jessica's birth, Justin had been a boisterous preschooler. Several days before the photo appointment, he had fallen flat in the yard and split his lip open. It had required several stitches, and the photo shoot had forever memorialized him with a fat lip and those stitches.

Diane shook her head, smiling at the memories as she lingered over the album. After a day, he'd been his usual lively self. Without the signs of injury, no one ever would have known there had been something wrong. Her smile slowly faded. It had been so easy to fix problems in his little world at that age.

She suspected it wouldn't be nearly so easy to fix his problems now that he was an adult.

Chapter Eight

On Wednesday morning, the weather was chillier, more typical of an April day in Maine. Aiden awoke early, and Shelley heard him clattering down the steps with Prize, his puppy, close behind.

"Good morning, honey." Shelley smiled at her son as he and the dog came into the kitchen. Aiden immediately crossed to the back door, wrestled with the doorknob for a moment, then pulled it open and held the door wide for Prize. When they'd gotten the puppy, they'd told Aiden he had to help take care of her, and this morning ritual was well established.

Prize hadn't had an accident in the house in longer than Shelley could remember. She was just over a year old now and probably close to her full size. Part beagle and part cocker spaniel, she was a darling little thing with a beagle's black, brown, and white coloring but a longer, silky, wavy coat.

"What do you want for breakfast?" Shelley asked her son as he closed the door. Aiden considered his answer as he came over to her side, yawning. Shelley knelt and hugged him, running her hand up and down his warm back, and he laid his head on her shoulder briefly before pulling back and asking, "Can I have a egg-in-a-basket?"

"You sure can. Why don't you go get dressed while I get breakfast ready?" She had organized Aiden's dresser drawers so that he could easily find pants and shirts, and he'd begun choosing his own clothes.

Aiden headed for the stairs just as Dan entered the kitchen. The two males paused for a good morning hug, and then Aiden went on upstairs.

Shelley smiled at Dan as she set the table. "Good morning."

"'Morning." He didn't smile back. Ever since Monday evening when she'd fussed at him about his trip idea, he'd been withdrawn and quiet.

"Have you set the date for your visit to the IBEW guy?" Shelley asked.

Dan nodded. "In two weeks, just like I told you." She heard the silent rebuke in the statement; he'd told her already, and she hadn't remembered.

"Good." She tried to infuse her tone with optimism.

Silence.

Shelley cleared her throat. "Did he tell you where the company is that you'll be doing your internship with?"

"Apprenticeship. No."

Shelley sighed. She'd had enough of the silent treatment. "Dan, I'm sorry if I didn't react the way you wanted me to the other day."

"Aren't you happy that I'm finally taking some steps to make our lives more financially secure?"

"Of course I am."

"I couldn't tell from the way you acted."

That was a little unfair. Shelley thought she'd been quite supportive, but... "It's just that I don't really feel like I can take the time away from my business to go with you right now. Dan, I'm very proud of you."

"Thank you." He was scrupulously polite but no warmer than before.

Aiden returned then, wearing jeans and a red-and-blue striped shirt over which he'd pulled an orange sweater. Shelley forced herself to bite her tongue. It wasn't as if they were going anywhere right away, and she knew it was important for him to feel that he'd done a good job.

Breakfast was a quiet affair. Emma was still sleeping, and Aiden did most of the talking. Dan declined her offer of an egg and poured himself a bowl of cereal. As soon as he was done, he excused himself. He was soon out the door to his workshop in the garage, where he was working on a cutting board for his sister's birthday, leaving Shelley feeling like a huge failure.

At nine o'clock, Adelaide came over. Emma had finished her breakfast by then, and Adelaide played with her while Aiden was busy with a Lego construction. Sometimes Shelley used Adelaide to help with baking tasks now, but today she was swamped with orders and simply needed to move as fast as she could.

"Shelley, I went to visit my friends." Adelaide looked up from the floor, where she was entertaining Emma with kitten finger puppets she had brought from her own home. Her brown eyes were shining.

"You did?" That sounded like fun. Adelaide didn't do much without her parents other than her time at the community center, so Shelley assumed it probably was a family gathering or something to do with their church.

"Yeah." Adelaide nodded vigorously. "They live in a house. All by themselves."

"Wow. I bet that's exciting." Shelley smiled as she whirled away from the cookie dough she was making to knead the dough for the blueberry bagels Rusty, the owner of the Cove, had requested.

"Not with their moms," Adelaide clarified. "'Cept for one mom."

Realizing a response was required, Shelley said, "So they're all grown up?"

Adelaide nodded again. "They go to school with me."

Shelley's hands paused in the dough. "You mean friends from the community center?"

"Uh-huh." Adelaide's attention had turned back to Emma.

Shelley puzzled over that for a moment. The life skills class Adelaide was taking was for handicapped young adults with intellectual skills similar to hers. "And tell me again where these girls live?"

"On the corner."

Shelley had to smile. Adelaide was so literal sometimes. "Together?"

"Yeah."

"And their mothers or other family members don't live with them?"

"No. Just one mom."

That was puzzling. "Do you mean they live in a group home?"

"Yeah! An' I'm gonna live there too."

"Oh, you are?" Shelley grinned. "Have you told your mom that?"

"Not yet."

Adelaide chattered on throughout the morning. Her friends went swimming together at the Y in Rockland once a week. Her friends went to the grocery store. Her friends watched movies. Clearly, she was quite enthused about the notion of her friends living together.

Allan stopped by at noon to pick up his daughter. The two of them were going to walk down to the gallery and have lunch with Margaret. While Adelaide was putting on her coat, Shelley said, "This morning, I heard all about her friends who are living together."

Allan chuckled. "Oh yes. That's all she talks about these days. I think she has a very rosy picture of how those girls live."

★　　★　　★

Diane hadn't slept well. On Wednesday morning, she got up at seven and took Rocky for a walk along the beach, enjoying the gradual creep of color into the landscape as the sun rose higher. She took a longer walk than usual, going far down the beach past the boardwalk.

Rocky, of course, was pleased by this. She threw sticks for him, chuckling as he brought them back repeatedly for another toss, although she avoided the surf. Cleaning him up after their beach walks was work enough without having to dry him off. Besides, that ocean was still really *cold*.

Halfway back, though, she found herself hurrying, worrying that Justin would get up and she wouldn't be there. The thought made her laugh. Her son was thirty years old, soon to be thirty-one. With a start, she realized that his birthday was only a week away. Would he still be here then? It was unlikely, given that he'd just had a leave at Christmas.

Justin still wasn't awake—or at least, wasn't out of his room—when she returned from her walk. She left her Bogs and parka on the back porch, slipping into the Ugg scuffs she had left inside the kitchen door. He still loved blueberry pancakes, just as he had since he was too small to say "blueberry" properly, and she smiled, thinking of those days.

First she set the table for two. Then she hauled a mixing bowl from a lower cupboard and began to gather her ingredients. Fortunately, she had a bag of frozen blueberries in her freezer. Digging out a half-cup measure, she filled it with the fruit and set it aside to thaw while she sifted together flour, salt, baking powder, and sugar. She had made this recipe so many times through the years that she had no need of a recipe; her memory guided her through the steps.

She got out a second bowl, smaller than the first, and beat together an egg and milk before stirring the mixture into the bowl of dry ingredients. When it was thoroughly integrated, she added a bit of melted butter and then drained the blueberries before folding them into the batter.

"Hey, Mom."

"Justin!" She put a hand to her heart. "You scared me."

"Sorry." He smiled. "Am I interrupting something?"

"Just blueberry pancakes." She indicated the griddle. "I was going to make them and keep them warm in the oven, but since you're awake, you'll get them fresh."

"Great. No one makes blueberry pancakes like you."

Diane glowed. "Butter and syrup are in the fridge. You can heat the syrup in the microwave if you like."

As he moved to comply, Diane studied her son surreptitiously. He had dark circles beneath his eyes, as if he hadn't been sleeping well. She had to bite her tongue to keep from blurting out questions, but she knew that he would tell her what was wrong eventually. Justin had always done things on his own timetable, no matter what the rest of the world was up to. She'd been surprised by his choice of the army as a career because of that, but he seemed to love being a soldier.

Quickly, she poured circles of pancake batter onto the griddle, flipping them over, then piling them on a serving plate as soon as they were browned to make room for more. In minutes, she had a steaming plate of blueberry pancakes, and after turning off the stove, she carried the platter to the table and set it down beside her son. "Here you go."

"Wow. Thanks, Mom." He had gotten the butter and syrup; he'd also poured each of them some juice.

Diane picked up the serving fork and filled his plate with three pancakes.

"That'll do for a start."

She laughed, placing two on her own plate. She suspected he probably could polish off the rest of the platter. Quietly, she picked up her knife and began to prepare her meal. Justin did the same, and they began to eat in silence.

"I guess you want to know why I'm here, huh?"

Yes! "If you want to tell me," she said.

He sighed, and the deep, unhappy sound tore at her heart. If only she could still fix everything that went wrong in his world.

"You know I started OCS after Christmas, right?"

OCS...Officer Candidate School. She nodded.

Justin took a deep breath. "Well, I failed."

Diane absorbed the blunt statement for a moment, trying not to show how taken aback she was. "All right. Do you know why?"

"That's the stupid part." He stabbed at a bite of pancake, clearly disgusted. "I met this girl, another soldier, who was in my class. She wasn't in my platoon, so I didn't see her every minute, but when we studied for classroom tests and things, we studied together. I met her at mess the first day. Her name's Dani."

He stopped and took the bite on his fork. "I worked hard, Mom. All the classroom stuff went fine. Tactics, Methods of Offense and Defense, Operations... I usually had one of the highest scores in the class. And I did okay with the stuff in the field. I had to retest on Land Nav because I lost my log sheet in the woods before the last checkpoint."

Diane made a sound of sympathy, and he nodded. "I couldn't believe it. I backtracked, but I never did find it." He grimaced. "So I got to do the whole thing over again the next day." He chuckled. "But it could have been worse. One guy got treed by wild hogs and the cadre had to rescue him. And a bunch of guys had trouble figuring out the grid coordinates and never did find all eight checkpoints."

Fascinated despite the fact that she hadn't quite understood all the army-speak, Diane asked, "So it wasn't your leadership skills that were lacking?"

"No, ma'am." He grinned, the first real smile she'd seen. "I mean, no, *Mom*. Even when my team didn't manage to get everyone through the obstacles in the Leadership Reaction Course, I still scored max points on leadership skills. A bunch of guys got recycled for leadership fails, stuff that happened in the field, but that was no problem for me."

"So what was the problem?" she asked gently.

Her son screwed up his face and mimed gagging. "Military History. I did good—"

"Well." The correction was second nature as a mom.

"I did *well* on the early ones, but the final was horrible. I hadn't spent as much time studying as I should have because I was with Dani." He looked utterly miserable. "I guess I got cocky."

"What happened to your . . . friend? Did she fail too?"

Justin shook his head. "She's a whiz with the classroom stuff. PT—that's physical training—is a little tough for her, but that's all."

That just didn't seem fair, Diane thought. The girl had led him astray and then didn't even suffer any consequences. But she refrained from saying that.

"Oh, honey, I'm sorry." She reached over and squeezed his shoulder sympathetically. Then, despite herself, she laughed.

"What?" He looked at her as if she were crazy.

"It's just really strange," she said, "to touch or hug you and realize that this tall man with muscles like concrete is the same little boy I used to rock to sleep."

Justin grinned, lifting his arm in a bicep curl. Despite the chill, he wore a short-sleeved T-shirt, and the size of the muscle that rose was indeed impressive. "All grown up, Mom."

"I know." She could barely hide her regret.

While they finished their pancakes, Justin asked her questions about her upcoming book publication. "Oh, wow," he said, "I guess I didn't realize what a big deal it is. Can I come on Friday night?"

"Of course you can." His interest pleased her. "I have a signed copy for you and one for Jessica. Would you like yours now?"

"Cool. I need something to read."

She gave him the book, and while he settled down on the couch to read, she decided to walk downtown. She felt jumpy and unsettled, disturbed by Justin's story, and she had some letters to mail anyway. She might as well go to the post office.

Rocky was lying on the floor beside Justin when she went for her coat, and he showed no signs of wanting a second stroll. Justin was lying on the sofa with the book propped on his chest while he lazily stroked Rocky's exposed belly with his free hand.

"Traitor," she told the dog. "Just remember who feeds you."

CHAPTER NINE

Although she'd already walked in that direction once earlier that morning, Diane moseyed along the promenade before making the short journey to the post office. And as she walked, she prayed for wisdom. She didn't know much about Justin's chosen career, but she prayed that she could be a sounding board for him and possibly offer some guidance, if he seemed inclined to accept advice.

After she turned onto Main Street and stopped in at the post office, she began to head back to Newport Avenue. Then, instead of going home, she decided she would stop in at the Shearwater Gallery and say hello to Margaret. She continued straight down Main instead of turning onto Newport Avenue, and as she crossed the street, she saw a familiar figure making his way along the street. Their paths would intersect.

Augie Jackson didn't see her at first. But she was certain of his identity. He had a ragg wool watch cap snugly pulled over his bald head, but there wasn't another short man with that bushy white mustache in town, particularly not one who would wear a green parka with yellow corduroy trousers and

Doc Marten slip-ons that were the next thing to red she'd ever seen in a men's shoe.

"Diane! Hey, I was going to give you a call." Augie beamed when he spotted her.

She grinned at the old man. "Oh? You want to ask me on a date?"

Augie cackled, laughing until he coughed. Diane thought he sounded even more congested than he had the other day. "You sound terrible," she said. "You should be home in bed."

Augie waved a hand impatiently. "I don't have time to lollygag around in bed."

Diane grinned. She didn't know if she'd ever actually heard anyone use the word *lollygag* out loud.

"I found a book that might help us with that map you brought by," Augie informed her.

"Really?" She smiled again at the inclusive pronoun "us." Augie, it appeared, was on the mystery-solving team.

"Don't have it with me though," he told her. "You want to come by, and I'll show it to you?"

"Sure." She thought of Margaret, who was so determined to figure out why the two maps of the area differed. "I'll bring Margaret along, if that's okay."

"Fine by me."

Diane and Augie arranged a time for Margaret and her to stop by Friday morning, before Margaret opened the gallery. If she couldn't make it, Diane would go alone. But she knew if her friend was available, she'd be interested.

As she reached the gallery, she realized her encounter with Augie had calmed her. She'd done such a good job of downplaying her reaction to Justin's dismaying news that she hadn't even let herself see how agitated it had made her.

Talking to God had helped too. She knew He just wanted her to love her son and give him the room to grow as an adult. It was long past the time when she could solve his problems for him.

Resolving to "let go and let God," as the saying went, she took a deep breath and then pushed open the gallery door.

★   ★   ★

The bell over the door of the Shearwater Gallery jingled, and Margaret looked up from her task. She was dusting every item in the gallery today before she allowed herself to sit down at her easel. Once she began to paint, it was all too easy to tell herself it was more important to produce new work than it was to spend time cleaning when she'd just have to do it all again.

"Hello," she said when she saw Diane coming through the door.

"Hi." Diane smiled as she unzipped her coat.

Margaret eyed her, wondering how her friend was doing. She was smiling, but Margaret recalled the worry in her face when she'd found her son on her doorstep last night. He wasn't scheduled to be home, Margaret was certain. What she knew about the army would fit on the tip of one of her liner brushes, but she did know the surprise visit probably wasn't great news, particularly given Justin's sober demeanor and the speed with which he'd disappeared. Still, she wasn't going to mention it unless Diane did. "What are you up to this morning?"

"I had to run to the post office," Diane replied. "But I'm glad I did. I just ran into Augie, and he told me he found a book that might reference our map."

"Really?" Margaret was diverted immediately. "What does it say?"

"He didn't tell me that. But I set a time to go visit with him Friday morning, and he promised to show the book to me then."

"Can I come? I could open the gallery a little later."

Diane laughed. "Actually, I already told him you and I both would be there. I figured you'd want to hear firsthand if you possibly could."

"You figured right!" They chuckled together.

"So have you been by the bookstore?" Diane asked.

"Not yet," Margaret said. "I got totally sidetracked yesterday, but I'm planning to stop by there at lunch."

"Why don't you go now?" Diane glanced at the time on her cell phone. "The bookstore should be open, and I have a few minutes to hang out and dust while you run over there."

"Really? You wouldn't mind?" Margaret was already reaching for her coat.

Diane took the dust cloth from her hand and made a shooing motion toward the door. "Not a bit. Go."

So she did. As she walked toward the bookstore, Margaret wondered if there was something—anything—she could have brought along that would help her verify whether the painting was her work, as she suspected. *Like what?* She asked herself. *A paintbrush?* Or what if she couldn't tell for sure?

Margaret had never been in a position where she'd had to try to identify her own work. And a book cover was, at best, a poor reproduction of a painting, no matter how well done the cover was. What if she couldn't tell?

Realizing she was practically trotting along Main Street, Margaret forced herself to slow down and take several deep, calming breaths. It would never do for Beth Levesque to see how upset she was. Beth was a sweetheart, but she didn't know the meaning of the word "secret." Margaret would prefer Beth have no idea that there was anything wrong.

"'Morning, Margaret!" Beth sang out as she entered the bookshop. "What can I do for you today?"

Margaret shrugged and smiled. "I need something new to read. I'll just browse a bit."

She made a show of starting at the opposite side of the store, checking the cover copy on several best sellers, before she reached for the book that had her painting on it. With her back to Beth, she took the book in her hands and carefully studied the cover. *There!* In the right corner was the tiny dab of russet where she'd considered brightening the darkness of the rock with a touch of some reddish shade. Ultimately, she'd decided not to go that route, so she'd painted most of it out, leaving one little spot where dappled sunlight fell.

Just to be certain, she glanced at the copyright page of the book. Her name was not there; in fact, no illustrator name was given. They could have at least given her credit for the work they'd stolen, she thought sourly.

Margaret felt as if she'd been punched in the stomach. It was definitely her work. How could she have thought for one minute that she wouldn't recognize it?

She carried the book to the counter.

"Find what you wanted?" Beth scurried behind the counter to ring her up.

"Yes. This one." Margaret's voice sounded odd, even to her own ears.

Beth glanced at her as she took Margaret's debit card. "You all right? You look like you don't feel so well."

Margaret made an effort to smile. "I'm fine. Maybe catching a cold, that's all."

Beth winced, holding up a bottle of hand sanitizer she kept behind the counter. "This stuff has been my best friend all winter." She handed Margaret her receipt. "You want your book bagged?"

Margaret shook her head. "No. I'm just going back to the gallery. Thanks anyway, Beth. Have a great day."

"You too. See you soon."

Margaret hurried back to the gallery with the offending novel beneath her arm. She felt as if she should hide it from sight, which was really silly. The book was a best seller. It was being seen all over the country.

"Did you see it?" Diane demanded the moment Margaret returned, setting the bell jangling as she pushed it open with perhaps just a bit more force than necessary. Her eyes widened when Margaret held up the book. "Is it yours? It must be yours—why else would you have bought it?" she answered herself.

Margaret nodded in dejection. "It's mine."

"You're positive." Diane snatched the book from her and scrutinized the cover.

"Oh yes. Without question."

Diane opened the book and found the copyright page, as Margaret had done. "No illustrator listed?" she asked.

Margaret shook her head. "Somehow that makes it even worse."

"Have you contacted your agent?"

"I didn't sell these through an agent, remember. Lighting the Way, that greeting card company, bought the rights directly from me."

"Is there anything in your contract that would permit them to let your work be used like this?"

"I certainly don't recall anything like that." Margaret sighed. "To be honest, there's an awful lot of legalese in there that I'm not certain I understand. But Matt Beauregard, the man who owns the card company, explained it all to me when we made the agreement, and I don't remember anything like that in the contracts."

"Maybe it's in that amended agreement you made for the merchandising rights." Diane sounded excited, as if she'd solved the problem.

Margaret shook her head. "I checked. There's not a word about books of any kind."

Diane's face fell. "You need to call Matt right away, Margaret."

"I know." Margaret sighed, almost wishing she'd never seen the stupid book cover. She hated confrontation with a passion. Making that phone call was going to require all the fortitude she could gather.

Chapter Ten

Beverly parked her car in Old First's lot that evening and took a deep breath. Tonight would be the moment of truth.

It was the season of Lent, but her church offered Lenten services on Thursday evenings, rather than on Wednesdays, as many other churches in the area did. She was looking forward to the service tomorrow night, at which a six-foot-high cross draped with cloth was featured at the front of the sanctuary.

Tonight, however, she had choir. She took another deep breath, swung her bag onto her shoulder, and headed for the wooden church doors.

Inside, there were lights on in the choir room, but no one was around yet. She hung up her coat and then set her music on the piano. After adjusting the bench to suit her, she began to play a few scales and followed those with finger exercises.

Midway through her warm-ups, Maddie walked into the room. She had a pencil stuck behind one ear and carried a sheaf of papers. "Hi, Beverly." She waved a hand in a vague gesture toward the door. "If you ever need me, and I'm not here, check in my office. Three doors down on the left."

Beverly nodded. "Thanks." She wanted to tell Maddie how overwhelmed she was by the idea of playing Handel, but the words wouldn't come.

"Tonight, we're going to start with 'Because He Lives.' Then we'll work on 'Christ Is Risen' and 'Crown Him with Many Crowns' and finish with the *Messiah*. Oh, I almost forgot to tell you: I'll probably just have you play voice parts for that until we've got the harmonies down properly."

Beverly blinked. "Really?"

Her relief must have shown on her face, because Maddie chuckled and said, "Really," with a warm smile.

"How's your son?" Beverly asked her. "The last time we spoke, you were heading for the hospital."

Maddie rolled her eyes. "He's okay. He didn't appear to be concussed, so they released him. But I can guarantee you he won't be swinging upside down on the jungle gym any time soon. Thanks for asking," she added.

Choir members began to trickle in then, and Beverly returned to her warm-ups. The moment she paused, a tiny silver-haired woman popped up beside her and held out a hand. "Hello. I'm Peggy Ivers. Welcome to the choir!"

Several other people followed suit, and Beverly realized she was going to have to try to get everyone's names and faces fixed in her head. Thank goodness for pictorial church directories.

Maddie stepped up to the podium then. Beside it was a music stand that she had locked in its highest position, and she held up a piece of music briefly. "Good evening, folks. We're starting with 'Because He Lives' tonight. Make sure you have a pencil because we're going to spend a lot of time on dynamics." She turned and made a graceful gesture toward the piano. "And this wonderful lady is Beverly Wheeland. She's a relatively new member of our church and an absolute godsend in our time of need. I'm sure you've all heard what happened to Linda last week."

Heads bobbed, and someone said, "We should put her on our prayer list tonight."

"Good idea." Maddie leaned over to the podium and scribbled something in a notebook. "As I was saying, Beverly is going to help us out until Linda gets the okay from her doctor to play again. Let's give her a warm Old First welcome."

"Welcome, Beverly!" the whole group said in unison.

Beverly raised a hand with a nervous smile. "Hello, everyone."

Maddie tapped the music stand with her pencil. "All right, vocal warm-ups first," she told the group, and everyone turned their attention to her again, to Beverly's relief. Being the center of attention always discombobulated her.

Beverly was only called upon for the occasional chord initially because the group warm-ups were a cappella. As the evening wore on, she was more and more impressed with Maddie Bancroft. The choir director was well organized and firm, expecting nothing but the best, and the choir rose to her expectations. Maddie occasionally had a twinkle in her eye, and Beverly could see what a great relationship she had with her singers. Each and every one of them wanted to please her.

The work was engrossing and rewarding, and when Maddie said, "Okay, time to put away our music," Beverly was astonished at how quickly the hour and a half had gone. Maddie concluded the evening by soliciting prayer requests from anyone who cared to speak, recognizing an older man in the bass section whose birthday was coming on Saturday, and offering a prayer. She was a very likable woman, and Beverly was almost glad she'd agreed to accompany for her.

If it wasn't for that complicated "Hallelujah Chorus," she thought. She'd dodged a bullet tonight, which gave her an entire week to work through the rough spots and continue to improve, but she had a feeling a week was going to be far too little time to tame that piece of music.

★　　★　　★

Shelley was being eaten alive by guilt.

As she made cherry pies in her beautiful new kitchen Wednesday evening after putting the children to bed, she remembered all the hard work Dan had put into it to help her realize her dream. True, their family was benefitting from the career she was building in her kitchen...but Dan was trying to put himself in a better position to support them as well.

She set down the rolling pin she'd been using to flatten the pie crust dough and picked up a fluted pastry wheel to make the long strips for the latticework she intended to weave over the top of each pie.

She hadn't meant to hurt his feelings or to indicate that this opportunity wasn't important, she reflected, running the little wheel through the dough. It was just bad timing.

Obviously, he couldn't see how difficult it would be for her to rearrange everything and take time away from work. He should remember how panicked she'd been when she had hurt her knee in January. Was it really so important to him that she go along?

Probably, she conceded. Dan had struggled to figure out a new career path. Right now, he was probably feeling a little insecure, worrying about whether or not he could learn to do everything he needed to. On that score, he should have no worries. She had never met anyone so handy in her life—unless it was his dad. Dan and his dad both could pick up a tool and start using it like a pro in a matter of minutes.

Mentally, she catalogued what she would need to do in order to go along. First, she would have to talk to Rusty at the Cove and see if he could do without her work for a day—or maybe make things a day ahead. They wouldn't be fresh, though, and she didn't want to get a reputation for delivering stale food.

She couldn't call the wholesaler who had helped when she hurt her knee because they had a minimum number of days for which they required a business to contract them. She was well past that deadline, and besides, they'd never consider doing a single day's work. If only Tami were still here.

She'd also need to find someone to take care of Aiden and Emma, she thought. She'd much prefer to have someone stay here overnight, rather than taking them to Dan's parents. Frances and Ralph would enjoy them, though, and she felt a little ashamed of herself for the mean-spirited thought.

And then there was Prize. If Aiden and Emma went to a relative's, maybe Diane would come over and let Prize out and feed her.

She'd also have to get online and search for a decent yet inexpensive hotel near their destination. That was definitely not Dan's forte. He'd book them into the first cheap place he could find.

She set the pastry wheel aside. Carefully she placed each strip on a baking sheet and placed it in the refrigerator for a few moments. The secret to success with latticework was not to let the dough get too warm, or it would tear. She set a timer for ten minutes. Too cold, and it would break when it was folded back.

She untied the waist of the chef's apron she wore and pulled the neck loop over her head. She carried it out into the backyard and shook it to remove the excess flour, then went back inside and laid it over a chair before retrieving the large cookie jar on her counter.

Tugging off the lid, she withdrew a resealable bag full of giant-size chocolate chunk cookies and got one out. After putting the jar back, she slipped out the back door again and walked out to the garage. Dan had his workshop there, and since he'd been laid off, he'd been keeping himself occupied with small projects. Today, he was cutting the wood for a set of cabinets he was completing for a couple from their church.

Easing open the door, she saw her husband at one of his electric saws. A miter saw? A jigsaw? She could never remember which was which. "Dan?"

He jumped, clearly startled. "Hey, Shell. What are you doing out here?"

She smiled and crossed the floor to hand him the cookie. "I brought you a treat."

"Oh, wow. Thanks." A smile lit his face as he accepted the cookie and took a huge bite. Closing his eyes, he gave a blissful moan. "The smartest thing I ever did in my life was to marry an amazing baker."

Shelley laughed, looping her arms about his waist when he reached for her, cuddling her with one arm. She had to tilt her head back to see his face because he was so much taller than she. "You didn't know I was a baker at the time."

"No, but I knew you could cook," he reminded her. He took another bite of cookie. "What brings you out here at this hour?"

Shelley smiled sheepishly. "I owe you an apology."

"Oh?" Even though he hadn't moved a muscle, Shelley sensed his sudden withdrawal. No doubt about it, she had hurt him when she'd refused to go along on his trip.

"I'm sorry for being such a wet blanket when you asked me to go along to meet the electricians." She bit her lip. "I get so focused on growing my business, that sometimes it's all I think of. I wasn't considering your feelings at all, so I apologize."

"Thanks." He was very still.

"And if you still want me, I'd like to go with you."

His arm shifted, and he drew her around to face him. "You would?" He looked so eager that she felt even worse than she had earlier.

"Yes. Shall I find a hotel?"

"That would be great." He looked down at her, eyes searching her face. "But what about your work? And the kids?"

"The kids—and the dog—are no problem. And I'll either find someone to step in for me at the Cove or I'll bake them something ahead of time." She shrugged. "I can make it work."

The smile on Dan's face, she thought as she made her way back to the house, was worth every minute of the hassle it was going to be to pull all this together.

Back in the kitchen, she pulled the baking sheet of dough strips from the refrigerator. She picked up the first strip of lattice, laying it carefully across the center of the pie before laying a second one across the middle to form an X. Then she worked methodically out to the edge, lifting every other row, laying down a strip and unfolding, lifting the next row, laying down a strip and unfolding and unfolding. When she got to the end, she spun the pie and repeated the process quickly and efficiently. It really didn't take long at all once she got started. The secret was to chill the lattice before beginning.

While the pies were baking, she got online and began to look for a hotel they could afford. The prices made her wince, but she finally found a good deal at a modest hotel that got excellent reviews. Just as good, it served a continental breakfast, which would save them money. Mentally patting herself on the back, she made the reservation.

Now only kids, dog, and baking help to figure out, she thought. *I'll think about that tomorrow.*

★   ★   ★

Margaret was having trouble working on Thursday morning. She had tried to reach Matt Beauregard several times yesterday, to no avail. She'd read over the merchandising addendum to her contract carefully, and there wasn't a word in there about book covers. She just couldn't imagine his neglecting to mention that to her.

The telephone number she had was not Matt's personal cell, which she had not realized until yesterday. Instead, it was a company line, because each time she called, it rang four times and then went to voice mail, instructing her to leave a message. Someone would return her call as soon as possible.

She'd left a message. She'd left *several* messages. But no one had called her back yet.

She glanced at her silent cell phone, checking the time. She and Allan were scheduled to have a parent conference with the teacher who ran Adelaide's class at the community center. She still had about thirty minutes before she had to be there, and the drive would take less than ten minutes. Maybe Matt would call before she left.

She walked back over to her easel. She had been trying something new with oils earlier, and now she had to let it dry before she could begin the next section.

She'd forgotten why she preferred acrylics, but she remembered now. Oils took *so* long to dry.

Across the studio, her cell phone rang. Margaret made a mad dash for it. "Hello?" *Let it be Matt, let it be Matt.*

"Hi, Margaret."

"Hi, Diane. How are you?" The adrenaline left Margaret's body in a whoosh, leaving her feeling like a balloon with a hole in the rubber.

"I'm fine, but I'm afraid I have bad news."

"Oh?"

"When I went to the post office this morning, Bernie Lanninger told me he heard August Jackson is in the hospital with pneumonia." Bernie was the postmaster. "One of the postmen lives across from Augie, and I guess he talked to the EMTs."

"Oh no. Poor dear man."

"I feel terrible. He's been coughing the last few times we spoke, and I wish I'd insisted he go to the doctor. He's so lively it's easy to forget he's closer to ninety than eighty, you know?"

"I do know," Margaret assured her. "But you can't blame yourself, Diane. Augie sees a lot of people in the course of a day, and apparently no one else intervened either."

"He didn't *look* sick," Diane said. "He just sounded bad."

"Pneumonia can be sneaky. I guess we'll have to postpone our visit to look at that book now."

"Yes, I guess we will," Diane agreed sadly. "And boy, do I hate waiting!"

Margaret chuckled at that. "You and me both!" After a few more exchanges, they ended the call.

It was time to go to Adelaide's conference. Margaret was intensely disappointed that she hadn't heard from Matt yet, but she was going to have to put it out of her head, she decided as Allan parked the minivan in the community center parking lot.

On the sidewalk he took her hand and they walked together to find the meeting. "What do you suppose they're going to tell us? I had no idea they had parent conferences for these types of workshops."

"I don't think they do," Margaret said slowly. "When I received the call, I got the impression this teacher wanted to speak specifically with us."

"Oh boy. That doesn't make me feel better. You don't suppose she could have gotten into some sort of trouble, do you?" His tone suggested the idea was unthinkable, and Margaret agreed.

"Of course not. Our Adelaide? When have we ever been told something bad about Adelaide?"

"You have a point." Allan smiled and squeezed her hand. "Thanks. I feel better."

"I don't," Margaret told him. Despite her best intentions, she hadn't been able to put the book cover fiasco out of her head. "I've called Lighting the Way at least four times, and no one ever answers the phone, not even during normal business hours. I've left messages, and not one has been returned."

Allan frowned. "That's really odd. I liked Matt, didn't you?"

Margaret nodded. "I trusted him. This is terribly disappointing."

"Hi, Margaret and Allan," Penny Tyler, the director of the special-needs program, greeted them as Allan pulled open the glass doors. "It's nice to see you again."

There was a second, younger woman in a pretty leaf-pattered blouse neatly tucked into a knee-length khaki skirt with her. Seeing them, she held out her hand. "I'm Annalee Sutter. I'm teaching the life skills class that Adelaide is enrolled in."

"Is something wrong?" Allan blurted out the words, and Miss Sutter looked surprised. Margaret smiled and patted his arm.

"Oh no. Not at all." Annalee looked chagrinned. "I'm sorry if you've been alarmed. I should have told you this was to discuss something good."

"Oh, that's a relief," Margaret said.

Annalee nodded. "Adelaide is very adept. She's catching on really well in the budgeting class." Annalee went on to describe how several of Adelaide's recent assignments had impressed her with their thoroughness. "In fact, she's far more skilled than most of our students and we thought you might want to consider looking into classes for her at the community college in the fall. I think she could handle some of the special classes offered there—beginning finance, computer skills, office management, things like that. Another thing I'd like to discuss with you is driving—"

Driving? "No," Margaret said in a definite tone. "She's enjoying this class. It's been great for her and I'd be happy to consider these other classes, but I just can't imagine Adelaide driving."

"Her capabilities might surprise you."

"But what about her reflexes? Her reaction time isn't the best."

Annalee nodded. "That's true of many of our students. But practice often improves that."

"I'd be concerned about her decision-making skills under pressure," Allan said, frowning.

"Again, that's a good reason to give her plenty of practice."

Margaret and Allan both were silent for a moment. At last, Margaret said, "I don't think we're quite ready to consider a class that teaches driving. Why don't we finish the finance courses before we make any other decisions?"

"That's a good idea." The teacher inclined her head. She gathered her papers and got to her feet. "Thank you for coming in." She extended a hand and shook each of theirs. "It was nice to meet you. I'm sure I'll see you at the end-of-session open house we hold for parents."

Margaret nodded, and Allan said, "Yes, we already have it on the calendar."

But as they walked back to the car, Margaret looked at her husband. "I feel like a student who disappointed the teacher."

Allan laughed, but it quickly faded. "I know. I never thought of teaching Adelaide to drive."

"I know the finance classes are very useful, but she's never going to get a driver's license."

Allan, oddly, didn't respond. He got in and fastened his seat belt in a thoughtful silence.

Chapter Eleven

Beverly had made plans to walk with Shelley at noon on Thursday.

She had just come out of her house in time to see Shelley walking down the street with Prize gamboling at her side. The young blonde wore jeans and a hooded sweatshirt that read: "Go ahead, bake my day."

"Good afternoon," Shelley called. "Isn't it a glorious day?"

It was indeed. "It's so nice not to have to wear three layers plus a heavy coat." Beverly knew it would be chillier on the beach, but the navy fleece peacoat over her roll-necked casual cotton shirt should keep her plenty warm.

"No children?" Beverly had expected Shelley to have a stroller and a preschooler as well.

"Adelaide's with them," Shelley replied. "And Allan is right down the street if she needs help."

Beverly smiled, thinking back a year to when she'd first met Shelley. The younger woman wouldn't have left her children at all, much less with a babysitter with Down syndrome. "Adelaide's very capable. I'm sure she'll be fine."

"So what's new with you?" Shelley asked.

Beverly thought for a moment. "I survived my first choir rehearsal. And thank goodness I didn't have to play the *Messiah*. I have another week to practice."

"How was it working with Maddie? She's so...so capable."

"That she is," Beverly replied. "She's very focused, but we got a lot done. And the choir members adore her."

"Figures," Shelley said glumly. "Just one more thing Maddie does well. When God was handing out gifts and talents, she must have gone through the line twice. At least."

"I'm sure it seems that way, but I imagine there are things Maddie doesn't do well either," Beverly said gently.

"Such as?"

"Relax," Beverly said promptly. "Would you want to take a vacation with her?"

"Never," Shelley said in a horrified tone.

Beverly chuckled. "Me either. I like her, but she's really driven."

"I was going to say competent."

"That too, but she almost seems to feel compelled to plan, organize, and succeed. I don't think it's a very comfortable way to live. Anyway, choir rehearsal went much more smoothly than I'd feared."

"That's great." Shelley sounded genuinely delighted. "Did I tell you Dan has finally found a career he wants to pursue?"

"A career?" *Not just a job, thank goodness.*

"He's decided to become an electrician."

"Won't he have to go to school for that?"

Shelley shook her head. "That's the great part." Beverly listened as Shelley explained the apprenticeship program to her.

"You're kidding," she said when Shelley had finished. "That's amazing. What a great program. I'm so happy for you both."

Shelley nodded. "It's certainly a relief knowing that we won't have to cut our budget back any further." She grimaced. "When he first told me, he asked me to go with him to visit the electrician he's going to apprentice with..." Her voice trailed off miserably. "And I said no."

"You said no?" Beverly tried to keep her voice neutral, but it seemed to her that it would have been a very supportive action if Shelley accompanied him.

They crossed the promenade and walked into the sand, but instead of walking up the beach as they often did, Shelley asked, "Can we walk the other way?"

"Sure." Beverly turned and they began walking just above the tide line. It was low tide, apparently, because the sand was wet and packed from wave action for several yards farther back than the water was presently reaching.

They walked in silence for a moment, and then Shelley said, "When you get married, nobody tells you how hard it can be."

"I know. There should be a manual." She thought of her deceased husband Will and the strain that had been between them so often.

Shelley giggled. "This visit he's making is an overnight trip, and I didn't want to take time away from my business.

But I changed my mind when I thought about it, so I'm going to go with him."

"I'm glad you changed your mind. I'm sure Dan appreciates all the support you can give him. A completely new career is a little intimidating." As she well knew.

"Maybe." Shelley sounded doubtful. "He's really excited. I'll get excited once all the arrangements are made. I still have to find a babysitter."

"Overnight? Why don't you ask Dan's parents? Frances seems to love having them." Beverly had gotten to know Dan's mother a little when they worked together on a fund-raiser.

"She does. I just don't want to always rely on her."

Beverly suspected Shelley's reluctance had more to do with her prickly relationship with her mother-in-law, but it wasn't her business.

"I also have to figure out what I can bake that won't get dry or stale for two days. And I'm going to have to work some extra hours the day before we leave so I have enough baked goods to get the Cove and my other clients through two days."

A seagull wheeled overhead, and Beverly eyed him narrowly, all too aware of the bird's potential to drop a bomb on her head. She was certain they flew off laughing when they did it too. The gull landed and followed them along the beach for a bit, until Shelley gave Prize more lead. The dog rushed the bird, which launched into the air with a loud screech and flew off.

During the action, Beverly had been considering Shelley's last statement. "Are there any bakeries in the towns around us?"

Shelley's forehead wrinkled as she thought out loud. "There's Atlantic Baking Company, there's the Pastry Garden, there's the Brown Bag...there might be more, but I can't think of them."

"Are any of those very small businesses just starting out?"

Shelley shook her head. "Not really. They're almost all located in an actual bakery with a café right there." She laughed. "As opposed to little ol' me in my kitchen."

"Little ol' you is doing just fine," Beverly assured her. "Is there anyone similar to you in Rockland?"

Shelley shook her head. "I'm pretty sure they're all bigger. They would provide baked goods, but they'd probably charge me for it. Wait a minute." She held up a finger. "There's a woman in South Thomaston who works out of her house. She does a lot of wedding cakes, I believe, but she also caters events. Why?"

"I was thinking that perhaps you could approach another baker about an exchange of goods. If she provides pastries for you for this one day, you'd do the same for her."

Shelley was silent for a moment. Then her smile bloomed, wide and pretty. "That's a *great* idea! Oh, I hope she's willing. An exchange of services. Why didn't I think of that before?"

Beverly had to laugh. "Because you've got a million other things to juggle?"

"Oh, right." Shelley joined in her merriment.

They had walked quite a way down the beach by then. "Shall we turn back?" Beverly asked.

"Sure, but hold on a minute." Shelley pointed to the dunes. "Isn't this roughly the place on the map that the other Marble Cove was located?"

Beverly paused and looked toward the lighthouse, measuring the distance with her eyes. "Probably. Why?"

"Just wondering. I thought maybe there'd be some sign if there had been buildings here before."

"What kind of signs did you expect to find?"

"I don't know. Foundations, maybe? Just part of one little wall, would that be too much to ask?"

Beverly laughed. "Jeremiah Thorpe drew that map in the eighteenth century. I doubt there'd be much left."

"You never know," Shelley said stubbornly. "Like Diane said, the shoreline would have been out much farther— you've seen maps of how much it's eroded. Down on Hatteras Island in North Carolina, they actually moved the lighthouse about three thousand feet inland a decade ago."

Beverly had forgotten Shelley was a font of lighthouse knowledge. "They *moved* it? How do you move a lighthouse?"

"*Ve-e-e-ry* carefully." They both laughed, and Shelley said, "I'll show you sometime. Dan gave me a book about it for Christmas the year we were engaged."

"I'd love to see it."

"And I'd love to find some sign of that town, if it really existed. But we can't disturb the dunes, anyway, and there's probably tons of sand on top of anything that remains."

★   ★   ★

When Margaret got home from the gallery that evening, the house smelled delicious. Allan had made a lentil casserole. "Dinner's going to be in about ten minutes," he said.

"Perfect," Margaret said. She shucked out of her coat and hung it up, then headed for the filing cabinet in the room she used as a home office. She knelt and pulled open a drawer, removing the folder that contained her contract with Lighting the Way. Such as it was.

The contract was only three pages. It was couched in such legal mumbo-jumbo that Margaret wasn't sure she even understood it, but she didn't see one word about permission to use her work on book covers. A fourth page contained a separate agreement for the merchandising to which she'd agreed.

Sighing, she carried it down to Allan. "Read this." She thrust it at him, taking the pot holders from him just as he prepared to slide the casserole out of the oven.

She carried the casserole to the trivet Allan had placed on the table and carefully set it down. It needed a few minutes to cool, the recipe had said.

Behind her, paper rustled. "I don't see anything pertinent, but maybe I'm missing something," Allan said.

Margaret sighed. "I sure wish Matt would return my calls. Do you think he could be avoiding me?"

"I can't imagine that. He's a great fellow," Allan reminded her. "It's only been three days since you discovered that cover. He might be on vacation or taking personal time for something."

"He should still check his voice mail," Margaret grumbled.

"Then it wouldn't be a vacation," Allan pointed out, smiling. Raising his voice slightly, he called, "Adelaide. Dinner!"

There was a thump from overhead, and they could hear their daughter walking toward the steps. In a few moments, she appeared, going to the sink to wash her hands. Margaret and Allan did the same, and then they sat down to offer grace and have their supper as a family, a practice they had begun when Adelaide was a baby and continued. Unless something interfered, they made it a habit to eat together and share the details of their days.

Tonight, the casserole was barely on their plates when Adelaide said, "Mom and Daddy, I want to ask you something."

Both parents gave her their attention. Margaret could see Allan smiling, and she braced herself for the inevitable "Can I get another kitty?"

"I want to live with my friends. Can I move in with them?"

Margaret was stunned. "Of course not. Honey, you already have a home here."

Tears sprang to Adelaide's eyes. "But I want to live in my own place, like my friends." A fat tear rolled down her cheek.

Allan cleared his throat. "Honey, your mom and I will need some time to think about your question. That would be a very big change for all of us." He paused. "You wouldn't have supper with us every day, like you do now."

"I'd have supper at *my* house, with roommates." The tears began to flow. "Even after you think, you're going to say no." She pushed back her chair, awkwardly pushed it in to the table, and walked from the room, head down, shoulders even more slumped than they normally were.

There was a hush in the kitchen after she left. The clock on the wall ticked loudly; Adelaide's footsteps could be heard as she ascended the hall and went back into her room. No door slammed, for which Margaret was grateful.

Allan's eyes met hers. "I didn't see that coming."

"I didn't either. But I suppose we should have," Margaret said. "All she talks about is her friends who live together in that group home. I imagine it sounds very exciting to her."

"Probably." They lapsed into glum silence.

Margaret felt absolutely terrible about hurting Adelaide's feelings. She hadn't intended to blurt out that edict, but she'd been so shocked.

"I want to live with my friends. Can I move in with them?"

No! You're my baby, was her first instinctive thought. Unfortunately, that had translated itself into an equally thoughtless response. Hesitantly, Margaret said, "It has never occurred to me that Adelaide wouldn't always live with us."

Allan's face looked so sad. "I never thought about it either. We've always been so happy."

"I suppose we have to accept that Adelaide is growing up. We wanted her to be as normal as possible..."

"So we shouldn't complain," Allan finished the thought.

"She's twenty-five years old," Margaret said. Adelaide's birthday was less than two weeks away. "This is a good thing, really."

"A good thing," echoed Allan.

Then why did it feel so bad?

CHAPTER TWELVE

Diane had worked on Thursday. She and Justin had lunch together and spoke of nothing important. Certainly not the questions that were burning on the tip of her tongue. ·

In the afternoon, Justin did PT on the living room floor, ending with one hundred push-ups and one hundred sit-ups. "I don't have to do quite that many for the APFT—"

"Whoa. Civilian here."

"Army Physical Fitness Test. But if I do a hundred of each every day, it feels a little easier when I stop at seventy-seven or eighty-two."

Diane stared at her son. "You do this *every day*?"

"Just about. Some days I also do weight training, and every day but Sunday I run."

"You make me look like a sloth."

Justin laughed. "I never saw a sloth that looked like a whirlwind of energy when she got moving."

He looked like his former carefree, happy self again for a moment, teasing her. But then the moment was gone, and he was too serious, too sober. She might have asked him to talk to her then, to tell her more, but he went for a run.

That evening, however, there was no place for him to run *to*. She finished up the supper dishes and walked into the living room to find him desultorily flicking through the television channels, stopping at an early season baseball game between the Red Sox and the Orioles.

She sat down in a chair adjacent to his seat sprawled on the couch, and they watched the game in silence, punctuated only by Justin's occasional critique of the Sox. *Armchair quarterback,* she thought fondly, even though football wasn't the sport in question.

Three and a half hours and nine innings later, the Sox squeaked by the Orioles 4-3 in a game that mirrored their last encounter of the season before.

"Yes." Justin pumped a fist. "Take that, O's. Now who's crying?"

Diane laughed as he turned off the television. "It's a good thing I moved out here and not south. What would you have done if I'd pulled up stakes and moved to Maryland?"

Justin mimed good-bye, and she chuckled again. But moments later, their light expressions faded, as did their mirth.

Finally, Diane rose and came to the sofa, sitting on the far end with one leg beneath her so she was turned to face her child. "Talk to me."

Justin stirred, hunching his shoulders as if he was uncomfortable in his skin. "I love being in the army, Mom. I'm good at being a soldier, and I think I'd make a good leader. I really felt that becoming an officer was the perfect career choice for me."

Diane noted his use of the past tense. But she only nodded encouragingly.

"Goofing this up..." He swallowed, and his eyes were full of misery. "Messing this up has totally messed with my head." He gave a short, unamused bark of laughter. "*And* my career, *and* my entire future."

"What about your girlfriend?"

He shook his head. "That wasn't anything serious. She couldn't run away fast enough when she found out I was going to have to recycle." But there was a hint of bitterness in his tone that told Diane the relationship had meant more than he was willing to admit.

He stood and stretched restlessly. She wanted to ask if he'd considered other directions for his life, but she sensed it was too soon for that. With a great deal of chagrin, she acknowledged that she had no power to fix this for him. She'd been so successful at helping solve several of her friends' dilemmas that now she felt as if she was failing.

Even worse, tomorrow was Friday, and her reading began at 7:00 PM. She had a lot to do tomorrow, largely making herself look professional, but she wanted to practice reading the selection she'd chosen and make sure it was perfect.

She hated that she was so busy right now when her son needed her. But Justin was a grown man. He'd come to her because home was where she was, but also because he needed space and time away to sort out the kink in his life plan. She hadn't asked, and he hadn't volunteered, when he was leaving yet, but he was welcome to stay as long as he liked.

*   *   *

First thing Friday morning, Shelley got out of her white station wagon in front of the Cakery. She had called Liza Cramble, the owner, as soon as she and Beverly had returned from their walk yesterday and made an appointment to come meet with her.

The Cakery had a simple sign. It wasn't a café or a doughnut shop. Like Shelley, Liza had created her bakery as an Internet business. It also sounded as if a good portion of her business consisted of wedding cakes and confections, unlike Shelley's. Still, she was hopeful that they could help each other.

She knocked on the door and then stuck her head inside. "Hello?"

"Hey! Are you Shelley? Have a seat and give me just one minute." A woman leaned her head around a portable screen and grinned at her. Shelley got a glimpse of vivid blue eyes and a *very* long braid of hair flicking back briefly, before Liza disappeared again.

Now this was an interesting concept, she thought, looking around. Liza had several portable walls or boards onto which were affixed large posters of a lovely variety of wedding cakes.

Simple mahogany pillars scattered around the perimeter of the space displayed actual cakes, clearly preserved for show but striking nonetheless. In front of the large, single window hung an enormous fern. The front part of the room looked like the place where Liza spoke with clients. Two glass-fronted bakery display cases partitioned the front from the back, with several smaller palms and tall Dracaena to complete the blockade. The wooden floors had been sanded and refinished to a high sheen.

There was a pretty mahogany table and six chairs in the center of the small area. Pads of paper proclaiming the company name and contact information and a few pens were scattered over its surface, and there were several photo albums of wedding cakes and accompanying confections.

It was gorgeous. Shelley wished she had a space like it. But while it was almost necessary for this business, it certainly wasn't for Shelley's. She didn't do wedding cakes as a general rule, and she usually went to speak to her clients rather than asking them to come to her. Maybe someday . . .

But doubts crept in as she waited. What could she possibly have to offer someone with a business as successful as this? She shifted the brand-new briefcase Dan had given her at Christmas and pulled out the proposal she'd put together last night. Her little plan to swap services suddenly seemed much less feasible.

"Hi, Shelley. Sorry to keep you waiting." The woman behind the screens popped out with an enormous smile and an extended hand. "I'm Liza. Welcome to the Cakery."

Shelley smiled. "Love the name." She indicated their surroundings. "And your shop. What a pleasant place to sit and look at wedding cakes."

"Yeah, I enjoy doing cakes. It gets a little crazy sometimes, but I have so many ideas in my head that I want to try, you know? And every bride is different. Some know exactly what they want, some give you carte blanche. Most are somewhere in the middle. They sort of have an idea, but they're interested in hearing my opinion. Which is good, since I tend to have a lot of them."

Shelley had to laugh. "Brides or opinions?"

"Both!" Liza grinned, flicking her braid back over one shoulder. "So tell me what you have in mind."

"After seeing your shop, I'm not sure it's something you'll be interested in," Shelley told her. "I'm looking for someone I could trade services with. My husband wants me to go on an overnight trip with him, but I supply baked goods to a couple of locations every morning, and I don't want to miss a day."

Liza had picked up Shelley's notes and was glancing at them. "Lemon tarts, assorted breakfast pastries, chocolate chunk cookies...this wouldn't be a big deal. And yeah, I'd love to trade. I have three places with standing orders not too different from these, actually. I haven't had a day off in..." She stuffed a pencil deep into her thick hair and scratched her head. "Can't remember. So when do you need me? I don't have a specific date in mind yet, but I'll look at my calendar and see. And hey, if this works out, maybe we could do it again quarterly or something. You know, just to give ourselves a little break."

"That would be great," Shelley managed to squeeze in.

"Do you work alone? I do." If Liza paused for breath, Shelley missed it, so she just nodded as the other baker babbled on. "My nephew helps me with the wedding deliveries that I can't manage by myself, but that's it."

Half an hour later, Shelley had managed to steer Liza through all their arrangements for next week and slide out the door. With one final enthusiastic wave, Liza vanished behind her screens again.

Shelley shook her head, giggling as she walked back to her car. Now *that* was an energetic person.

At home again, she braced herself and picked up her phone. Her mother-in-law was a wonderful person but often just a little...abrasive. Shelley had really hoped not to have to call her, but it just didn't make sense to pay a babysitter for an overnight when Dan's parents would love to have the kids and wouldn't charge them a cent.

Frances was predictably thrilled. "We'd love to! When should we pick them up?" In fact, she was so delighted that Shelley felt pangs of guilt for not letting her keep them more often. They made arrangements to drop the children off at Dan's parents' house on their way out of town.

When she ended the call, Shelley set down the phone and dusted her hands together as if removing the last of something unpleasant. Now all she had to do was tell Dan.

*   *   *

By Friday afternoon, Margaret was convinced Matt Beauregard had received her messages and was deliberately avoiding her. At the gallery that afternoon, she drafted a letter to Matt and put it in an envelope. She'd give it to the postman when he came in tomorrow.

She also sent an e-mail, although she had little hope that it would be answered. And, of course, tomorrow was Saturday, and she was quite certain she'd hear nothing until the weekend had passed.

Allan had run some errands and offered to stop by the gallery to get her after picking up Adelaide from the community center. Although she usually preferred to walk for the exercise, she was anxious to get home, get dinner, and get dressed for Diane's reading tonight.

"Hi, Mom." Adelaide welcomed her the minute she climbed into the van.

"Hi, honey." She turned to Allan. "Thanks for picking me up. I'm starting to get butterflies on Diane's behalf. I want to get to the library early."

"Any word from Matt today?"

Margaret sighed. "No. I wrote a letter that I'll mail tomorrow, and I sent an e-mail."

"I guess that's all you can do for the moment," Allan said. "Unless you'd like to drive down there and try to see him in person."

The greeting card company was headquartered in Albany, New York. It was a tempting thought...but it was entirely possible that they wouldn't be able to connect with him after driving all that way. "No, I don't think so."

Glumly, she added, "We don't even know if the company still exists."

Allan gave a surprised burst of laughter. "Why don't we try to think positive? It hasn't been a week yet. I'm sure you'll hear from Matt soon."

Adelaide began to chatter then, telling them about her day. As she listened to her daughter, Margaret was struck, as she often was, by how happy her child was. Adelaide appeared to have forgiven and forgotten their tiff of the other day. Still, Margaret had been thinking about it ever since. When Adelaide paused for a breath, Margaret said, "Adelaide, I owe you an apology."

"For what, Mom?" Adelaide sounded puzzled.

"You remember when you asked about living with your friends?"

"Yeah." Adelaide sounded subdued. "You were grumpy."

Margaret almost chuckled. Trust Adelaide to distill it down to the bottom line. "Yes, I was, wasn't I? I'm sorry I was grumpy. That wasn't fair to you."

"It's okay, Mom."

"I wasn't prepared for your question," Margaret admitted. "I've been thinking about it since then. Would you like me to arrange a visit to your friends' home?"

"Yeah!" Adelaide was enthusiastic. "That would be great."

Yes, Margaret reflected. It would be, if only so that she could see this group home for herself and get a sense of how well run and clean it was, how well the girls were supervised— She cut off the thought, mentally shaking a finger at herself. Their whole tiff had begun when she'd forgotten to acknowledge that Adelaide was becoming a grown woman. That idea was going to take some time to adjust to.

CHAPTER THIRTEEN

Diane hadn't been this nervous since her wedding day. Even that hadn't been as bad. Then, she'd been walking toward the love of her life, her future. Today, she was walking toward the possibility of a lot of criticism.

What if no one liked her book? Oh, friends would say they did. But friends were required to say things like that. She'd had a few early reviews that were positive, but what if they'd lied?

What if they had? she asked herself. She had many more important concerns in her life, and the largest one was walking right beside her. It was going to be hard to set aside her worry for her son tonight.

She and Justin walked around the front of the library, where a large sign had been placed in a window earlier in the week. Now there was one on the door as well. It directed attendees along the well-lit sidewalk to the door at the left side that led to the door of the multipurpose room. Justin held open the glass door and gestured for her to precede him. Gilda Harris, the librarian, spotted them immediately. "Hello, Diane," she said warmly, walking toward them. "Please, let me take your coats. Beth is dying to show you how we've set this up."

Gilda escorted them to the front of the large room, where bookstore manager Beth Levesque was adding final touches.

"Diane!" cried Beth. "This is so exciting!" The reading was a joint effort between the Crow's Nest and the Friends of the Library. Beth originally had intended to hold it in the store, but she and Gilda quickly agreed that there simply wouldn't be enough floor space for all the people they expected. Diane wasn't so sure about that. She pressed a nervous hand to her stomach. There certainly were a lot of chairs to fill.

It was a great setup, she had to admit. Rows of chairs had been placed in a long, curving arch in front of the podium. Hiding much of the podium was a tall, gorgeous flower arrangement. Beside it were chairs for Diane and Beth, who would introduce her.

At the other side was a folding table draped in linen, with lovely gathers flowing to the floor. An arrangement of pink and lavender flowers sat at one side; an enormous stack of books at the other. A little thrill rushed through Diane as she realized those were all hers.

Leading her around to the back of the table, Beth said, "Here are pens, and I'll keep a pitcher of ice water and a glass for you. Beneath the table are more books, in case you run out."

Diane was speechless. There had to be fifty books on the table. She couldn't imagine running out!

She thanked Beth and laid her book on the podium. She'd practiced it so much that she probably didn't need the novel, but she wasn't about to be without it and suddenly go blank.

"Mom, this is great!" Justin whispered as Beth went off to tidy up the already-perfect stacks of books.

"It really is, isn't it?" Diane was dazzled.

Her son took her arm. "Check out these flowers. Aren't they pretty?"

Diane cast him a puzzled look, letting him lead her. "Yes, they are. I hadn't expected you to notice."

Justin only smiled. He reached into the arrangement and withdrew a small envelope that he handed to her.

Diane's eyes went wide. She slowly opened the envelope and withdrew the little white card. She read the short sentiment:

Congratulations, Mom! So proud of you. Love, Jessica and Justin.

Diane reached for Justin, hugging him close as her eyes filled with tears. "Thank you," she whispered. With all the worries and concerns eating at her son, he'd made this moment unforgettably special.

Justin chuckled. "You're welcome. We wanted you to know how proud we are of you. Jess is so sorry she can't be here. She's working on a big case for one of her firm's top attorneys, and he scheduled a meeting for tonight." Justin made a face to show what he thought of that. Then he sobered. "Dad would be proud too, I know. He's probably driving every angel in heaven crazy, saying, 'Look down there. That's my wife!'"

Diane smiled through her tears, thinking fondly of Eric. Justin was right. He would have been so proud. She wanted to sob, but she pressed her hand against her mouth until the urge passed. "Thank you," she said again, squeezing Justin's arm. "Now you have to excuse me. I've got to go to the ladies' room and repair the makeup I'm sure just ran all over my face."

In the restroom, she blotted her eyes, carefully touching up her mascara and eyeliner with the emergency kit she'd thrown into her bag at the last minute, powdering her nose and making certain there were no telltale streaks from tears. Maybe tonight would take Justin's mind off his problems for a little while. He seemed to be carrying such a heavy burden.

She had barely returned when Margaret, Allan, and Adelaide entered. "Look, Adelaide, we're Diane's first fans," Margaret said.

Adelaide immediately ran to Diane and hugged her. "I'm proud of you."

She hadn't realized, maybe hadn't permitted herself to think, that this might be an emotional night for her. Momentarily too touched to speak, Diane rested her head atop Adelaide's for a moment before kissing the crown of her head and stepping back. "Thank you."

Shelley was right behind Allan and Margaret, and they and Justin helped Shelley carry in the light refreshments she had made. Margaret efficiently helped to set up a table at the far side of the room for the cupcake tower Shelley was creating, the platters of vegetables and fruits and accompanying dips, and the crackers and cheese. The punch bowl went at the far end, where Adelaide began setting out stacks of cups.

"Hello, Diane."

She turned at the sound of the deep, familiar voice. Leo Spangler, her veterinarian and admirer, stood right behind her holding a single incredibly lovely lavender rose just beginning to open. "Hi, Leo." She smiled as he handed her the bud. "Thank you. This is beautiful."

"As are you."

She smiled and dropped her gaze, butterflies fluttering in her stomach at the look in his eyes. Touching a petal gently with one finger, she said, "What a delicate color. It matches the arrangement my son and daughter gave me."

"Are they here?"

"Justin is. He surprised me on leave from the army." *And wasn't that the truth?*

"What a great surprise." Leo cleared his throat. "I'm looking forward to reading your book."

Diane was about to respond when she realized Justin was approaching. She drew him closer. "Honey, this is Dr. Spangler, Rocky's veterinarian."

Leo extended a hand, and she watched as the two men exchanged a firm handshake. "Call me Leo."

Justin smiled. "Justin Spencer. Nice to meet you."

"So you're a soldier." When Justin nodded, Leo said, "I did a stint in the marines. When I got out, I went to school on the GI Bill."

"I didn't know that," Diane said.

"We haven't spent a lot of time exchanging life stories." Leo sent her a quiet smile. "Yet."

"Diane?" Beth was calling to her, and it was a good excuse to leave the men. Justin had arched an eyebrow, grinning at Leo's comment, and she could feel a blush rising as she hurried away.

The room filled quickly. Diane greeted people for a time, surprised and delighted when two friends from Boston and the woman who'd been her next-door neighbor walked in.

"It was in the paper," Dolly Fleisher said. "We couldn't believe it, but when we thought about it, we could. Congratulations!"

More people poured in: Beth's husband Ham Levesque, Sara Silverthorn, and a large contingent of ladies from the Friends of the Library. Lee Waters from the Pet Place and his mother Evelyn, mayor of Marble Cove. Brenna McTavish and Shelley's boss Rusty from the Cove, her neighbors Fred and Cindy Little, and Gerald Kimball from the newspaper. A large group from Diane's church, Marble Cove Community, also arrived to support her.

And then Diane saw Justin holding the door wide. Beverly escorted her father in, with Mrs. Peabody flitting along right behind them. Beverly winked at her as she directed her father and Mrs. P. into places in the front row where Margaret had reserved seats for them all. Leo, she noted, slipped into an outside aisle seat next to Justin.

The room filled quickly. By the time Beth rose to introduce Diane, every seat was filled and there were people standing in the back. Polite clapping filled the room as Beth sat down and Diane took the floor.

She took a deep breath, seeing so many familiar faces sprinkled through the crowd. "Thank you, Beth," she said. She turned to face the room, wishing she could preserve the moment forever. "And thank you all for coming. The selection I've chosen to share with you tonight..."

Chapter Fourteen

Shelley made chocolate chip pancakes on Sunday morning. She always tried to do something special for her family on Sunday mornings, and this was among everyone's favorites.

Aiden was the first to join her in the kitchen. "Good morning," she said to her son, smiling at his still-sleepy eyes.

Aiden made no reply, climbing into his seat, crossing his arms on the table, and laying his head on them. He would be asleep again, right there, in minutes, if she didn't engage that sharp little mind. "Hey, Aiden," she said, "knock-knock."

"Who's there?" His voice was muffled by his position.

"Cargoes."

"Cargoes who?" He sat up. Aiden had recently discovered knock-knock jokes and thought they were the funniest thing in the world.

"Car goes beep-beep!"

Her son began to giggle. "Knock-knock."

"Who's there?" Shelley smiled. Mission accomplished, it seemed.

"Jimmy."

"Jimmy who?" It had taken her several explanations to make him understand he needed to wait for his victim to respond before blurting out the answer.

"Jimmy some food, Mama. I'm starving!"

Shelley laughed, genuinely delighted. "Okay. I'm making chocolate chip pancakes, but if you don't want those, I can mix up some mud-covered waffles."

Aiden made a face, bouncing in his seat and shaking his head wildly to let her know what he thought of that idea. "Pancakes!"

"All right. Pancakes it is."

Dan entered the kitchen then, carrying Emma, who smiled and began to chatter and hold out her arms when she saw her mother. He came over and transferred the baby to Shelley.

Emma said, "Mama," and gave her a wet, sloppy kiss on the lips, then immediately began wriggling. "Lemme down." At nineteen months, she could say more than two dozen words and was beginning to string them together, as well as attempting to repeat nearly everything they said to her.

Shelley laughed and set her down. "Go get in your seat."

"My seat," Emma repeated as she toddled off. "My seat. My seat."

"Good morning." Shelley stretched up to give Dan a kiss; he'd been catching just a few more minutes of shut-eye when she'd gotten up to feed Prize and start breakfast.

"Good morning. What's this?" Dan picked up a piece of paper on which she'd printed out the US Army emblem with the eagle in the center.

Shelley grinned. "Diane asked me to make an army cake for Justin."

Dan whistled. "And you're going to try to reproduce this?"

Shelley shook her head. "No, dear. I *am* going to reproduce that."

"I can't wait to see how this turns out," Dan said. "He's going to be blown away."

"My seat?" Emma had turned and was looking at her father expectantly.

Dan grinned. "Sure, I'll help you get in your seat." He picked her up and set her in her booster seat. She'd begun to protest the high chair not long ago, so now she sat at a big-girl seat.

"Hey, Emma," said Aiden. "Knock-knock."

Emma clapped and looked across the table at her big brother. "Nah-nah."

"No." He shook his head. "You say, 'Who's there?'"

"Who's there?" Dan asked, intervening before there was trouble. Aiden recently had begun having conversations with Emma, but he got frustrated very quickly when she didn't respond as he expected.

"Cargo."

"Cargo who?"

Aiden frowned. He cocked his head and thought for a minute. "Mama, what's next? I forget."

Dan and Shelley exchanged a smile as she came over to whisper in Aiden's ear.

Aiden finished his joke, and the four of them sat down to breakfast.

It didn't take them long to demolish the pancakes. Dan wiped Emma's face and set her on the floor. Aiden already had slipped down and carried his plate to the sink before heading out of the kitchen.

"Dan." She waited until he looked up at her. "Your folks said they'll keep the kids overnight when we go away."

Dan glanced at her then. "What about your work? You said you can't get away." Studying his face, she realized that he hadn't really believed her when she'd told him she'd try to make arrangements so that she could go along.

Shelley picked up her plate and utensils. "I've made arrangements with another baker to swap services. She's going to provide the things I need, and at a date to be determined, I'm going to do the same for her. So I went ahead and made a hotel reservation."

Dan's whole face lit up. "That's great. I didn't think you were going to be able to work it out. Thanks, honey."

"You're welcome." Was she so married to her work she was ignoring the needs of her family? She resolved to try to be more aware of things like that in the future.

★   ★   ★

Beverly enjoyed church even more than she normally did on Sunday. For some reason, knowing so many familiar faces in the choir made her worship experience feel much more personal. Several of the choir members made a point to speak to her before or after the service, and when she told Maddie how much she had liked the offertory anthem, Maddie gave her a hug and said, "Thanks. I'll see you Wednesday night."

Beverly's father had attended church with her, and afterward, he insisted on treating her to lunch.

"You're making my favorite supper," he said, "so it's the least I can do." They went to Captain Calhoun's. There was a short wait since they weren't the only people in town who'd thought going out to lunch after church was a good idea.

Each of them had a bowl of lobster chowder, and they decided to split a lobster roll. Right after the waitress refilled Beverly's lemonade, her cell phone rang. Checking the readout, she saw it was Jeff. "Excuse me, Father."

She slid from the booth and walked out to a quiet corner near the reception desk. "Hello?"

"Hi, Beverly." Jeff's voice was warm. "How are you?"

"I'm fine, thanks. How are you?" She hadn't heard from him since Monday evening, when he'd extended the invitation to go with him to his convention. Truthfully, it had been a bit of a relief. She wasn't ready to make that decision.

"Busy," he said. "And apologetic. I thought I had to go out of town today, which is why I didn't call you. But my plans changed, and now I don't have to go away. Would you like to have dinner with me tonight?"

Beverly had promised her father pot roast; there was enough for Jeff, but she didn't feel quite ready yet to respond to his invitation "I'm sorry," she said, "I already have plans for tonight."

There was a short silence. "Shucks," he said. "How about the weekend after next? I'll be in town again then."

"I'd like that," she said. And it was true. She would miss seeing him, even though she had mixed feelings. Still, the time apart would be good. It would allow her to really think about where she wanted their relationship to go.

And about how to respond to his invitation to travel with him in the summer.

★   ★   ★

On Monday morning over breakfast, Justin grilled Diane about Leo Spangler. "He seems like a great guy, Mom," he told her. "I liked him."

"He's a very nice man," Diane said primly.

"You should go out with him next time he asks," her son advised, leaving her smiling and a little surprised that Leo had apparently shared his pursuit of her with her son.

When she entered her office and booted up her computer, she found she had gotten several e-mails from fans—she had *fans!*—in the two days since her book signing. In addition to knowing she'd given someone several hours of enjoyment, the contacts inspired her to work more steadily on her current manuscript. So steadily, in fact, that she'd barely come out of her office the rest of the day except for meals. It wouldn't do to keep her readers waiting too long.

On Tuesday, however, she took time away from her work in the afternoon to head to Sailors Memorial Hospital, several miles outside town, where August Jackson was still a patient. His illness had temporarily brought their quest for information about the old map to a screeching halt, but Diane was hoping he could tell her more about what he had found.

Sailors Memorial was a pretty building as hospitals went. Made of red brick with sparkling white painted trim, the exterior had been renovated several years ago, when they'd extended and updated the emergency department. Diane recalled what it had looked like before. She'd had to bring Jessica here with a bad case of bronchitis during one memorable summer vacation, and the large windows and long planters filled with live greenery made it a much more inviting place to visit now, she decided.

Augie's room was at the far end of a general care wing. Diane knocked at the partially open door and heard a gruff "Come in."

Pushing open the door, she found her aging friend was in a two-bed room. He didn't have a roommate at the moment.

"Hello there," she said. "I was sorry to hear you were in the hospital." She walked over to the bed and leaned down to hug Augie before pulling a visitor chair around to face the bedside so she could sit and be more at his level.

"Hi, Diane. What's the news from out there?" The old man jerked his thumb at the window. Before she could respond, he grimaced. "I'm sorry I missed your reading Friday night. I was planning to come and buy one of your books."

"No problem." Smiling, Diane reached into her bag and withdrew a copy of her book. "Here you go. I thought it might help to pass the time. When are they going to spring you from this joint, anyway?"

"I'll be here another couple of days." He gestured at the tubes and wires to one side. "IV antibiotics and nurses checking my breathing every time I yawn." He flipped over the book and began reading the back cover copy, beaming. "Thanks."

"You're welcome."

"How did the reading go?"

Diane grinned. "It was amazing. I didn't realize I had so many fans in Marble Cove."

Augie chuckled. "Of course you have fans here. That's what we do. We support our own."

Diane nodded her head. "So I've learned." She cleared her throat. "Augie, I wanted to ask you some questions about that book you found with historical information in it that might help us solve our map mystery."

"I have a better idea. Why don't you take the key to my house and get the book? It would be easier to show you than to tell you, and I don't know for sure how much longer I'll be stuck in here."

The old man shifted and pointed to the closet along one wall. "Find my wallet. My key's in there."

Diane rose and opened the closet, holding up a key a few moments later. "Is this the one?"

"That's the one," Augie declared. "It's the key to the back door. Go in through the kitchen, through the doorway to the right, and that's my living room. The book's on the table right beside my chair."

"What's the title? I don't want to bring the wrong book."

Augie chuckled, but quickly stopped, as the action made him begin to cough. Breathless, he held up a finger. "That hurts," he said when he'd gotten his breath back. "Anyhow, you shouldn't have trouble recognizing it. It's called *A Pictorial History of Marble Cove*. It was published in 1922, but it contains photographs from the mid-1800s as well as a couple of illustrations, and people's recollections."

CHAPTER FIFTEEN

When Diane left the hospital, she only drove about a half mile before making another stop. The Butcher Shoppe was a large, one-story white building with a green-and-white striped awning above the front door. It offered prime beef, pork, veal, lamb, and poultry, and organic options of all of the same. Homemade sausage, smoked meats, specialty sauces for baking and grilling, homemade soups and breads, and a terrific selection of imported cheeses were also available. Locally caught seafood had its own display case, and the shop boasted an unusual selection of beverages.

She'd discovered it years ago while vacationing, and she'd been delighted to see that it was still open and apparently thriving. Even through the winter, she had noticed a steady stream of customers, and she knew in the summer that one could wait in line for twenty minutes or more to be served.

Today was Justin's thirty-first birthday, which just seemed impossible. It seemed only yesterday, sometimes, that she'd had two young children, a busy career, and a loving husband. Had she appreciated how lucky she had been? She liked to think so, but until she had been diagnosed with cancer, she suspected she had taken an awful lot of life's little joys for granted.

First she stopped at the meat counter for Porterhouse steak, which she knew was one of Justin's favorites. Then wild rice and chanterelle mushroom soup caught her eye, as did a loaf of sweet raisin bread she knew Justin would love.

Loaded down with her purchases, she returned to the car and headed homeward. She had bought Justin an e-book reader and a gift card so that he could download some reading material immediately, as well as a Dresden blue T-shirt with a silk-screened image of the lighthouse with "Marble Cove, Maine," written across it in block letters. It was becoming more and more difficult to shop for her son, who lived in barracks on post so he could save his money. She thoroughly approved of that, but it certainly limited any purchases of house, garden, or kitchen types of gifts.

When she got home, she went into the house with her purse and the groceries, setting them on the counter. Justin wasn't in the living room, so she walked back through the hallway and peeked into the guest room. Her son lay fast asleep with Rocky curled up on the rug by the side of the bed.

Concern rose. It seemed to her that Justin had been sleeping an awful lot lately. Could he be struggling with depression? Or was it simply that when he was home he felt free to relax in a way he probably didn't have time for in his normal routine?

She turned and walked back to the kitchen, hearing the soft pad of Rocky's paws across the floor as he rose and followed her. "You hungry, buddy?" she asked.

It was nearly five o'clock. She had no idea how the dog knew what time it was, but when she worked past five without taking a break, he invariably would come and shove his head beneath her arm. Normally, it would indicate that he wanted her to pet him, but at that time of day, it was clearly more of a "Hey! Get up and get my supper," type of nudge.

After filling Rocky's bowl and setting it down, she got on with her own dinner. She'd found an interesting-sounding recipe for a steak marinade using soy sauce and cocktail sauce. It got rave reviews on a cooking Web site, and she thought it would make a nice birthday dinner. Quickly mixing up the marinade, she placed both steaks in a zippered plastic bag and poured the marinade in, then placed the bag in the refrigerator.

Next, she walked over to Shelley's and rang the doorbell. Prize began to bark, and as Shelley approached the door, she could hear her telling the little dog to sit and stay. They'd been working hard on her obedience training, and it was paying off.

"I was expecting you!" Shelley said when she opened the door. "Come and see. I think it turned out really well."

Diane followed Shelley back to the kitchen. When she'd realized Justin would be home over his birthday, she'd begged Shelley to make her a cake with an army theme.

"What kind of army theme?" Shelley had asked immediately.

Diane had looked at her blankly. "I don't know...he branched military intelligence. I do know that much."

"What does that mean? 'He branched'?"

"There are different specialties, I guess you could call them. Different branches, like aviation, field artillery, infantry. A soldier 'branches' one area to concentrate on." Diane had laughed ruefully. "I'm ashamed to admit I know very little about what my son does."

"Military intelligence. He probably can't talk about most of his work. Let me do some research," Shelley had said. "I'll come up with something and run it by you if I'm unsure."

"Okay. I'm sure whatever you do will be wonderful," Diane had assured her friend.

Now, as she stepped into Shelley's kitchen, Dan was standing in front of the counter holding up a piece of poster board.

Diane looked at him, puzzled, until Shelley came in behind her and said, "We both wanted to be here when you saw the cake."

"Shell did an awesome job," Dan volunteered. "Take a look." He swept the poster board aside with a flourish. When Diane got a look at the cake her friend had designed for Justin, she was speechless.

It was a round layer cake. The entire top was decorated with an army insignia, an eagle in the center on an army-green background. Shelley had reproduced the design in stunning detail. In the center, the eagle held items in each talon. His wings were outstretched, and there was a snake in his beak. Above his head was some sort of round star emblem. The eagle was surrounded by a double row of gold icing. Not yellow, Diane noted, but shiny gold, inside of which UNITED STATES ARMY was printed in official-looking block letters with two stars placed at the four and eight o'clock positions. The gold wasn't just a line, but an incredibly detailed design that looked like braid.

And then she noticed the sides. On a field of ivory, American flags waved. Not decals, but flags that Shelley had painstakingly recreated in icing. In between the flags were the blue and gold insignia of military intelligence, a four-pointed star beneath something that looked vaguely like a flower—although she would never say that out loud. Diane recognized the emblem because she, Eric, and Jessica had flown down to Fort Huachuca in Arizona when Justin completed his training, and she had "pinned her son," attaching the symbol of his success to his uniform. They'd been so proud.

Tears rose, partly at the sweet memory, and partly at the unbelievable amount of work her dear friend had put into a simple birthday cake. "This is..." Her voice wavered, and she stopped. "Shelley, this is incredible. Amazing. I've never seen anything to equal it." She turned and embraced her friend, still fighting tears. "Justin will never believe you created this right here in your own kitchen. It looks so professional!" And then she realized what she'd said. "Oh.

Duh. You *are* a professional. Even so, this is much better than any other decorated cake I have ever purchased."

Dan nodded. "She's got a gift, doesn't she?"

"She sure does. Margaret isn't the only artist in our gang."

Shelley flushed pink with pleasure. "I'm pleased with the way it turned out."

Diane smiled at her friend's modest statement. And then panic rose. "We can't eat this!"

Shelley and Dan both laughed.

"Of course you can," Shelley said. "It was meant to be eaten."

Dan held up a digital camera. "Besides, we took a million pictures of it."

"You have to let me pay you," Diane said. "This is too much work to do for nothing."

"Oh no. No payment of any kind. No cash, no goods, no services." Shelley shook her head adamantly. "I'm going to add this to my portfolio. I need more things like this, so it was just an excuse to play."

Shelley set the cake in a large box, and Dan carried it across the street, with Diane holding the doors open. Justin was sitting on the couch when they came in, and Diane pointed a stern "Mom" finger at him. "Do not move."

Justin grinned. "Gee, Mom, what's in the box?" He pretended that he was going to rise, and Diane shrieked, giggling.

"Don't you dare! I haven't had a chance to surprise you in *years,* buddy."

Dan had already ducked into the kitchen with the box, which he'd set on the counter. As he came back out, he walked over and extended his hand to Justin. "Happy birthday. Thirty-one isn't so scary when I see what's on the other side."

Justin laughed. "Thanks, man. Double thanks, I guess."

As Dan took his leave, Justin rose and followed Diane into the kitchen. "I won't look in the box, I promise. I was going to go for a run. Do we have a dinner plan?"

"We do," Diane said. "We can eat around seven. That should give you plenty of time for a good run and a shower."

While he was gone, Diane scrubbed two large potatoes and put them in the oven to bake. Then she chopped and tossed a baby spinach salad, put it in two plates and sprinkled each with hard-boiled egg and bacon. She set the covered salads in the fridge and checked her watch. Good.

She had a gorgeous Fostoria Candlewick pedestal cake plate and dessert plates that had been a wedding gift thirty-odd years ago. Getting them out, she washed them in warm soapy water and dried them gently. Then she very carefully lifted Shelley's masterpiece and set it on the cake plate.

She stood back and shook her head. No way could she bear to deface that with candles. It would just have to be a candleless birthday this year. Placing the platter in the back corner of the counter, she set the box in front of it to shield it from Justin's eyes. It was almost too tall to be concealed, but if she kept Justin out of the food prep area, he wouldn't see it.

Quickly, she set the table, checking the time again. She didn't want it to feel too formal, so she used her everyday ceramic plates and flatware. She had some leftover birthday napkins, so she dug those out and, with a grin, added them as well.

Next she returned to the potatoes, pulling them from the oven, cutting them lengthwise in half and scooping out the potato. Quickly she added butter, Parmesan and American cheeses, sour cream, and a touch of garlic salt. When the potato mix was thoroughly blended, she spooned it back into the potato halves, garnished them with paprika, and returned them to the oven to finish baking.

Justin came in the front door then. "Hey."

"Hi, honey. Nice run?"

"Yeah. I passed your friend Beverly. She looks like she's serious about running."

Diane nodded. "She gets in a couple miles several times a week, at least."

"Does she do marathons?"

"Not to my knowledge." But Diane knew that there was probably a lot she had yet to learn about her friend. Beverly was a very private person. Pulling information out of her was like mining for gold. A whole lot of work for a very small result most of the time, although occasionally you hit pay dirt.

Justin headed for the bedroom. "I'm going to grab a shower. How long do I have?"

"About fifteen minutes," Diane said.

"Perfect."

While Justin was still occupied, Diane got into her bedroom closet and got out the gifts she'd wrapped for him, piling them at the far end of the kitchen table from their place settings. Next, she went out to turn on the grill to high.

Retrieving the steaks from the fridge, she carried the bag outside and used tongs to pull each steak out and place it on the grill. After five minutes, she turned them over.

Justin came into the kitchen just as she carried the steaks in on a platter she'd warmed in the oven. Rocky came over, his nostrils twitching, clearly interested in helping her. "Go lie down, boy," she told him. "This meal isn't for you." He watched for another moment, but eventually, he went and lay down on the new dog bed he'd received for Christmas, one filled with polyfiber and cedar that smelled a lot better than *eau de dog*.

She set the platter on the table and laid a meat fork to one side, then got her salads out, uncovered them and added croutons. Finally, she drizzled a honey vinaigrette over the top and set them on the table, retrieved the potatoes in a pretty serving dish, and said, "Voilà. Let's eat."

"Mom, this looks amazing." Justin had taken his seat and was silently watching her buzz around the kitchen. "You didn't need to go to all this trouble."

"You're right," she said. She kissed him on top of the head, and then seated herself to his left. "But I wanted to."

"I *love* a good Porterhouse," he said.

"I know. Happy birthday, but don't get used to it." They laughed together. She noticed, though, that Justin's amusement faded quickly, and he was back to his too-silent, too-sober self again after the moment.

She filled the silence throughout the meal by catching Justin up on the friends and neighbors he had met, her last chat with his sister, the latest lighthouse news, and the progress of the new book she was writing. He responded, but she could see that his heart wasn't in it.

So she forged ahead. She cleared the table and moved the pile of gifts closer to him. Then she got the cake. Justin looked at her, a half smile on his face as she approached.

"Ta-da! Happy birthday." She set the cake in front of him.

Justin's mouth fell open. "Holy—*cow*, Mom, where did you get this?"

Diane smiled, appreciating that he remembered to moderate his "army barracks" language. "Shelley made it. Can you believe it?"

Justin was shaking his head. "This is...I've seen a lot of people get army cakes from their families, but I've never seen *anything* like this. She's a genius."

"I agree. Although she'd never believe you."

Diane had gotten out her camera and taken several photos. Justin had a smartphone, and he had her take a few shots of him with the cake that he could send to friends. When they had finished, both of them were still studying the cake, noting detail after detail of exquisite workmanship in silence.

Justin touched one gentle finger to the eagle. "The thing is," he said in a low voice, "I may not stay in the army, Mom."

To say Diane was shocked would have been a massive understatement. For a moment, she struggled for words. "Really? I thought you said you could retake this test."

"Recycle," he corrected. "I'll have to take the entire course again."

"Oh." She was taken aback. "When you said it before, I guess I thought that if you retook the test and passed, you'd be fine."

He shook his head. "I'm due back from leave on the first of May. After that, I only have two months before I reenlist. If I do. I don't know, yet, if I decide to try OCS again, whether I can get into a class right away or whether I'll have to go to the end of the list and wait my turn."

Diane sighed, touching his arm. "I'm so sorry, honey. I had no idea you were wrestling with this. Are you really considering leaving the army?"

Justin shrugged miserably. "I don't know."

Diane let the silence lay for a moment, and then she asked, "What would you do if you got out?"

He shrugged again. "I don't know. I've got strong computer skills, so I could probably get a job somewhere...but ever since I joined the army I've felt that it was my calling."

Diane nodded, smiling as she remembered her relief when he'd finally chosen to pursue a military career. "I know."

"I don't want to go back to enlisted for the rest of my career. I really wanted to be an officer."

"You still can, right?" she asked softly.

He nodded. "If I don't mind wasting a couple of months doing the entire course again." He leaned forward and put his head in his hands again, scrubbing them over his face after a moment. "I just don't know what to do."

"Well, you don't have to decide right this moment." Diane picked up the cake knife and held it out, handle first. "Would you like to do the honors?"

Justin was aghast. "I can't cut that!"

That made her laugh, despite her concern for her son. "That's what I said to Shelley. She says it's just cake. Plus, if we don't eat it, it'll go to waste. And after she worked so hard, I wouldn't dare disappoint her. You know she's going to ask how it was."

Justin nodded and took a deep breath. "Okay. Here goes." He made a smooth slice to the center of the cake and down, then withdrew the knife and made an intersecting cut. "Got a plate?"

Diane pushed one of the dessert plates toward him. "That's huge," she objected. "I only want about half that much."

Justin grinned and snapped his fingers. "Shucks. I guess I'll have to eat this big one then."

They savored every mouthful of cake, finding it as delicious as it was beautiful. Beneath the astonishing exterior was a deep, rich chocolate cake, and the buttercream icing was sweet and smooth.

As they ate, Justin shook his head and looked at her. "I don't know, Mom. I can't imagine myself not being a soldier." His cell phone rang, and when he pulled it out of his pocket and glanced at the readout, his face lit up. "It's Jess." He punched the button to answer the call. "Hello there."

"Happy birthday to you..." Diane could hear her daughter singing.

Justin was grinning, and when she had finished, he said, "Thanks!"

Diane got up and headed for the sink. While her kids were talking, she placed dirty dishes in the dishwasher, put away the one half of her potato that was the only food left over, other than the cake, and began to wash the things she hadn't gotten cleaned up before the meal. Justin's deep voice in the background was a pleasant counterpoint to the splash of water.

A few minutes later, Justin scraped his chair back and rose. "Jess wants to talk to you," he reported, holding out his phone.

"Okay." Diane dried her hands on a dish towel. "Would you like to throw Rocky's ball for him for a few minutes? He didn't get as much exercise today as usual."

"Sure. C'mon, boy." Justin beckoned, and after glancing at Diane and getting a nod, Rocky scrambled for the door. Justin laughed as he followed the dog.

Diane lifted Justin's phone to her ear. "Hello, honey. Thanks for calling."

"Is he outside now?" Jessica's voice was a half whisper.

"Yes." Diane glanced through the window over the sink. "He's giving Rocky a much-needed run."

"All right. So tell me what's wrong. All he would tell me is that he's soon up for reenlistment and he's trying to decide whether or not that's what he wants to do."

"That's true," Diane said cautiously. If Justin hadn't confided in his sister, it really wasn't her place to explain.

"There's more to it than that," Jess said with certainty.

Diane blew out a breath. Her daughter always had been perceptive. Very little got by Jessica. "I think," she said, "he had a disappointing or upsetting experience, and that he'll talk to you as soon as he's ready."

"Okay." Jessica sounded satisfied. "I'm glad he came home to you. I'll pray for him."

"Excellent idea. Thank you, honey." They spoke briefly of a few other matters before exchanging "I love you's" and ending the call.

Diane laid Justin's phone on the corner of the counter where he'd be sure to see it when he came in. She had never imagined him changing careers midstream.

CHAPTER SIXTEEN

Beverly's hands shook as she loaded her music into her shoulder bag on Wednesday evening. She'd been working on Handel diligently since last week's choir rehearsal and the unexpected reprieve, and she prayed that she had mastered it sufficiently. Maddie was a demanding taskmaster, despite her pleasant manner, and Beverly would feel terrible—and embarrassed—if she let her down. Thank goodness there was only one more week left after this before the regular accompanist returned.

When she stepped out the door, she groaned. It had been spitting rain off and on all day, but it had increased to a steady shower. She ducked back inside and grabbed her umbrella. All she needed was for her music to get wet!

Arriving at rehearsal, she received an even warmer greeting from the choir members than she had last week. Maddie started with a cappella warm-up scales and exercises, as she had the previous week, but soon enough she launched into rehearsal. After a quick review of some trouble spots in each piece, Maddie attacked them quite a bit more vigorously than she had last week. The choir seemed to take it in stride, and Beverly suspected that last week's gentle rehearsal had been for her benefit. This Maddie needed up-to-tempo accompaniment, and Beverly had to concentrate closely to be ready to review any time Maddie stopped the choir and announced the measure at which she wanted them to pick up and review again.

All too soon, Maddie announced, "All right, everyone. Put 'Crown Him' away and get out your *Messiah*. We went over parts last week. This week, let's give it a try." She glanced at Beverly. "Half tempo," she said, demonstrating a slow, sedate beat while the choir rustled music around.

Beverly nodded. Okay. She could do half tempo.

The first time through wasn't bad at all. Maddie stopped them frequently, making corrections and reviewing sections, adding dynamics where they weren't already noted. But all too soon, they had finished, and the choir director was giving Beverly a much faster beat. It still wasn't quite up to tempo, but fast enough that Beverly could feel her heart racing as she prepared for the opening chord.

"Haaa-le-lu-jah!" And they were off.

Beverly didn't have time to think for the rest of the rehearsal. It was all she could do keep up with her responsibilities. By the time the rehearsal finally ended, she felt like a trembling wreck.

While Maddie took prayer requests, shared two birthdays that would occur in the upcoming week, and closed with a final prayer, Beverly sat quietly, willing her hands to stop shaking.

When Maddie dismissed the choir, a number of people came up to congratulate Beverly on what a good job she was doing. So many, in fact, that she suspected Maddie might have mentioned that she was feeling a little insecure.

Maddie was still busy answering questions and chatting with people when Beverly gathered her music and her jacket and headed for the door. But as she slipped by the choir director, Maddie shot out an arm and gently caught her elbow. "Beverly. Can you give me a moment?"

"Of course." She waited until Maddie was done discussing the remaining Lenten services with Peggy Ivers.

The moment the older woman turned away, Maddie grinned at Beverly and stuck out her hand. As Beverly met the extended palm with her own, Maddie said, "Terrific job tonight!"

"Thank you." Beverly shook her head. "I was worried about the *Messiah*."

"You played it beautifully," Maddie said. "You match my tempo, and you pick up the music at whatever measure I spit out as fast as Linda does. I had no idea we had another musician so talented sitting in our congregation."

Beverly didn't know what to say. "Thank you. Have you spoken to Linda?" *Is she coming back next week for sure?*

"Not this week," Maddie told her. "She goes to the doctor next Tuesday. But she assures me that she's coming along just fine. She's expecting to be back in time for Holy Week."

Beverly stiffened her knees to prevent herself from sagging. She didn't want Maddie to see just how relieved she would feel when the regular accompanist took over again.

But Maddie must have noticed something, because she laughed and put an arm around Beverly's shoulders for a brief squeeze. "You're doing great. Stop worrying."

Easy for you to say, Beverly thought to herself as she headed for her car. Maddie Bancroft probably never worried about anything for long.

* * *

On Thursday morning, Shelley bundled Aiden and Emma up, fastened Emma into the stroller, took Prize's leash to her left hand the way she'd been shown at obedience class, and headed downtown.

Aiden would be whining about how tired he was by the time they got back, she knew. But she also knew that if the little boy didn't get some exercise, he was going to be a demon later in the day. It had rained off and on all day yesterday, and they'd been stuck inside. Today, more rain clouds were supposed to roll in by midafternoon, so if she wanted to get a walk in, they had to go this morning. If she was lucky, maybe it would wear Aiden out enough that he'd take a little nap.

There was a day when she would have felt guilty for that thought, she realized. A day when she would have spent an enormous amount of time worrying about being a good mother. She'd been fairly isolated until Diane had moved in and shaken her out of her little cocoon. Hard to believe that she hadn't even known her neighbors, Allan and Margaret and dear Adelaide, very well.

They had a delightful, pleasant walk downtown. She was teaching Aiden the difference between daffodils and tulips, and they certainly had a great many opportunities for him to identify flowers...although she had to laugh when they saw a bed of pretty pink and lavender hyacinths that completely stumped him.

Once on Main Street, she turned toward the Cove. Since she had Prize with her, she didn't want to walk into the restaurant, so she waved at Brenna, who indicated that she'd go into the kitchen and tell Rusty Shelley was outside.

Moments later, Rusty Garrison poked his head out. Friendly and low-key, Rusty had gotten his name from his hair, although there was now a good bit of silver sprinkled in with the "rust." He smiled warmly, blue eyes crinkling. "Hey, Shelley, come on in."

"No, no, I've got the kids and the dog," she demurred. "I just wanted to tell you—"

"Wait a sec." Rusty vanished, and the door banged shut.

Shelley raised her eyebrows but waited patiently.

Rusty was back in a moment, holding up two lollipops. "Sweets for your sweeties, okay?"

"Sure. What do you say?" she prompted Emma, as Rusty crouched and handed her a lollipop. Shelley saw that he'd been smart enough to bring two of the same flavor. There would be no fussing about who got what kind.

"Dank you," Emma mumbled, making Rusty chuckle.

"You're welcome, Emma."

She helped her daughter peel off the paper, while Rusty did the same for Aiden, who, she was happy to see, recalled his manners.

When the children were happily sucking on their lollipops, Rusty rose. "Sorry."

"That's okay," Shelley said smiling. "I just stopped to tell you that I found someone to fill in for me next Thursday when I go away with Dan." Although they'd be leaving on Wednesday, Thursday morning would be when Rusty needed baked goods delivered.

"That's terrific," he said. "Who'd you find? I have to confess I hadn't even started looking yet."

"Liza Cramble from over in South Thomaston. She has the Cakery."

"Oh, right. She did my cousin Helen May's wedding cake. Did a nice job too, as I recall, and it was tasty. Does she do pastries?"

Shelley nodded. She pulled a list from the diaper bag affixed to the back of the stroller. "Here's a list of the things she's going to provide. Her phone number is on here in case you want to make any changes."

"Great." Rusty glanced over the list. "Thanks, Shelley. This looks like it'll work out fine. You want me to cut her a separate check, or do you want to pay her?"

Shelley shrugged. "Go ahead and pay her. Seems easier."

Rusty nodded. "Thanks again for taking care of this. See you tomorrow."

Shelley nodded. She usually made her deliveries early in the morning before the kids were out of bed. Sometimes Dan helped her out when he had time. "See you then. Blueberry muffins are on the agenda."

"Yum. My absolute favorites." Rusty grinned and reentered the restaurant.

As Shelley paused to make sure the diaper bag was still firmly in place, Aiden wandered a few steps away and squatted, looking at something on the ground. "Mama, when do ants come back?"

Shelley hesitated. "I don't know. Probably when it gets warm. I think they hibernate in the winter." *Maybe?* She'd never really thought about it.

"Like bears hi-hi-hiberate?"

Shelley laughed. "Yes, like bears *hibernate*. Are you ready to go visit Miss Margaret?"

Aiden nodded, taking the hand she held out.

They walked to the Shearwater Gallery. As they passed one of the plate glass windows, Shelley saw that Margaret was in the display space creating a new arrangement. The theme appeared to be rain and flowers, very appropriate for mid-April.

She had hung two paintings that looked like they had been done by the same artist. One was a planter of pansies, and one with complementary colors was a basket filled with daffodils and crocus. Another, sitting on an easel, was of a bed of blue, yellow, white, and midnight irises, and propped against the easel's legs was a fourth painting—a gorgeous watercolor of a cottage garden on a rainy day. Low pedestals of various heights held other mediums: a blown-glass vase with a dried bouquet; a wood sculpture of a watering can done in some beautiful light wood that showed a fascinating grain; and a wooden rack with three handmade bud vases, in which she had pretty pink, white, and lavender hyacinths blooming. On the floor she'd set another sculpture of life-size ceramic barn boots with an umbrella stashed in one.

Shelley knocked on the window, and when Margaret turned, she gave the older woman a thumbs-up seal of approval.

Margaret grinned and backed out of the exhibit, waving and gesturing for them to enter.

As Shelley opened the door and maneuvered the stroller, the dog, Aiden, and herself through the entrance, Margaret asked, "Would you like me to hold the door for you?" in a wry tone.

Shelley laughed. "Sorry. I'm not used to waiting for help."

"Come on back," Margaret invited. "It's a party."

"Oh?" It wasn't until Shelley got several steps inside the door that she realized Diane and her son Justin were there as well. "Hi," she said. "Are you two having a good visit?"

"It's always good to be with one of my babies," Diane said, laughing as the tall man beside her grimaced.

Justin stepped forward, handed extended. "It's nice to see you again, ma'am."

Intellectually, Shelley knew that Diane was old enough to be her mother, and she knew that Diane had children of her own that were older than Shelley herself. But Diane seemed so lively and youthful that it was easy to forget her age, and it was always a shock to realize she had grown children. "Thank you," she said, returning the handshake. "It's nice to see you again too, Justin. But please don't call me ma'am. I always wonder who you're talking to for a moment."

Justin laughed. "Sorry. Force of habit."

Diane was smiling, but Shelley thought her expression seemed a bit strained. More than a bit, actually. What could be wrong?

"What brings you downtown this morning?" Margaret inquired.

"Just letting Rusty know I found a substitute for next week," Shelley told her.

"Oh, great," Diane said. "So you'll be able to go with Dan?"

Shelley nodded. "Would you be able to let Prize out and feed her Wednesday from noon to Thursday around the same time? We'll be home by supper time Thursday."

"No problem," Diane said. "Would it be all right if I brought her over to my house to play with Rocky?"

"Sure. You can keep her there the whole time if it would be easier," Shelley said, and Diane nodded, making an effort to smile.

"Rocky would enjoy that. They get along so well."

By now, Shelley knew Diane well enough to know that something was definitely bothering her. But it didn't seem like the time to ask. She'd have to try to catch her later.

"Shelley," Justin said, "thank you so much for that awesome birthday cake. You did an incredible job. Those emblems looked exactly like the real ones."

"You're welcome." Shelley smiled, pleased that her efforts had met with approval. "It was fun for me too, and it gave me a chance to add something new and unique to my portfolio."

"She keeps a display notebook with photos of all of her offerings," Margaret told him. "I love looking through it, but it always makes me feel like I need to go get a brownie from the Cove!"

Everyone laughed, although Shelley noticed Diane's laughter was subdued, as Justin pulled out his phone and shared some photos of the cake with Margaret.

Shelley chatted for another minute before both Aiden and Prize got restless. "I'd better get these guys out of here." In a whisper that didn't reach Aiden's ears, she said, "I'm hoping that if I wear him out enough"—she pointed at her son—"he'll N-A-P this afternoon."

Diane smiled and nodded. "I remember those days." She elbowed her son in the ribs.

Justin shrugged. "I nap in the afternoons now," he pointed out, and they all chuckled again.

Shelley crossed her fingers. "Let's hope my strategy works." She looked around the room until she saw her son. "Aiden, are you ready to go?"

CHAPTER SEVENTEEN

While Justin held the door for Shelley and her entourage, Diane turned to Margaret. "We should go too. I want to get that book from Augie's house. Would you be able to take a lunch break or meet me at the hospital sometime in the afternoon?"

"How's one o'clock? I'll get Allan to take over here for a little while."

"One sounds good. We're heading over there now. Thanks for letting us interrupt your work. I thought Justin might like to see some of the new things you've gotten in."

"Thanks for stopping by," Margaret said. She hesitated for a moment, and then she asked, "Diane, are you okay? You seem...I don't know, maybe a little 'down.'"

Diane did her best to smile. "I'm okay." But the tears that suddenly welled up from nowhere told the truth.

"Sure you are." Gently, Margaret patted her shoulder. Then she reached behind the counter and withdrew a tissue. "Here."

Diane glanced at her son, but Justin was out on the sidewalk now, still talking to Shelley. "I don't want him to see I'm upset," she said, dabbing at her eyes.

She didn't know why, but she didn't feel that she could talk about Justin's dilemma with her friends right now. She felt almost a little guilty, because most of the time they shared their tribulations as well as their triumphs. Even Beverly had begun to confide in the other three.

But this wasn't really her story to tell, and something stayed her tongue.

Margaret had been looking at her expectantly, but after a moment, she lowered her voice and said, "Justin's coming back."

Diane quickly blotted her eyes and stuffed the tissue in her pocket. She knew Margaret was curious, but she simply couldn't talk about her worries right now. Not without breaking down, which she was determined not to do in her son's presence.

"We're heading over to Augie's house now to get that book," she said to Margaret, summoning her usual smile. Or something close to it, she hoped. "I'll pick you up here at one, all right?"

"Sounds like a plan." Margaret leaned forward and hugged her. "Hang in there," she whispered. Drawing back, she said, "Justin, thanks for coming by. I'm glad you liked those new sculptures."

He nodded. "Mom will have to let me know how they sell. I'm predicting a big hit."

"I hope you're right. See you later," she called as Diane and Justin headed for the door.

As they walked along Main toward Newport Avenue, Diane said, "I'm going to walk a couple of blocks to my friend Augie Jackson's house. He's in the hospital, and he asked me to pick up a book for him. Want to walk along?"

Justin nodded. "Sure."

The two of them walked in silence for a few minutes, and then Justin said, "So Shelley's baking business is going well?"

Diane nodded. "She's been quite busy, and you saw the quality of her work yourself at my reading as well as with your cake."

"And I know Margaret is happy with her gallery and her painting."

"Yes. It was a little stressful financially early on, but I think she's got her feet under her now."

"How about your other friend, Beth? No, Beverly. Beth is the short lady from the bookstore." He grinned, shaking his head. "Since you live here now, I figure I'd better make an effort to get to know all these people you talk about so much. Beverly was at your house the night I came home, right?" He looked down. "Sorry if I was rude that night."

"You weren't rude. Beverly is leaving a government job in Augusta near the end of the month to become a full-time self-employed consultant. She'll be working from home, advising small-business owners and helping people who want to start businesses."

"That's bold."

Diane smiled. "Yes, I think she's more nervous about it than she's let on. Plus I'm sure it's going to be difficult leaving friends she's worked with for years."

They walked in silence for a moment as Diane tried to decide what to say next.

Justin beat her to the punch. But his voice sounded flat and defeated as he went on. "I thought that if I got out of the army, I might be able to start a software consulting business, or tune up computers and fix virus problems."

"That's certainly a growing market," she said carefully.

"Yeah."

They walked in silence again until they reached Augie's house. Diane didn't quite know what to say. She didn't want to be a pushy mother. After all, he was a grown man. But she did want to be there for him if he needed her input. She would wait, she decided, and not offer advice unless advice was specifically asked for.

In the week since Diane had visited Augie's house, even more of his flowers had bloomed. Tulips were beginning to show, and the garden, which had been largely whites, lavenders, and yellows, was now a riot of red, pink, orange as well.

Justin whistled when he saw it. "Whoa. And I thought you were addicted to flowers," he said, laughing.

Diane grinned. "I prefer a little more method and a little less madness. Although it does make quite a statement, doesn't it?"

Justin waited while she ducked into the little cottage. *A Pictorial History of Marble Cove* was right in plain sight where he had said it would be. Diane had to restrain herself from opening it right then and there. Augie had been such a dear to find this for them, and she knew he wanted to be "in on" any discoveries it might yield.

"Got it," she announced, holding up the tome as she emerged from the home.

They made the short walk home to Newport Avenue. Diane forced herself to set the book aside and make lunch: open-face lump crabmeat smothered in cheddar cheese, applesauce she'd made from locally picked apples last fall, and celery sticks filled with peanut butter. The latter had been one of Justin's favorites since he was a child. And leftover birthday cake, of course.

When they'd finished, Justin sat back and sighed. "That was delicious. You're going to spoil me, Mom."

It made her so happy to see him smile. "That's the idea."

"Since you made it, I'll clean it up, okay?" He pointed toward the clock on the wall. "I know you have to meet Margaret at one."

"I do. Thanks." She kissed Justin and practically danced out of the room, eager to pick up Margaret and head for the hospital. Then she turned around and backtracked. "Would you like to go along?"

Justin, hands full of plates destined for the dishwasher, shook his head. "Thanks, but you can tell me about it later. I need to work out and run, and then study a little."

"Study?"

He shrugged. "Just in case I decide to recycle. Figured I might as well increase my knowledge base of military history, you know?"

Diane nodded. "Good thinking." She waved. "See you later."

★   ★   ★

Allan had come down to the gallery and had lunch with Margaret, so when Diane pulled up out front, Margaret went right out to meet her.

"That was fast," Diane commented as Margaret fastened her seat belt.

Margaret grinned. "I can't wait to hear what Augie found. Have you peeked?"

Diane shook her head, making her dark hair tumble over one eye. "No, I could tell Augie really wanted to unveil the discovery, so I restrained myself." She glanced over. "Any news on the book jacket?"

Margaret shook her head glumly. "I called directory assistance to see if the company had another number. I even asked about a personal listing for Matt Beauregard, but no luck. I've been reduced to sending e-mails and leaving phone messages, none of which have been answered."

"Oh, rats. What now?" Diane turned the corner and headed toward the highway and Sailors Memorial.

"I don't know." Margaret was so frustrated she could scream. "I don't have the time—or the money—to go track him down. At least I'm not getting a 'this number is no longer in service' message, which would scare me even more. What do you think I should do?"

Diane was silent for a moment, her lips pursed in thought. "I hate to even suggest this," she said, "but it might be time to talk to a lawyer about your options. Even if you choose not to do anything at this time—or ever—at least you would know what to do legally."

Margaret sighed. "I was afraid you were going to say that. I hate the thought. Matt seemed like such a good person...but I sure don't understand this lack of communication." She paused. "I don't think that just any old lawyer will do, though, do you? I'm almost going to have to find someone that knows a little something about artists' contracts." She lifted her hands helplessly. "How do I do that? Google it?"

"Maybe, but why don't you start by asking some of your contacts. Louellen Lumadue or Bernadette Lassiter, perhaps?"

"Louellen might know," Margaret said. "And if not, I bet she knows people who do. Good idea. Thanks."

"Anytime." Diane smiled.

"I do not need more stress in my life right now," Margaret told her friend. "Adelaide has made friends with some girls from her class at the community center, and several of them live in a group home setting together. She thinks that sounds fantastic, of course."

"I'm sure she does."

"I told her that we would take her to visit, and I think we're going to go this Sunday. Allan and I are really interested in seeing how this whole setup works."

"Oh boy." Diane smiled sympathetically. "You do have your hands full, don't you?"

"Her birthday is next week, and I'm having a little party for her. It's Tuesday evening, and I'd love it if you could attend. Justin, too, if he's still in town. I invited Adelaide's new friends."

"Tuesday evening," Diane repeated. "I have no idea whether or not Justin will still be here, but I'll come."

Margaret waited a beat, hoping Diane would share her worries about her son, but when the silence stretched on, she realized Diane still wasn't ready to discuss it. "Shelley's going to make a cat cake. I can't wait to see it."

"Oh my gosh, I forgot to show you pictures of the cake," Diane said. "It was incredible."

"I saw the ones on Justin's phone this morning, remember?" Margaret shook her head. "It was way beyond incredible and well into unbelievable. Shelley has no idea how good she is, does she?"

Diane laughed. "No. Absolutely not. The cat cake ought to be fabulous. It'll be interesting to see what she comes up with."

Margaret nodded. "She was worried, wanted to know if I had pictures or an image in my head, but I told her whatever she comes up with will be great. And I know it will be."

They arrived at the hospital a few moments later, parked, and went directly to Augie's room.

When Diane knocked on the door, Augie immediately called, "Come in!" Clearly he was expecting them.

"I have your book." She walked in smiling. "How are you feeling?"

"A lot better," he admitted. "I can breathe again. Doctor says maybe tomorrow he'll spring me."

"Do you have anyone who can help you when you get home?" Diane asked.

Augie shook his head. "The doctor was talking about some kind of home care, but I don't want strangers tramping in and out of my house."

"What about a young person?" Margaret asked. "Coral Peabody's granddaughter helped Harold Wheeland for a while last year. Belinda seems like a very nice girl."

"That's a good idea," Diane said. "I've met her. Quiet, but very competent. I think she's about seventeen now. I believe she even made some meals for Harold to heat up in the evenings."

Augie shrugged. "I might consider that."

"She'd be delighted," Margaret said. "That's how she makes her pin money."

Augie nodded slowly. "Maybe I could help her earn a little then."

"Great," Margaret said. "I'll call Coral and get Belinda's phone number for you."

"Thanks." Augie leaned forward to take the book from Diane. "Did you find what I was talking about?"

Diane shook her head. "We didn't have time to look. Why don't you show us?"

Margaret knew that was a little white lie. Diane would have loved to dig into that book, but letting Augie share the information was the type of kind gesture that typified her friend. It had been a lucky day for them all when Diane had decided to purchase the old Benton cottage.

Augie leafed through the old book, handling the pages with care. "There are some old photographs in here, but there's something even more interesting. It's an interview with a woman who was in her eighties at the time—ah, here we go. She's talking about her childhood here, and she references something odd. Listen:

"'Of course, when I was a little girl, the old town was still there. But almost everything was washed away in the big storm of September 1815. Only some foundations remained.'" Augie looked up over the top of his glasses at them. "In 1815, a major hurricane struck New England. I looked it up."

"What old town is she talking about?" Diane's voice had risen with excitement. "Past the lighthouse...! That's where the map indicates the town—a town—was built."

"Although not *our* Marble Cove," Margaret said.

Augie shut the book and handed it to Diane. "I read the whole thing, but I didn't find out anything else. There are a couple aerial views of the lighthouse and Marble Cove, but they're too recent. All that shows below the lighthouse is scrub and swamp."

"Diane," Margaret said, suddenly recalling something, "remember all that information you found in the Maine Room when we were trying to find the historical background on the lighthouse?"

Diane nodded. "But it seems to me that if there was information about this, someone would have read it or heard about it."

"Maybe. But we weren't looking for information about a whole different location for the town then, either. If no one's ever heard about this before, why would they have tried to find the information?"

"True," Diane admitted.

They visited with Augie for awhile longer, until the elderly man's eyes began to droop. They said quiet farewells and tiptoed out.

In the elevator, Margaret said, "I'm going straight home to call Mrs. Peabody about getting Belinda's number." She sighed. "And then I suppose I'd better e-mail Louellen and see if she can give me the names of any lawyers who deal with art issues."

"I'll try to find some time to check the Maine Room for information about this." Diane tapped the book. "But between Justin, my story, and the doings with the new book, I'm not sure how much time I'm going to have."

Margaret chuckled. "Well, time isn't really an issue," she pointed out. "It's waited more than two hundred and fifty years already. A few more days won't make a difference."

Chapter Eighteen

The group home was an unassuming white Cape Cod on a corner at the other end of town. The front was nicely landscaped with large holly bushes trimmed into slim pyramids at each corner of the house. Each bush was covered with red berries. Low-growing rhododendron and azalea huddled beneath the windows, and Margaret saw masses of buds that would soon put on a lovely spring show. A little bed in front contained a half-sunken wagon wheel and many of the spring-flowering bulbs common to the area. A wicker love seat and two chairs graced the small porch, and she wondered if the girls sat out there much in the summer. A brick walkway led to a one-car garage on the far side away from the street.

As she, Adelaide, and Allan mounted the low stoop and knocked on the door on Sunday afternoon, Margaret was impressed despite herself. The paint was well maintained and the exterior looked to be in good repair.

The sound of giggling and running feet could be heard, and a moment later the door flew open.

"Addie! Hi!" The speaker was a Downs girl whose hair was cut in a cute bob. She looked to be about Adelaide's age.

Behind her was a shorter blonde girl. Or woman? Margaret thought she might be a little older, perhaps thirty to forty. She wore glasses and had a disproportionately small head, but she also wore a broad smile.

"Hi." Adelaide turned to her parents. "This is Chloe and Tina. This is my mom and dad," she said to her friends.

"Wanna come in?" asked the shorter girl whom Adelaide had called Tina.

"Yes, please." Adelaide started forward, and Allan and Margaret followed.

They entered into a small foyer. Straight ahead was a flight of stairs, and a living room stretched to the left. Through the living room, Margaret could see a large eat-in kitchen.

The living room had comfortable-looking blue couches and recliners. There was a piano on the interior wall against the stairs, and a fireplace opposite. In an entertainment center beside the fireplace was a large flat-screen television, and another Downs girl with a long ponytail was seated on one of the couches watching *The Sound of Music*.

"This is our living room," announced Chloe, the taller greeter. "That's my twin sister. We're identical. Cassie! Say hi!"

The dark-haired girl on the couch turned and gave them a fleeting wave and greeting, and Margaret saw that the two girls did indeed look alike. Moments later, she was absorbed in her movie again.

"We'll give you a tour," announced Chloe.

"Thank you," Margaret said. "We'd like that."

The girls led them into the kitchen, where a woman about Margaret's age was helping another young woman to pull a tray of cookies from the oven.

"Hello," she said. "The girls are excited to have visitors today. Welcome to Bayview House. I'm Elsa Kling. This is my daughter Maryann."

Maryann's face lit up when she saw visitors. She turned to Elsa, fingers flying, and Margaret realized the girl was signing.

Elsa laughed, signing back. "Maryann would like to know if she can hug you."

"Of course." Margaret held out her arms, and the young woman hurried around the table and very, very gently, cuddled close and laid her head on Margaret's bosom as Margaret embraced her. She kept her arms down at her sides, and Elsa laughed again. "What she really means is that she wants a hug from you."

"Hey, Addie, wanna see my room?" Tina asked.

Adelaide said, "Yeah!" and all four of the girls went rushing back through the living room to the stairs.

Elsa held out a plate. "Would you like a cookie?"

"No, thank you," Margaret said, while Allan said, "Sure," and accepted a huge sugar cookie. "This is a lovely home." She looked around, noting the modern kitchen and the large oak table with six chairs around it, and two more positioned by a smaller table in the far end of the room.

"Thank you." Elsa indicated a door at one end of the room. "Since Chloe seems to have abdicated, I'll continue your tour. Let me show you the basement. The girls talk about Adelaide quite a bit," she said as she started down the enclosed stairway. Margaret noted the handrail with approval. "Chloe says Adelaide wants to live here."

"Adelaide thinks it would be fun," Margaret corrected, "but we're not really looking for a placement right now. We would like to see how you run things, though, in case that changes in the future."

Elsa nodded. "Sure. Let's start at the beginning." She paused at the bottom of the steps. "I'm a widow. My husband died very suddenly ten years ago, and Maryann and I did not have a large cushion to fall back on. We sold our home, which was much larger and needed more than two lonely ladies to fill it, and purchased this with the intent of turning it into a private group home for girls like Maryann and your Adelaide." She laughed. "I'm skipping the mountains of red tape, both financial and regulatory, and giving you the short version. This is the laundry room, by the way," she pointed to the left. "And a half bath. Each girl does her own laundry, including sheets and towels, every week. And this is a recreation room." She turned right into a large space with a sewing corner at one end, and a large seating area with an even larger television at the other. "This is where we come when we all want to watch a movie together." Off to one side was a puzzle table with a half-completed jigsaw puzzle on it, and along one wall was a desk holding a laptop computer. "This is connected to the television too. Sometimes Chloe and Cassie Skype with their parents. They are retired and travel a good bit. Occasionally the girls go with them, but for the most part, they prefer a settled life here. Tina's parents are deceased. Her brother has custody, but they have several children and weren't able to fit Tina into their schedule." A single lift of her eyebrows told Margaret what Elsa thought of that excuse. "This is a great fit for Tina, though. She's very happy here."

She started back the way she had come. "But back to the story of the house. As I said, it's a private residence. The girls pay rent. I am fairly particular about the girls I permit to join us. No promiscuity, no foul language, no running away." She laughed. "I don't mind being a housemother, but I don't want to be the police."

Upstairs again, she pointed down the hallway. "That leads to the garage. Maryann's room is the last door on the left and my suite is on the right. We share a full bath in there. Upstairs are three bedrooms and another full bath. Right now each girl has her own room, although if girls don't mind rooming together, I can take as many as six. I supervise meals, although all the girls take turns cooking and cleaning up afterward. The same with housework. We have a rotating schedule, and we all participate."

Margaret was too impressed for words.

Allan said, "We had no idea anything like this was available. No wonder Adelaide wants to come live here!"

"Do you take pets?" Margaret asked, thinking of Adelaide's cats.

Elsa shook her head regretfully. "We do have one very sweet hairless guinea pig. You may not have noticed his cage in the kitchen. But Maryann is allergic to both cat and dog dander."

Elsa showed them the fenced-in backyard, with its picnic table on a sunny patio, sturdy adult-size swing set, vegetable garden, and several fruit trees at the far end. "We make preserves," she told them. "And pies, and anything else we can think of to use all the fruit we get off those trees. And everyone helps with the garden and yard work as well."

The girls came to find them and dragged them upstairs for a tour of every bedroom. Every room's bed was made, every girl's clothes in relatively good order. Margaret found herself imagining Adelaide in this setting, a disturbing thought, since she and Allan had intended that Adelaide would live with them as long as they were capable of giving her the help and supervision she needed.

They stayed nearly an hour, and when it was time to depart, Adelaide protested. Margaret and Allan gave her a few more minutes with her friends while they waited outside in the car for her in silence.

"So what did you think?" Allan finally asked.

Margaret sighed. "It's a dream home. I couldn't find a single thing to criticize."

Allan chuckled. "Did you want to?"

"Criticize?" Margaret looked sheepish. "Deep down, probably. I'm so afraid Adelaide is going to move away, Allan."

"I know," he soothed. "Me too."

"I imagine there are people who think we'd be glad to have an empty nest, people who consider Adelaide a burden..." Her eyes welled with tears. "But they'd be wrong. She's our sunshine."

"That's an apt description," Allan said, smiling. "Our little ray of sunlight. She brightens everyone's day when she walks into a room."

"She does. And I don't know what I'll do if she leaves us." Margaret lapsed into dejected silence while at the same time Adelaide emerged from the house and then joined them in the car.

They drove home quietly and when Allan pulled into the driveway, Margaret saw Shelley coming out of her front door.

"Hi." Shelley waved and started across the street. "Beverly and I are going to take a walk. Want to come along?"

No, I want to go have a good cry. But... "That would be nice, if you don't mind waiting until I change." Margaret indicated the church clothes she still wore.

"No problem," Shelley said.

Margaret hurried to her room and slipped on jeans and a T-shirt with a flannel shirt over it. Adding sneakers and a zip-up hoodie, she hollered, "Back in a little while," to Allan and Adelaide, and met her friends out front.

Beverly had joined them by then. "I texted Diane, but she said she was working and the words were flowing."

Margaret chuckled. "I know that feeling, although mine's with a paintbrush. We definitely should not interrupt."

"I wanted to talk about Diane, anyway," Shelley said.

Beverly and Margaret both laughed. "Tell it like it is, Shelley!" Margaret said. Just being with her friends had already lifted the gloom that had enveloped her.

"Aw, you know what I mean." Shelley elbowed Margaret. "I'm worried about her. She hasn't said a word about Justin coming home out of the blue like that. At Christmas, he told Dan he was about to start some officer's training. What do you suppose happened?"

"I don't know," Margaret said. "She hasn't confided in me either."

"Nor me," added Beverly. "But I agree, she does seem troubled."

"Justin too," Margaret said. "He's been pretty lighthearted the other times I've seen him. He's not happy." All three of them contemplated that for a moment. Then Margaret said, "I suppose all we can do is pray for them."

"And be there," Shelley added, "if they need a hug or a shoulder."

★　　★　　★

Midmorning Tuesday, Beverly was upstairs sorting the contents of office boxes. She had less than two weeks of work left at the State House, and she had begun bringing most of her personal items home. Yesterday had been difficult—it seemed everything she touched reminded her of something she enjoyed about her job. Was she making a huge mistake, quitting a perfectly good job?

The doorbell of the Wheeland house rang, interrupting her fit of worry. "Father, are you expecting anyone?" she called.

"No. Shall I get it?"

She knew he was sitting in his recliner. "No, I'll do it." She dashed down the stairs. Through the wavy glass in the old front door, she could see a blurry figure that looked like it might be a woman. One of her friends? With a smile, she pulled open the door.

"Hi, Beverly." Maddie Bancroft stood on the front porch, beaming at her.

"Hi, Maddie. I wasn't expecting you."

"No, and I'm sorry for not calling first."

"Oh no, it's fine. I just thought it was probably one of my neighbors asking if I wanted to walk along the beach."

"Like Shelley. You two are close, aren't you?"

"Yes," Beverly said, only now realizing how very close to her three friends she had grown. "There are four of us neighbors who have gotten to know each other rather well."

"That must be nice. Sometimes I get the feeling that Shelley is trying to avoid me." Maddie looked surprisingly distressed.

Beverly put a hand on Maddie's arm. "Shelley is not a very confident person. It may simply be that you intimidate her."

"What? That's ridiculous. I could never intimidate Shelley. She's gorgeous, she's turning her baking business into something the whole town is talking about, she's got the most adorable *and* well-behaved kids on the planet. Why on earth would she find *me* intimidating?"

Beverly almost laughed out loud. "You're very, uh, capable."

Maddie frowned. "You're very diplomatic, Beverly. I'm overbearing, totally obsessive, and rigid. At least, that's what my husband tells me. But I can't imagine people finding me intimidating. Most of the time, I feel as if they're laughing behind my back."

Beverly felt an unexpected stab of sympathy for the other woman. She knew a little bit about having a critical spouse. "Oh, Maddie, that's not true. You're efficient and organized, and there is nothing wrong with either of those traits. Who's the first person people call when they need to get something done right?"

Maddie smiled, but there was sadness lurking in her eyes. "I would rather people call me because they want to do something with a friend," she said quietly. "I don't get those kinds of calls."

Beverly didn't have a clue how to respond to the forlorn words. While she mentally groped for and discarded response after response, Maddie squared her shoulders and drew a deep breath.

"Well, no matter. I didn't come here to whine." She grimaced. "I came here to beg."

Beverly was startled enough to forget about consoling the other woman. "For what?"

"Linda Hayford went back to her doctor yesterday. He won't let her try to play yet, especially something as demanding as the *Messiah*. He wants her to give it at least three more weeks before she plays again."

Beverly blinked. "Three more weeks? But that's—that's after Easter!"

"I know." Maddie was watching her closely. "Beverly, I'm going to need you through Easter."

"For rehearsals." Her stomach was flip-flopping, and she swallowed.

"Not just rehearsals." Maddie's voice was gentle. "For Easter Sunday."

"But—but—I don't play in public. I can't play the 'Hallelujah Chorus' in church. I just *can't*." The last word was almost a wail. "Maddie, you don't understand. I get nervous. My fingers freeze. They tangle. I—"

"Beverly. Breathe."

She stopped speaking, abruptly realizing that she was practically hyperventilating.

"Slow down," Maddie said. "Now. Can you tell me exactly what it is that frightens you?"

Beverly shook her head. "I just get so nervous. I'm terrified I might foul up and then the whole choir would have to stop—"

"And then we'd begin again. No one would die. The world would not end. We'd just find the right measure together and start from there."

"But the choir would be so upset. You..." Beverly closed her eyes and covered her face with her hands, pressing tightly.

"I can't play the piano," Maddie said. "I'm hopeless. Took lessons for six years, but I was terrible. Your playing, on the other hand, is a thing of beauty. You handle dynamics, key changes, tempo changes, and anything else without a hitch. If, by some improbable chance, you did make a major mistake, all your friends in the choir would be supportive."

Beverly didn't have a choice. She could see that. There wasn't another accompanist available that wasn't already playing for an Easter service somewhere. If only she wasn't so terrified.

CHAPTER NINETEEN

Margaret's phone rang a few minutes before seven that evening. "Hello?"

"Is she gone?" It was Shelley, inquiring about Adelaide.

"Yes. Allan took her to the store. She has no idea we're having a party. We had a very small celebration this morning."

Shelley giggled. "I *love* surprise parties! I'm bringing the cake over right now, so watch for me."

Margaret went to the door, holding it wide when Shelley arrived so that she could edge inside with the large bakery box she cradled in two arms.

Shelley went directly to the dining room, where Margaret had cleared off her sideboard for the party layout. Together, the two women lifted the cake from the box and set it in the place of honor.

"Oh, Shelley," Margaret breathed. "You have truly outdone yourself." The cake was nothing like Margaret had expected. It wasn't a standard layer or sheet cake. It was a cat, shape and all. And there was absolutely nothing cartoonish about it.

The cake was a larger-than-life-size mold of a long-haired cat, curled up fast asleep. The brown tabby striping was composed of several shades that bled into each other perfectly, and there was white on the face and paws. Shelley had cleverly used a fine-toothed comb or some other tool to texturize the cat's coat, ensuring that the "fur" all lay the right way, clear to the tip of the tail. There were even lifelike white whiskers made of some type of stiff monofilament.

As if that wasn't enough, Shelley had covered the cake board on which her creation lay with a rumpled piece of pink fleece, making it appear that the cat snoozed on a blanket.

"I didn't write 'Happy Birthday' on it," Shelley said anxiously. "There didn't seem to be a place that it wouldn't detract from the effect. Will it matter, do you think?"

"Oh no," Margaret said, still agog. "I agree with your artistic impression. It wouldn't be right for this masterpiece. Oh, Shelley, thank you. I was expecting a cat that looked sort of like Garfield, but this kitty looks like she might open her eyes any second. It's beautiful. Adelaide is going to be so thrilled!"

Through the window, she caught sight of an unfamiliar minivan pulling into the driveway. As it stopped, the doors opened and Elsa Kling and Adelaide's four friends poured out.

"My goodness," Shelley said. "It's a pink invasion!" Presumably in honor of the birthday girl's favorite color, every one of the five wore some shade of pink. "I think," Shelley said, "I'll go home and put pink sweaters on Emma and me before we come over. See you in a few." And she left, giggling.

Margaret hurried to the door to admit the first guests. She was still greeting and gathering coats when Diane, Beverly, and Mr. Wheeland arrived. Diane quickly took over coat duty so that Margaret could attend to her guests, while Beverly got her father seated.

"No Justin?" Margaret inquired the next time she and Diane had a moment to breathe.

Diane shook her head, her face troubled. "No. He, ah, he had some things to do. Did you get any information about lawyers yet?"

Margaret didn't miss the change of subject, and her heart ached for her friend. She wished Diane could share her burden. She was always quick to help out when anyone else was having difficulties, but she didn't seem able to ask for it when she herself needed assistance. Even, Margaret thought, if the only thing they could do was listen and be supportive.

Out loud, she said, "I e-mailed Louellen, and she forwarded it to a couple of other artists she thought might have suggestions. I got two names, so I suppose I'll have to call them and ask about their experience with copyright law."

Shelley, Dan, and their children came in then.

Margaret set her concerns aside and played hostess after texting Allan to tell him all the guests had arrived. Aiden and Emma, she saw, were charming Adelaide's friends. Chloe and Aiden were having an intense conversation about Spider-Man, while Emma was sitting in Elsa's lap, beaming as Tina sang nursery rhymes to her. Chloe's twin had found a quiet corner, while Maryann was getting and giving hugs to anyone within reach.

A few minutes later, Allan shepherded Adelaide into the house, and her expression when everyone yelled "Surprise!" tickled Margaret to no end.

Adelaide was thrilled that her friends had been invited. She kept saying to Shelley, Diane, and Beverly, "Those are my friends!"

When it came time to cut the cake, there was general agreement that it would be a crime to ruin Shelley's creation. She was charmingly embarrassed by all the praise, and by Allan's insistence on taking her picture beside the cake, before Adelaide made the first cut. "But not his head," Adelaide said. "I wanna save the head." Margaret couldn't imagine why, but she carefully avoided that end of the cake. Even though she cut generously sized slices, there was still half the kitty left afterward.

Beverly rolled her eyes when Margaret handed her a dessert plate. "I already ran today, but after eating this, I may have to go out a second time."

"Oh, you," said Margaret. Beverly was very, very slender. One slice of cake would never harm that figure. "I'm going to enjoy it and worry about my diet some other day."

Diane and Shelley gravitated toward them in time to hear the end of the conversation.

"Ugh." Diane made a face. "No diet talk allowed." She gestured to the table where Adelaide and her friends had gathered and were giggling and chatting. "I love Adelaide's friends. They all seem very sweet."

"And I'm incredibly impressed with Mrs. Kling," added Shelley. "I was talking with her about living with all the girls. She seems to love the 'controlled chaos,' as she called it." She made quote marks in the air.

"We visited with them on Sunday afternoon." Margaret ran a finger around the edge of her pink paper cup. "It's a wonderful place. All the girls help with housework, meals, and gardening, and everyone does her own laundry, but they have plenty of time to pursue other things. And it feels like a home."

"Are you thinking of placing Adelaide there?" Diane cocked her head, eyebrows rising.

"No. Absolutely not." Margaret didn't know why she felt defensive. Diane's tone hadn't been accusatory in any way, just curious. "We just wanted to meet the friends she talks so much about." *Which we could have done today.* "The things Adelaide said about their living situation sounded awfully rosy, so I was interested in seeing it for myself. Turns out, the girls are absolutely right. It's a marvelous place."

★   ★   ★

The big day had finally arrived.

"What do you think I should wear?" Dan asked as he and Shelley packed for the overnight trip. He held up a tie, eyebrows raised. They would be leaving at noon, dropping off the children with Frances and Ralph, and then driving to Dan's appointment with the IBEW fellow in Augusta.

Shelley nodded. "A button-down shirt with a tie and a vest. You probably don't need a suit, but it can never hurt to look nice."

"I probably don't need the tie tomorrow to meet with the electrician."

She laughed because he sounded so hopeful. "No, you could probably just go with a shirt and vest. But no jeans," she warned him.

Packing took very little time, and all too soon, they were pulling into Dan's parents' driveway.

Frances must have been watching for them, because she was opening the car door and freeing Emma from her car seat before Shelley could even get her seat belt off and step out of the car.

"How's my sweetie pea?" she cooed, snuggling Emma close.

Emma squirmed and wriggled. "No!" she insisted, pushing at her grandmother's arms.

"Well, what's this?" Frances continued to hold her, and Emma started to wail. Loudly.

"She's becoming very independent," Shelley said, resisting the urge to say, *Put her down!* "She prefers to walk."

Clearly reluctant, Frances finally set Emma down, and the wailing cut off in midstream. Shelley handed the children's suitcase and Emma's diaper bag to her mother-in-law. "Here. Everything you should need is in here. Please don't forget to put Desitin on Emma's bottom if she looks at all red."

"Isn't she potty-training yet?" Frances looked askance.

"No," Shelley said. "She hasn't shown any interest yet." *So please don't put her on a potty chair and make her sit there.* She'd witnessed Frances doing that to Aiden once and stopped it immediately.

"All my children were potty-trained by the time they were two," Frances observed.

Ralph chuckled. "Not the way I remember it, Shelley. Don't you believe it."

"They were!" Frances rounded on her husband.

"Mom." Dan sighed. "Please. Just…stop, please?"

They didn't linger long after that inauspicious beginning. As Dan turned onto Route 17 west and headed for Augusta, he reached over and covered one of Shelley's hands with his. "I want to thank you for not yelling at my mother when she provokes you."

Shelley smiled, laying her other hand over his and squeezing. "She sure does seem to enjoy that, doesn't she?"

"You have to know it's not just you," Dan reminded her. "She does it to almost everyone in my family too."

Shelley did know now, and that's what made it bearable. Dan's sisters sometimes teased their mother when she made one of her sweeping pronouncements. To hear her tell it, she'd raised seven perfect children—perfectly. To hear them tell it, the Bauer home had been more…what had Elsa Kling called it? *Controlled chaos.*

The memory made her smile, and she took a deep breath. The last thing Dan needed was to stress about how much his mother upset her. "So tell me again what we're doing today. Tell me everything he said."

Dan's excitement showed. Typically a man of few words, he talked practically the whole way to the meeting about the things the training director had told him.

They arrived a few minutes early and were shown straight into the office of the training director. Jeb Raines was a tall man with a warm smile who made them feel at ease.

"Your scores on the qualifying exam were high," he told Dan. "The reading, math, and mechanical skills all were excellent, so you should do fine with the coursework. As I told you in the e-mail, I have an electrician who has agreed to take you on as an apprentice. He's a master electrician named Wayne Stover, and his business is just up Route 1 outside of Marble Cove."

Dan nodded. "Stover Electricians. I've seen it."

Jeb handed Dan a folder. "In here is all the information about the coursework portion of the apprenticeship. Pellissippi State Technical Community College has two different online programs. You did say you preferred that?"

Dan nodded. "We have small children. If I'm doing an apprenticeship and going to classes on a campus somewhere, I'll never see my family. But does an online degree mean the same thing to a potential employer?"

"The online programs are excellent," Jeb assured him. "People are so mobile now that a lot of them find it impossible to commit to attending college classes. An online degree is perfectly acceptable."

"So he'll actually be taking college classes?" Shelley was a little surprised.

"Our electricians receive an associate's degree in science or applied science. I recommend the science degree because if you're at all interested in further education, these credits all transfer and can be applied to the bachelor's degree in construction management technology at Middle Tennessee State."

Shelley shook her head. "Wow. That sounds weird. We live in Maine, but he'd have a degree from Tennessee."

Mr. Raines chuckled. "The world is definitely getting smaller."

Dan had opened the folder and was perusing its contents. "So what's the difference between the applied science and science degrees?"

"The applied science degree is not something from which you could easily transfer your credits, if you should change your mind and decide you want to get a four-year degree down the road."

Dan shook his head. "I doubt it. I'm more of a hands-on type of person."

The other man laughed. "You would not be the first person to sit in that chair and utter those words." He sobered, looking from Dan to Shelley. "But I would encourage you to read through the information in the folder and discuss it together. You're young. You have a lot of years ahead of you to try new things. A lot of people change careers more than once in their lifetime now."

Shelley immediately thought of Beverly, who was mere weeks away from taking the plunge and opening her consulting business. Then she thought of Diane, who'd also been in a business that was somewhat related to her current occupation. And look at Margaret—she hadn't even started painting until she "retired" and now owned an art gallery. Shelley didn't count herself in the "second-career crowd," because really, she hadn't had any major skills before she became a wife and mother and now a baker. She hadn't changed careers so much as discovered hers.

Dan had more questions for Jeb Raines, and they spent another quarter hour with him. At the end of the meeting, the man said, "Your meeting with Wayne Stover is scheduled for nine tomorrow morning." He hesitated. "Wayne's a...strong personality, but he's one of the most skilled electricians I know, and his apprentices always know their stuff by the conclusion of their time together. You'll be learning from the best." He rose and held out a hand. "Great to meet you, Dan, and you too, Shelley. Your support will be important to Dan. The next couple of years are going to be busy ones."

CHAPTER TWENTY

Thanks to their GPS, finding their hotel was a breeze. Shelley was a little apprehensive about the accommodations. It had received a good rating and boasted some amenities despite the modest price. But until she actually got into the room and saw how clean and nicely appointed it was, she wasn't able to relax.

Fortunately, it was exactly as advertised. They put on their swimsuits and spent a pleasant hour in the heated indoor pool, and after returning to their room to shower and change, they headed for a little Italian restaurant the girl at the front desk had recommended.

Fiammetta's was a mom-and-pop place with only ten tables. It was almost clichéd, with red-and-white-checked tablecloths, candles with melted wax that had dripped down over the top of the squat wine jugs used to hold them, and overly ornate fake gilt embellishing the wooden trim.

Shelley didn't have high expectations for the food, and their waitress did nothing to change her mind.

"What can I getcha?" The girl was a bit too plump for her white blouse and black pants. She was snapping a piece of gum, and Shelley wondered how on earth she could manage without getting it caught on the silver stud that pierced her lip. Her hair was a deep black with red and purple highlights, and her fingernails also were black. Shelley never trusted black fingernails. It was just too difficult to see how thoroughly a person had cleaned their hands.

"What do you recommend?" Dan asked. They hadn't been given menus when they came in.

The girl shrugged. "Everything's good. We have three appetizers, two salads, three entrees and a couple of desserts, depending on what Carla feels like making." She rattled off choices so fast neither Shelley nor Dan caught any of it.

Finally, they had managed to order what Shelley hoped would be an edible meal, and their waitress brought them drinks and vanished.

They were the only patrons in the place. As far as Shelley was concerned, that was an ominous sign. Maybe it had been a mistake to order oysters for an appetizer. Spoiled oysters could make a person sicker than just about anything she could imagine.

When she said as much to Dan, his face paled. "Maybe we should leave." He looked so nervous she felt bad for even mentioning it.

"Let's wait and see how the appetizer is," she told him. "The Board of Health would have shut this place down if it was that bad."

A short while later, their waitress returned with the appetizer course. After the first bite, Shelley conceded she'd been far too quick to judge. They shared a delicately delicious plate of fresh oysters cooked in the half shell with garlic, breadcrumbs, and a touch of parsley. When their entrees arrived, Shelley dined on handmade pasta filled with cheese and herbs, while Dan had an enormous bowl of traditional Tuscan seafood stew. A steaming basket of crusty Tuscan bread brushed with garlic accompanied the meal.

Not another soul came into the small establishment throughout the evening. Despite the gingham-checked tablecloths and goth waitress, it was a lovely evening out, something they rarely indulged in anymore. They talked all through the meal about the apprenticeship program. Dan could hardly wait to meet Wayne Stover in the morning.

After the meal was cleared, they succumbed to icy lemon sorbetto, a perfect finish to the meal.

"I'm stuffed," Dan groaned. "You're going to have to roll me back to the hotel."

"And who's going to roll me?" Shelley patted her tummy. "I ate too much but I don't care. That was fabulous!"

Best of all, the bill was far smaller than Shelley could have imagined.

Dan put his arm around her as they walked to the car. "Thank you for making the time to do this. I was glad you were with me today."

She laid her head against his shoulder. "You're welcome." She too was glad she had come along. And it hadn't been nearly as problematic as she'd feared to find a substitute baker.

As they got into the car for the short trip back to the hotel, Shelley's cell phone rang. An unfamiliar number showed on the lighted display. Probably a wrong number or a political campaign. But the urge to know overcame mild annoyance, and she hit the "answer" button. "Hello?"

"Hello, may I speak to Shelley Bauer, please?" The voice was female but unfamiliar.

"This is Shelley."

"Shelley, my name's Polly Embley. Liza Cramble's my best friend."

"Oh dear." Shelley was filled with dread. "What's happened? Is Liza okay?"

"Liza has the flu," Polly said. "She got sick last night, and by this afternoon she was so dehydrated I drove her to the emergency room. They decided to keep her overnight for observation because she has a mild heart condition." Polly cleared her throat. "She gave me the name of every baker she could think of, and I've been calling and calling, and I'm so sorry, but I cannot find anyone who has time to help out for tomorrow morning." The woman sounded near tears, and despite the panic rising, Shelley felt the urge to comfort her.

"Oh, Polly, please tell Liza not to worry about it for one more minute. I'll figure it out. Tell her to just concentrate on getting better."

"I'm so sorry to have to dump this on you." This time Shelley definitely heard a sniffle.

"Polly," Shelley said, "you've gone way above and beyond the definition of friendship, and I appreciate your efforts. Don't you dare think about this for another second."

"Thank you, Shelley. You don't know how I've been dreading making this call."

"Now you've done it, and you can relax. You don't want to exhaust yourself and succumb to the flu as well."

"No wonder Liza liked you," the other woman said after a pause. "Thank you, Shelley. I'll pass your kind words on to Liza. We're both sorry to leave you in the lurch."

"It'll work out," Shelley said. "You take care, Polly."

When she ended the call, Shelley dropped her hands and the phone into her lap, hardly able to take it in.

"Honey?" Dan cast her a worried glance. "What's wrong?"

Shelley sighed, so overwhelmed by the development that even her panic had faded, giving way to dull acceptance. "My replacement baker is sick. In-the-hospital sick, so I will have no baked goods being delivered to Rusty or my other daily clients in the morning."

Dan's mouth fell open. "Holy cow. That's a problem."

"It is," she agreed. "It is indeed. And the woman who called said she tried and tried to find a sub, but no one is available. Liza's been in business longer than I have, and she's the type of friendly, outgoing person who knows everyone. If she can't get someone to help, then I have no shot."

"Oh, Shell," Dan said. "I'm so sorry."

"The only thing we can do," she said, realizing there might be a solution after all, "is to drive home right now instead of staying the night. If I bake when we get home, I should be able to get enough done to deliver right before the Cove opens in the morning. My other clients are retail and don't need them as early."

Dan glanced at his watch. "We could get there pretty quickly."

"I know." She felt tears rising and was torn between breaking plans with Dan and not fulfilling her business obligations. "Not delivering would be a huge blot on my reputation. Who will hire a baker they can't depend on? Dan, I *have* to find a way to get these orders done."

"Maybe my mother could—"

"No. She's got the children. And yes, they're in bed now, but your mom's probably tired. She's not used to keeping little ones full time anymore."

"How about Annie?" Dan's second-oldest sister, Annie Eddington, and her family lived on the outskirts of Marble Cove. Eleven years separated her from Dan, the baby of the family. Her children were eighteen and sixteen now. "She's a terrific cook. You know that."

Shelley opened her mouth to tell him it would never work. But then she remembered something Annie had referred to when she'd first heard about Shelley's business. "Didn't your sister used to make desserts for the Cove?"

Dan nodded. "She used to help out when she was in high school. But she's nowhere near your league."

"Yes," Shelley said, "but at least she has some idea of what I need her to do."

"Megan could help her, I bet," Dan said, referring to Annie's eldest child. Megan had graduated from high school almost a year ago and was working while attending college part time until she figured out what she wanted to study as a major. "If they get the key from my mom and go over to our house, you could talk them through everything they needed."

"But...it's after eight. I can't ask them to stay up half the night."

"Sure you can. And you can stay up with them, long-distance." Dan grinned. "Annie loves adventures, and this certainly would qualify. And if you go over each recipe with them, they can't go wrong. Besides, you can sleep in the car on the way home if you have to."

It would never work. But if it did... "Do you really think she would do that? It's an awful lot to ask of someone."

"Shelley, she's my sister. And yours, now."

It was true that Shelley felt closest to Annie. Although two of Dan's other sisters and another sister-in-law were closer to Shelley's age, they were much stronger personalities. A little intimidating, if Shelley was truthful. Although having them around to run interference with Frances on Sundays was usually a good thing. Vera, especially, didn't hesitate to call her mother out on some of her more critical comments.

Dan spoke again. "If Annie asked you for help, what would you say?"

"Of course." But that was different. Wasn't it? "Okay," she said, still not sure. "I guess I can call her and see..."

"Want me to call?"

Yes. Shelley took a deep breath. "No. My business, my problem."

Dan didn't say anything in response, but as he turned into the hotel parking lot, she saw his smile flash again.

She waited until they were inside the room to call. "Hello?"

"Hi, Annie, it's Shelley."

"Hi, Shelley." A worried note crept into Dan's sister's voice. "Is something wrong?"

Shelley sighed. "Yes. Nothing critical. No one's injured or sick or anything like that. But I have a business crisis, and I—I'm hoping maybe you can help me out."

"Sure. Whatcha need?"

Before Shelley even got done explaining, Annie said, "No problem! Meg, you wanna go over to Aunt Shelley's and help me bake some stuff for her business?"

Shelley could hear Dan's niece in the background. "Yeah! Cool!"

She had to laugh. "Oh, Annie, I am going to owe you big time."

"Two words: birthday cake."

Shelley laughed. "Best one ever, I promise!"

"I'll call you as soon as we get to your house, and you can help us figure out where everything is, okay?"

"Okay. You're awesome."

Shelley turned off the phone and flung herself at Dan. "Thank you, thank you, you brilliant man!"

"It was a pretty good idea," he said, waving modestly.

"It's a *terrific* idea. I never imagined I'd need a backup for the backup," Shelley said ruefully. "I sure hope this works."

★　　★　　★

Beverly arranged to meet the Old First organist in the sanctuary half an hour ahead of rehearsal so that they could put together the piano and organ accompaniment to the *Messiah*.

Estelle Baumgardner was a no-nonsense woman who looked to Beverly to be about Margaret's age. She had curly silver hair still laced with strawberry blonde that she usually wore in a loose bun. The high school vocal music teacher, the woman was reputed to be a strict taskmaster. Beverly hoped Estelle would forgive her mistakes. The mere thought of the duet was tying her nerves in knots.

After introductions, Estelle wasted no time getting down to business. "Let's hit that opening chord first." And they did.

Beverly's fingers were shaking.

"All right," Estelle said. "Let's take it from the top." She used her head to indicate the common time key signature and tempo. "One-two-ready-*aaaaaannnd*."

Beverly hit the wrong chord. Horrified, she fumbled along for a moment, trying to right her mistake.

The rich, resonant tones of the organ stopped abruptly.

Beverly closed her eyes, mortified. Mentally, she braced herself for a blast of criticism.

A moment later, she heard a soft, "Beverly?"

Her eyes flew open. Estelle stood beside the piano bench, a sympathetic smile on her face. "Are you as scared as you look?"

Beverly nodded, her throat tight, as tears threatened.

The organist perched on the end of the piano bench. "Why?"

Beverly swallowed. "I—I'm not used to playing in front of people. Accompanying terrifies me. If I mess up, it'll ruin the piece."

"Mess-ups happen," acknowledged Estelle. "But in this case, you and I can provide cover for each other. If you mess up, just stop for a bar or two, find your place and join in again. If I mess up, I'll do the same." She chuckled. "Although if I mess up, it will be a lot more painfully obvious than if you do."

Beverly had to smile.

Estelle reached over and picked up her right hand, gently shaking it to loosen the tense muscles. "Once," she said, "when I was in high school, I was accompanying the men's glee club. I reached over with my left hand for a quick page-turn—and I accidentally turned two pages."

Beverly gasped. "What did you do?"

"Well, of course I crashed onto the wrong chord. I didn't have the piece memorized, but I knew it well enough that I knew what I had done after about a measure. The choir director realized it too. He very calmly stopped the choir, quietly gave us a cue, and we started again."

"Oh my word. That's my worst nightmare."

Estelle nodded. "It used to be mine too. But after it happened and I survived, I was never as scared of making mistakes again." She shrugged. "We can always stop and start again."

"In other words, this isn't brain surgery."

The organist let out a peal of laughter. "Not by a long shot." She sobered a bit. "You have to remember, most of your listening audience has only a passing familiarity with music. Most of them don't read music or play an instrument. They may love a well-played piece, but they certainly aren't going to criticize our mistakes. I've missed a sharp or flat before, hit a wrong chord, and yes, it affects a moment in the music. But it's only a moment, and it passes."

"Thank you." Beverly felt better already. "You're right. If I mess up, I'll just pick up and get back on track."

"That's the spirit." Estelle rose. "Ready to try it again?"

Beverly nodded. "Absolutely."

Estelle slid back behind the organ and readied the music. On her cue, they began to play together . . . and it was flawless. Halfway through, Beverly realized she was smiling. And when they had finished, the choir members now gathered in the sanctuary began to clap.

Maddie came forward and said, "That was terrific, Beverly! You are truly the answer to my rather desperate prayers. When I found out Linda was injured, I prayed for someone capable of handling this music, but God did me one better. You're not just capable, you're remarkable."

Chapter Twenty-One

Shelley wanted nothing more than to rush home Thursday morning to find out how Annie and Megan's baking efforts had gone over. But Dan had asked her to go to visit the electrician for whom he would be apprenticing, and she knew how important that was to her husband.

They left Augusta bright and early, and by nine they were pulling into the parking lot of Stover Electricians, an old Victorian home that had been converted to the business. Going inside, Dan and Shelley were greeted by a cheerful receptionist, who directed them to have a seat while she walked back into a hallway to inform Mr. Stover that they were there.

She returned momentarily and asked them to follow her.

Wayne Stover was seated at his desk, but he stood when they entered. The office was masculine and clean and neat, as was the man himself. He wore dark blue jeans and a deep red thermal shirt beneath a denim button-down shirt with "Stover Electricians" in a patch above the breast pocket.

He advanced around the desk, hand extended. "Welcome to Stover's. I'm Wayne." Shelley saw that the electrician was easily as tall as Dan himself, with shoulders so wide it looked as though he'd have to sidle through the doorway. His eyes were a bright, steely blue, and his hair was gunmetal gray, although the hairline was receding.

Dan introduced himself and Shelley, and Wayne said, "Pleased to meet you, ma'am. Glad you came along. We're a family-oriented company; my missus will be glad to get to know you. Have a seat." His manner was brisk and businesslike. He eyed Dan from head to toe. "So you want to be an electrician."

It wasn't a question, but Dan said, "Yes, sir."

"Why?" The word was a bullet.

Dan seemed to flounder for a moment. "Um, well, I worked on the docks, but as you know that's not a very stable livelihood, especially for a man with a family to support. I enjoy making things. I've done some carpentry, and after looking at several lines of work, I thought being an electrician would appeal to me the most." He met Wayne's eyes head-on. "And I believe this career path will give me the best training to support my family."

Wayne grunted. His piercing gaze fastened on Shelley. "You're supporting him with this career move?"

She was surprised to be consulted, but she smiled and nodded. "Absolutely. Dan's very good with his hands. He and his father built me a gorgeous kitchen up to commercial code for my home-based baking business."

The man's eyes switched back to Dan. "If you come to work for me, I expect you to be at work on time every day. I expect you to keep up with your class work and get good grades. I expect you to demonstrate the skills you learn, not just adequately but with excellence. Stover electricians do superior work." He eyed Dan silently for a minute. "You think you're up to that?"

"Yes, sir." Dan didn't hesitate this time.

"I don't suffer fools, and I don't like to waste time. If you have a question while we work, ask. While you're apprenticing with me, I expect you to give 200 percent effort. Got it?"

"Got it."

"You won't be able to start your classroom studies until summer. And since it's April, you'd better get accepted and registered right away for your first courses. I'll expect an outline of your coursework no later than a month from today."

"Yes, sir."

"Okay." Wayne reached back to his desk and picked up a folder. "This is full of company employment paperwork: insurance, W-2s, and all that stuff. Get it all completed and be here at 8:00 AM sharp on Monday."

"*This* Monday?" Dan looked alarmed.

"That a problem?"

"No, not at all. I was just surprised . . . I didn't realize this would happen so fast."

Wayne shrugged. "I told Jeb Raines I'd take you on. No point in wasting time."

"No," Dan agreed. "That suits me."

Back in the car, Dan and Shelley looked at each other, slightly stunned at the speed with which the apprenticeship had come together. "Wow." Dan shook his head. "I guess I've got a new job."

Shelley grinned. "I guess you do."

"He's...I'm not going to be able to make a lot of mistakes."

"No, he's certainly got high expectations. I imagine you'll hear immediately if he's not pleased with something."

Dan gave a burst of nervous laughter. "That was pretty clear." He took a deep breath. "I hope I can do this, Shell."

"I have faith in you, honey. And Mr. Stover might have sounded a little scary, but remember what Mr. Raines said? You'll be learning from the best."

From there, they drove to Dan's parents' home to pick up Aiden and Emma. During the ride, Shelley called Rusty at the Cove. "Hi, how was the delivery this morning?"

"Smooth as silk," Rusty reported. "Except your sister-in-law made the drop-off. I thought that girl from Thomaston was going to bake for you."

"She got the flu, and Annie agreed to fill in. She used my recipes, and I coached her long-distance." She laughed. "It was...interesting."

"Well, she did a good job," Rusty said. "The baked goods didn't quite have your fine hand, but our customers seemed happy enough. Please tell her thanks from me."

Ending the call, Shelley wiped invisible beads of sweat from her brow. "Annie came through with flying colors," she reported to Dan. "I'd like to invite Quentin and her to dinner to thank them."

"That's an excellent idea. She'd like that."

When they arrived at the elder Bauers' home, Shelley found herself surprisingly eager to see her children. She rarely left them for this long. The three of them spent the best part of each day together, and she missed her little buddies.

They knocked on the back door, and Shelley's heart rose as she saw Aiden's little figure come padding toward the door. He was still in his Lego pajamas, and he wore his L.L. Bean "wicked good" moccasin slippers.

Then Shelley got a good look at him, and shock froze her in her tracks. Behind her, Dan muttered, "Oh man, what did she do now?" *She*, Shelley assumed, being his mother.

Aiden opened the door. "Hi, Mama! Hi, Daddy!" Throwing himself forward and locking his arms around his mother's waist, he said, "I missed you."

"I missed you too," Shelley managed.

"Meemaw cut my hair," he tattled in an aggrieved tone. "I told her you said I didn't have to, but she cut it anyway. An' I was mad, and she told me if I talked back, I couldn't have ice cream."

"I see," Shelley murmured. Her son looked like a shorn sheep, with a conservatively short haircut trimmed around his ears and buzzed close to his head. His hair looked like Diane's son Justin's, she realized.

Dan's father followed Aiden to the door then. "Frances is getting Emma dressed," he said to Shelley and Dan. Then, seeing the thundercloud expression on his son's face as Dan looked at Aiden, Ralph spread his hands. "I told her that was a bad idea," he said. He ran a hand over his own military-short hair. "Come on in. They'll be down in a minute."

Wordlessly, Shelley preceded the men into the kitchen. She was so angry she was afraid to speak. Her mother-in-law had cut Aiden's hair. Without even mentioning it, much less asking permission!

A few months ago, Aiden had announced that he wanted to let his hair grow. Shelley wasn't thrilled, but she had read an article on the development of decision-making skills in children, and she had decided that hair was not a critical issue on which to take a stand. Aiden could decide what he wanted to do with his hair, and they would respect that. She had been pretty certain he wouldn't let it get too out of hand.

His bangs had grown out until he was peering from beneath them or impatiently brushing them aside, and one day he'd asked her if the bangs could be just a little shorter. So she'd trimmed the bangs. The rest had been getting shaggy and noticeably longer, and she'd been hoping that soon he would tire of having to brush it and go back to a shorter style. But not like this.

The sound of footsteps preceded Frances and Emma into the room, and Shelley braced herself. Carefully avoiding eye contact with Dan's mother, she knelt and focused on Emma, who ran across the room and hurled herself into her mother's arms. "Mama!"

"Hi, sweet pea." Shelley kissed the top of her daughter's head, keeping her eyes on Emma. Thank heavens her hair didn't appear to have been cut.

"Hello," said Frances in an overly jolly tone. "How did the visit go?"

"Fine." Dan's tone was cool. "I see you gave Aiden a haircut."

"Yes. Doesn't it look much better?"

"Aiden doesn't think so."

"Oh for heaven's sake," his mother said defensively. "His hair was a mess. And I didn't do anything permanent. It'll grow back, won't it, Ralph?"

Her husband threw up his hands. "Oh no, you don't. You're not dragging me into this. I told you not to do it. Aiden didn't want you to do it. But you had to do it anyway." He held out a hand for Aiden. "Come on, kiddo, I'll help you get your suitcase." With a disgusted frown, he turned and walked from the room, his grandson in tow.

As the pair left, Frances said, "I don't see what the big deal is. It was just hair."

"If it was no big deal," Dan said, "why did you cut it? Aiden had gotten permission from us to let his hair grow for a while."

"It looked awful." Frances's face had grown red. "I was ashamed to take him anywhere looking like that!"

"You didn't even have them twenty-four hours. Where did you think you needed to take him?"

"I stopped by the church office yesterday afternoon," Frances said, her face setting in stubborn lines. "I had some business with Reverend Locke and thought I'd bring Aiden along since the pastor hadn't seen him in ages."

That jab scored a direct hit on Shelley. She knew it bugged Frances that she and Dan hadn't fallen into line and gone to "the family church," but she'd never felt comfortable there. And truthfully, the distance from Dan's mother was a welcome thing.

Shelley picked Emma up and climbed to her feet. She still hadn't said a word to her mother-in-law. "I'll be in the car," she told Dan. To Emma, she said, "Tell Meemaw good-bye."

"Bye-bye!"

"Shelley—" Frances's voice might have held a plea, but Shelley didn't care. Her throat was too tight and tears threatened.

"Thank you for keeping our children," she finally managed before she stepped out the door.

Dan followed moments later with Aiden and the children's overnight things. They buckled both children into their car seats and got into the front seat. Without a word, Dan started the motor and backed out of the driveway. He didn't speak until they were halfway home. "I'm sorry." He sighed. "She knows she was wrong."

Shelley swallowed. "I shouldn't be so upset. It's just hair."

"We have every right to be upset," Dan countered. "That wasn't her decision to make." He reached over and took Shelley's hand. "I don't know what gets into her."

From the backseat, a piping treble voice said, "Bugs."

The speaker wasn't Aiden; it was Emma. Shelley and Dan glanced at each other with identical expressions of surprise and mirth, and then they both laughed out loud.

"Maybe you're right, Em," Dan said. "Maybe you're right."

★   ★   ★

On Friday, Margaret met Diane at the library late in the morning, when Allan came down to take over for her at the gallery for a bit.

Margaret waved at Gilda Harris, the librarian, as she breezed into the old building. "Hi, Gilda. Is Diane already here?"

Gilda's blue eyes twinkled. She lifted her pencil eraser-end first and pointed at the ceiling. "Already up in the Maine Room."

Margaret headed up the stairs. The door to the Maine Room was usually locked, but since Diane was in there, it stood open, light spilling into the hall. "Hello," Margaret called quietly.

"Hey." Equally quietly, Diane called, "I was a little early."

Walking into the room, Margaret's eyebrows rose. "You certainly were."

Diane had stacks of books piled on the reference table in the center of the long room. "I got out everything that looked remotely like it might be helpful," she said, grinning.

"Guess I'd better get started." Margaret shucked off her corduroy coat and surveyed the stack. Choosing one, she took a seat across from her friend. "Refresh my memory. What, exactly, are we looking for?"

"Anything that might give us a clue about why the town was originally built south of here. And also, why it was moved."

"So that could be maps, photographs, or just narrative accounts." Margaret sighed. "Meaning we're going to have to skim each book."

"'Fraid so." Diane grinned. It was nice to see her smile.

The old book Margaret had chosen was fascinating, but it yielded nothing of import. Nor did the next three.

An hour into their search, Margaret stretched and stood. "I've got to take a break and move a little bit."

"Good idea." Diane placed a marker neatly in her book and rose as well.

"Justin still visiting?" There. That was general enough not to be nosy.

Diane nodded, subtly tensing up, and Margaret was sorry she'd even mentioned it. "Yes. I'm not sure yet when he's leaving."

"The army must be getting generous with its leave policy," Margaret commented, grinning.

But Diane didn't smile in return. "I suppose. I've enjoyed having him around." She bent down from the waist and stretched, touching her toes, then slowly rolling up.

Margaret's grin faded. "I bet. I've been thinking a lot about that lately, with Adelaide so enchanted by her friends living in a house together. I would miss her so much." Her throat clutched; her voice dropped to a whisper.

Diane seated herself at the table again. "I know you would." She looked sympathetic. "When my kids left home,

I didn't expect to miss them quite so much. I thought I was well prepared...Eric and I both did." She chuckled a bit. "We were pathetic."

Margaret took her seat as well. She picked up a book at random and began leafing through it. "I never really allowed myself to even consider that Adelaide would move out. 'Move out' isn't even a part of our lexicon," she said with a tremor in her voice. Tears threatened, and she sniffed. "I always assumed she would be with us until the day came that we couldn't care for her. I thought I'd have years before I had to deal with this."

Diane was listening with sympathy in her eyes. She nodded.

"She's only seeing the...the fun part of living with her friends. What happens when they disagree? When someone's grouchy? Adelaide is so sensitive. She'll cry if someone hurts her feelings even a little—oh my goodness!" She stopped abruptly, her attention focused on the book she'd been leafing through in an agitated fashion.

"What?" Diane's gaze sharpened.

"Here's an account of that hurricane Augie's book mentioned!"

"Seriously?" Diane leaped to her feet and rounded the table.

Margaret leaned over the book, pointing with her finger as she read. "It says that Marble Cove was flooded, all except for the church at the north end of town. After the water receded, so much damage had been done that they needed to completely rebuild almost everything, so they decided to reestablish the town on higher ground in a different location."

"They decided . . . that explains our map, Margaret!"

"It does, doesn't it?" Elation had wiped away the bleak sadness in which she'd been mired. "So the town once *was* south of its current location. And the church that was mentioned might be Old First. It's at the south end of our current town, and it sits on higher ground than that swampy marsh just beyond it."

"If this is true, then the treasure might well have been hidden or buried in the original old town." Margaret met Diane's eyes in dismay. "And it says right here it was flooded. It could be anywhere."

"If it's even still there," Diane said. She sounded more dispirited than Margaret usually heard her. "If there was a hurricane, it could be gone altogether."

Chapter Twenty-Two

Justin attended church with Diane on Palm Sunday. Afterward, they went to Shelley and Dan's house for dinner.

"I thought you went to your in-laws' house for Sunday dinner," Diane commented as Shelley put her to work setting trivets on the table and getting drinks for everyone.

Shelley shrugged. "We usually do, but today's a special day. We wanted to spend some time with you and Justin. He must be going back soon."

"I'm not sure yet when his leave ends." Diane tried not to show how upset she felt about Justin's unsettled future. "Would you like me to put two butter dishes on the table?"

As it turned out, going to Shelley's was a good thing. Justin got down on the floor and played Legos with Aiden while Emma toddled around them bringing toy after toy for Justin's inspection. It was the first she had heard him laugh in several days. If anything, he seemed more morose around the house than he had when he had first arrived.

She didn't understand it. She had assumed that once he'd had time to consider his options, he'd be able to make a choice and move on. But when they all sat down at the table, she noticed he encouraged Dan to talk about his trip last week and the apprenticeship he soon would be starting, rather than speaking much himself.

As they strolled along the beach with Rocky after the excellent meal, she couldn't stand it anymore. "So what are you going to do now?"

He didn't pretend to misunderstand her. "I don't know, Mom," he said with a sigh. "I just don't know."

"What, exactly, are your options? How many choices do you have?"

"Three, I guess." He sounded as if they were discussing the weather rather than a crucial decision that would affect the rest of his life. "I can recycle—go back through OCS again—and pray I don't fail this time. Or I can stay enlisted. I only have seven and a half years until I could retire. If I stay in for either reason, I'm due back May first. Option C is to get out and not reenlist when my re-up rolls around in November."

Diane nodded and listened intently, waiting for him to continue. But he didn't.

The sounds of the seashore washed over them—the constant dull rush of the waves where they broke on the sand, a dog barking at his master to throw his ball again, gulls wheeling and screaming where an early tourist down the beach was feeding them. She knew it must be a tourist because no local in his right mind would encourage those obnoxious birds.

Finally, she asked, "Is one more appealing than the others?"

Justin sighed. He picked up a small stone, edges rounded by the ocean's power. "Not really..."

Diane said, "I have faith in you, honey. You'll figure it out." But secretly she was quite alarmed. She'd worried at times that Justin seemed so dull, so depressed, but he would perk up each time. Case in point: he'd just been smiling and laughing with Shelley's kids.

But that didn't mean he wasn't struggling with depression. How long should she wait, she wondered, before dragging him to a doctor? If, of course, she was even able to convince him to go.

*   *   *

Margaret paced back and forth.

"You're going to wear a path in the floor if you keep doing that," Allan observed. He had brought her lunch to the gallery and stayed to share it with her.

"I just don't know what to do." Margaret ignored his humor. She wasn't feeling much like laughing at the moment. "I cannot believe I haven't heard from Matt." He'd seemed to be such a nice man. "Louellen says I was a fool to have signed any contract without an agent. Her agent handles everything she paints."

"And takes a hefty chunk of change for her efforts, I'm sure," Allan pointed out.

"True. She also said I should, at the very least, have some type of standard contract written by someone who is familiar with current standards and commission rates, whether it's an agent, an attorney, or a manager."

"That's reasonable, I think. Have you heard back from any of the attorneys you contacted?"

Margaret nodded. "I got nice e-mails from each of the first two I contacted, saying they'd like to talk with me." She walked away again, moving around a freestanding pillar to the far end of the room. "I haven't called either one of them yet."

"Because...?"

"I don't know." She gestured miserably as she walked back again. "I keep thinking I'll hear from Matt. And talking to an attorney intimidates me. I don't even know what questions to ask!"

"I don't think you have to ask a lot," Allan said gently. "You tell your story and let them ask the questions."

"*After* I find out what they're going to charge me for a consultation." She put both palms to her temples, realizing that she had a headache brewing.

"Well, yes. We could afford an hour at one-fifty, but two or three times that is probably out of our price range."

Margaret nodded as she went behind the counter to fumble around in her handbag for painkillers. "All right." She washed down the pills with water and then she started across the room again.

Allan cleared his throat. "Honey, we need to talk about something else."

Margaret stopped in her tracks and wheeled to face him, wary of his next words. He sounded serious. "What?"

"Elsa Kling called this morning. One of the girls who lives with her will be moving out in June. She will have a space available, and she wanted to offer it to us first. She says Adelaide would be a perfect fit."

"Adelaide would..." Margaret was stunned. "You did tell her we're not interested?"

Allan shook his head. He finished the last bite of the chicken casserole he'd brought and began to fold his napkin and store his dishes back in the lunch bag he'd packed.

"Well, you should have. Because we're not! Adelaide is happy with us, Allan. She would miss home terribly—"

"Possibly true," he acknowledged, holding up a spoon and gesturing for emphasis, "but Margaret, our daughter is a grown woman. Yes, she has some intellectual challenges, but if we want to encourage her to grow, to be independent and think for herself, we need to present her with this choice and let her decide what she wants to do."

Tears stung Margaret's eyes. "No. She's our baby. You know what her decision is going to be. She thinks that place is fantastic."

Allan didn't utter a word. But the steady brown eyes that had been her own personal beacon of strength and love for more than forty years were warm and understanding.

Margaret put a hand to her heart. "Oh, Allan, I don't know if I can do it." She covered her face with her hands, and Allan rose. Crossing the room to her, he drew her into his arms. Margaret laid her head on his shoulder. "Can we at least speak with Elsa privately before we take such a huge step?"

"That's an excellent idea. Would you like me to call her and set it up?"

Margaret nodded, unable to speak, and Allan gently rocked her, giving her time to regain her composure.

Chapter Twenty-Three

On Tuesday afternoon, Beverly got a call from Diane. Right away, she grabbed her peacoat and bag and headed for the Shearwater Gallery.

The bell jangled as she swung through the door, and she saw that all three of her friends were there. "What's going on?" she asked. "Are we having a powwow?"

"Margaret and I found some information about the map on Friday." Diane's eyes lit with excitement.

Shelley squealed. "Yay! What is it?"

"You did? Spill!" Beverly was pleased to see Diane looking a bit more like herself. Her friend had been busy with her book launch for the last few weeks, but Beverly was almost certain there was something wrong. Something to do with Justin's visit had put that little line of worry on her friend's forehead.

Margaret brought a piece of paper and the map from beneath the counter. "I wrote down the information we found." Quickly she explained about the hurricane and the town's move to higher ground.

"So you think Old First is the church the author is talking about?" Beverly tried to wrap her mind around all the facts.

Margaret tapped the map lying beside the copied text. "Yes, but we still don't know where the treasure—if there is any—might have been buried."

"Yeah," Shelley said, frowning. "The graveyard search was a bust."

"Let's go with what we *do* know," Diane said, eyeing the coastline on the map. "We do know that the old town was once south of the current town. Is there anywhere along the beach south of Old First that we could search without disturbing the dunes or slogging through the marsh?"

"There's a big outcropping of rock there," Shelley said.

"It's sort of a crescent, with the inner side facing the sea." Margaret's voice rose a bit as she thought about the place in question. "It would make sense that the town was inside that crescent. So the treasure could be somewhere along the base of those rocks."

"Maybe we should get out the metal detectors again," Diane suggested, "and check around that area."

Shelley shivered. "As long as we don't do it at night this time."

★　★　★

It was the Wednesday of Holy Week and the choir's last rehearsal before Easter Sunday. They warmed up in the choir room, and then everyone trooped over to the sanctuary so that they could sing the "Hallelujah Chorus" with the organ and piano accompaniment.

Beverly and Estelle's joint accompaniment on the "Hallelujah Chorus" went better than Beverly had expected. Twice she did as Estelle had suggested and simply stopped playing for a measure and got her fingers back on the right keys.

When they were finished, she unobtrusively drew a deep breath. With a little heaven-sent assistance, she just might make it through the Easter Sunday service without totally embarrassing herself.

"Prayer requests?" Maddie asked, pencil poised over her notepad.

Several choir members spoke up, mentioning members of the church who were ill or bereaved. One had a grandson serving in the marines in Afghanistan; another person was leaving a job to take a new one clear on the other side of the country.

"Anyone else?" Maddie asked.

Beverly cleared her throat. "Tomorrow's my last day of work at the State House in Augusta. I'm a little nervous about leaving a solid job to devote myself to my own business full time, so if anyone's inclined, a little prayer wouldn't go amiss."

"Prayers for Beverly tomorrow," Maddie repeated. "I'm sure that's going to be tough, saying good-bye to work friends and such."

Beverly nodded, her throat suddenly tight. She hadn't even really thought about it until just then, but she realized that it would, indeed, be tough.

She said good-bye to all her new friends in the choir as they took their leave. Everyone was hurrying. Outside the church, the wind was rising, and a mixture of snow and freezing rain was predicted to begin any time.

"Beverly, Estelle, that was wonderful!" Maddie came breezing back into the sanctuary; she'd been putting the music away in the choir room.

"Thank you." Estelle picked up her coat and slid her arms into the sleeves. "Beverly has done a fantastic job sliding onto Linda's piano bench." They all chuckled as the organist shouldered her large bag stuffed with music and departed.

As Beverly rose and walked over to the pew where she had laid her coat, Maddie came over and leaned against the end of the pew.

"Estelle's right. You have done an outstanding job with the music. Do you sing?"

Beverly shrugged. "Yes. I'm not really a solo voice, but I have a passable alto and good pitch."

A gust of wind rattled the windows, and the sleet hitting them momentarily sounded like balls of hail. The beams of the rafters creaked, and Beverly shivered. The drive home was going to be miserable. And then she heard a bell ring. It was not the usual bright, rich tone of the bell in the steeple. "Listen!"

"To what?" Maddie cocked her head. Her eyebrows rose. They listened together, and once again, Beverly heard the deep booming sound of a bell.

"What bell is that?" Beverly asked.

Maddie gave Beverly a strange look. "Bell? What are you talking about?"

"Can't you hear that?" Beverly could hear the sound clearly, repeated over and over.

"No." Maddie turned back to collect her coat.

"Could it be the bell in the old bell tower?" Beverly got to her feet.

"Old bell tower?" Maddie shook her head. "Beverly, you're not making sense. Where are you going?"

"To see if that's what it is." Beverly shouldered her bag and started back down the aisle toward the double doors that led into a spacious vestibule.

Grabbing her own things, Maddie hurried after her. "Beverly, wait for me."

"The entrance to the bell tower is this way." She turned and began to walk in that direction. The sound of the bell was louder here, nearly deep enough to be a gong. "My friend Diane and I were in there a couple of months ago."

Maddie shook her head. "I didn't even know we *had* an old bell tower."

"That's definitely where it's coming from, though." Beverly felt a strong sense of urgency. They were almost there when a tremendous crash made them both duck. "What was that?" Beverly gasped.

"I don't know." Maddie shook her head. "It sounded like it came from the sanctuary."

As quiet settled over the church again, Beverly realized that the bell was no longer ringing. And oddly, the feeling of urgency she'd been experiencing had abated. Suddenly, it no longer seemed nearly as important to get into the tower as it had a few moments earlier.

Abandoning the search for the sound, the two women walked back and opened the sanctuary doors. They hadn't turned off any lights, and yet the room was much dimmer than it had been before. Peering over Maddie's shoulder, Beverly strained to see what had happened.

"Oh my dear heaven." Maddie lifted a trembling hand and pointed. "Beverly, it's the light fixture. It—it *fell*!"

Sure enough, one of the three large chandeliers that had hung from the ceiling was now lying in a crooked heap near the front rows of pews. It had just missed the baptismal font and the old grand piano, but the first row of pews was smashed and damaged.

Maddie was shaking visibly. "Beverly, if you hadn't heard that bell and insisted on going to investigate, I would have been standing directly beneath that light when it fell."

CHAPTER TWENTY-FOUR

Shelley and Dan had just put their children to bed when someone knocked on the door. Fortunately, it was quiet enough that Prize, who was already up in Aiden's room, didn't hear and come barking down the stairs.

Dan went to the door. When he opened it, his surprise showed in his voice. "Hi, Mom. Is everything okay?"

"No. May I come in?"

Shelley tensed. She hadn't spoken to her mother-in-law since the hair-cutting debacle a week ago.

Dan stepped back and gestured for his mother to enter. "Come on in."

"I won't stay," Frances said. "I'm here to apologize." She twisted her hands together as she spoke. "I shouldn't have cut Aiden's hair, and I'm sorry for it."

Shelley opened her mouth. "I know you are." She sighed. "It was just a shock."

"I wish I hadn't done it."

"Mom, there's one thing that bothers me more than the fact that you cut his hair," Dan said quietly.

"What?" Frances looked stricken. "Dan, I didn't do anything else."

"Yes, you did. When Aiden told you he had permission to let his hair grow, you chastised him for arguing with you."

"I—I—" Frances had tears in her eyes.

"One thing we think is very important in our family"—Dan gestured to Shelley and himself—"is respecting other people's choices. Aiden made a choice, but you didn't respect that."

Frances bowed her head. "I don't know what else to say. I was wrong."

Shelley rose and went to her mother-in-law's side, taking a deep breath. "I'm going to be very honest," she said to Frances in a calm, quiet tone. "I was furious on Thursday."

Frances' tears overflowed. "I knew when I was doing it that it would be upsetting. I just...I just couldn't stop myself."

"Would you talk to Aiden, please? It would mean a lot to him if you apologized and told him you would listen to his feelings in the future."

"Of course. I'll come by tomorrow and talk to him."

"We know you love our children and want what's best for them," Shelley continued. She put her arm around Frances' shoulders. "And we hope you know how much we appreciate both your babysitting and your willingness to spend time with the children. We have far too many friends whose parents don't really have much of a relationship with their grandchildren. I don't want this to come between us. Any of us."

Frances swallowed and nodded. "I was afraid I had permanently ruined our relationship." She glanced over at Dan. "Honey? Will you forgive me?"

"Of course I forgive you, Mom." Dan sighed and raked a weary hand through his hair. "But please promise me you'll never do that again."

"Never," his mother promised fervently.

When the sound of her car had finally pulled out of the driveway a few minutes later, Dan was the first to move. "Way to go, Shell!" He held up a hand for a high five.

Shelley released the tension that had gripped her and met his palm in the air with her own. Then she sank down on the nearest chair and put her head in her hands. "Whe-e-ew. It's really hard for me to be that frank with your mom."

Dan nodding, grinning. "For a minute there, I was thinking, 'Where's my wife and who is this stranger talking to my mother?'"

She laughed. "Me too!"

Companionably, they headed into the living room to watch a television show they both enjoyed. Before they turned on the television set, Shelley said, "I've been thinking about when we went on our little trip last week. We should talk about what to do about my business the next time we want to go away."

Dan frowned. "Or if you get sick. We were lucky when you hurt your knee that it was January and local businesses were really slow. But if it had been July . . ."

"Exactly." Shelley drew her legs up to one side on the couch. "I think this thing with Liza was a fluke, and I'd like to try subbing for her when she needs a break. But if your sister is willing, I thought maybe I could ask Annie if she'd be willing to be on call as a backup in case of emergencies with the backup."

*   *   *

Margaret punched in Matt Beauregard's telephone number for at least the fifteenth time since she'd first seen the cover of that absurd book at the beginning of April. It was Maundy Thursday, the day during Holy Week when Christians commemorated the Last Supper, and she doubted she'd get an answer now. Even if Matt had been getting her messages, a lot of offices closed a day or two early for the Easter celebration.

But when she got the answering machine yet again, something inside her snapped. For days, she'd been leaving polite messages for Matt to call her. She was done being polite.

"This is Margaret Hoskins, Matt. I've been trying to reach you for days, and I'm growing quite concerned that you appear to be dodging my calls. If I don't hear from you by the end of April, I'm going to be forced to consider legal action regarding the unauthorized use of my painting."

She punched the "end" button with more force than necessary. "There," she said to Allan, who was putting on his jacket. "Maybe that will get a response."

"Maybe." Allan looked sympathetic as he picked up the keys to the van. "Are you ready to go?"

"No," Margaret said, "but I'm going anyway." They were meeting with Elsa Kling this morning to discuss the possibility of Adelaide living in the group home.

Allan patted her back as he ushered her out of the house. "It'll all work out, honey. We have to trust that God has a plan for Adelaide, even if it's not the plan *we* had."

"I know," she grumbled. "I just wish He'd come right out and tell us."

Allan laughed. They drove across town to the home of Elsa Kling and her little family of young ladies. Adelaide and the girls who lived with Elsa were all out for the day, either at the life skills class or some other activity. When Margaret had called to ask Elsa to meet with them, they had decided this might be best.

"Hi, Margaret. Hi, Allan. Come on in." Elsa answered the door and took their coats. "Why don't you come into the kitchen? I have some things written down that I want to share with you, and it might be easier to do it at the table."

They followed their hostess into the large kitchen and took seats at the dining table. Elsa had a Power Point presentation ready to share with them. Some of these things they knew from their first visit, but there was plenty of new information. After the presentation, she shared other things with them: a schedule showing everyone's task responsibilities and another showing everyone's activities and the times each girl needed to be a certain place. She showed them some of the field trips, including some weekend excursions they had taken in the past, and talked about some of the things she hoped to do with them in the upcoming year. Permission forms, insurance information, health records, rental and other costs...it seemed to Margaret that Elsa had it all, and she told her so.

"I try," Elsa said. "My goal is for each girl who lives here to feel that we are a family."

Adelaide already has a family. She doesn't need another one. But Margaret didn't say that out loud. Her less emotional, more rational side told her Elsa was trying to reassure them that their daughter would be well cared for.

"What about illness?" she asked. "And, heaven forbid, injuries that constitute an emergency?"

"Since you're local," Elsa said, "I assume you'd prefer to continue to be involved in Adelaide's medical care. And that's fine. For the girls whose parents do not live locally, I'm happy to act as a parent/guardian. Emergencies?" She shrugged. "My first call would be 911, and my second would be to you."

They asked a few more questions and got a more detailed tour of the home. Before Allan and Margaret took their leave, Elsa asked, "So you are seriously considering letting Adelaide move away from home?"

Margaret couldn't help it; her eyes instantly welled with tears. "If that's what she chooses to do, we'll support her." She had to stop.

Allan took over. "As you can see, this isn't an easy decision for us. We'll let you know as soon as possible."

Back in the car, Margaret gave way to her tears. When she could speak again, she said, "If only Elsa wasn't so out-and-out wonderful...!"

Allan laughed. But his laughter quickly died away. "I understand what you mean! This is terrible, but I was sitting there wishing I could find a reason not to tell Adelaide about the opening..."

"But you couldn't," Margaret finished. "Me either. Much as it hurts, we're going to have to present Adelaide with all of the options and let her decide what she wants to do."

*   *   *

Late on Thursday afternoon, Diane felt like a taking a break. She stood, moving away from her computer and stretching. A walk was what she needed.

"Justin? Want to go for a walk with me?" she called.

From the direction of the living room, her son's voice said, "Not really, Mom. I'm teaching myself how to do coding for the Web."

Well, that was good, wasn't it? "Sounds interesting."

"Not really. But if I get out, I'm going to need all the marketable skills I can get." His voice sounded so flat and depressed that she winced.

Diane dropped her head, her shoulders slumping. If only she knew how to help her son. He was front and center on her prayer list every day, and she *did* trust God to answer her prayers... she just wished He could move a little faster. Or at least give some little sign that He'd heard her?

Picking up her phone, she texted Margaret, Shelley, and Beverly. *Wanna walk? Meet me at the beach end of the street in ten.*

She walked into her bedroom and fished socks out of a basket of laundry that hadn't magically folded itself overnight, then found her sneakers. Her phone made the musical tone it played when she got a text message. Picking it up, she read, *I m in. C U there.* It was Margaret. Great!

And even better, by the time she had tied her sneakers and found her sweatshirt, Beverly and Shelley both had responded that they would meet her too.

Walking out to the living room, Diane said, "Okay, I'm headed out for a walk. I'll make us some supper when I get back." She patted her leg. "Want to go for a walk, Rocky?"

The big yellow dog sprang up from his place on the hearth rug with alacrity, although she would have sworn he was sound asleep.

"I think that's a yes," Justin observed. "See you in a bit."

"See you." She blew him a kiss on her way out the door, but her smile quickly faded as she walked briskly down the street.

Margaret had actually beaten her to their meeting place, she saw as she came down the street. And Beverly wasn't far behind. Just as she reached them, Margaret shaded her eyes with her hand and said, "Oh, good, here comes Shelley."

Sure enough, Diane saw, Shelley was coming...along with Aiden, Emma in her sand stroller, and Prize gamboling along on lead at her side. She grinned and waved at Aiden. "Hey, buddy. Are we going to find a sand dollar today?"

"Yeah!" Aiden cavorted along the sidewalk as if he was on a trampoline, hopping and leaping.

They all grinned at the little boy's energy, and Shelley said, "You saved my life with that text. I haven't spoken to another adult all day."

"Happy to oblige," Diane said. "Isn't it a gorgeous day?"

Indeed it was. Coastal Maine was experiencing a capricious spell in late April—sleet and wind one day, sunny warmth another, and today the sun was still shining brightly at three in the afternoon. Gulls soared overhead, and a light breeze assailed their hair, but no one cared. The incoming waves were quite small today, and the steely blue-gray surface of the ocean beyond the breakers was very calm, not a whitecap in sight. It was an *exceptional* day, Diane decided.

"I had a scary experience last night," Beverly said. "And another miracle."

Instantly, all of the others' eyes were glued to her face. "Tell us!" Diane demanded.

They listened, agog, as Beverly described the ringing of the bell in the old bell tower, and how investigating the sound had saved Maddie and her from injury or worse.

"Oh my word," breathed Shelley. "That *is* a miracle. Interesting that it wasn't a light this time."

"And even more interesting that only you heard it," Diane added. "I wonder if there's any significance to the fact that the old bell was the instrument of your escape from harm, or that the first time we heard it was when we found the letters?"

Beverly shrugged, and Diane saw that her friend was becoming uncomfortable with the talk of yet another miracle.

"Beverly," she said, "wasn't today your last day of work?"

Beverly nodded. "It was. I just went in for the morning. My coworkers held a good-bye breakfast for me."

"How was it? Did you cry?" Shelley asked.

"I'm not much of a crier, but it was...hard," Beverly said. "I've worked with several of those people for a decade or more. You get to know someone pretty well in that amount of time, you know?"

Diane nodded. "I do know."

"It was sweet, though. They gave me a really lovely fancy-leaf begonia for my home office, and a care package kind of box, with different teas, a mug, crackers and cookies, hand lotions, and little soaps...and a card every single person had signed." She sniffed, looking close to tears.

Diane knew Beverly well enough to know she would hate breaking down and crying in front of them all on a public beach. Quickly, she said, "And right after Easter, you start working on growing your own business. That's so exciting!"

Beverly nodded. "I am looking forward to that." Then she glanced over at Margaret. "How did you get away from the gallery, Margaret? It's not even four yet."

Diane almost smiled. She was getting good at reading Beverly; she could have predicted that there would soon be a change of subject.

"I didn't go in today." Their friend sounded subdued. "Allan opened up late and is staying until five."

"What's wrong?"

"Nothing," Margaret said. And then she burst into tears.

It took all three of them to get the story out of her as they left the boardwalk and crossed the beach to walk on the hard-packed coarse sand near the water's edge. When they heard that Adelaide might be moving out, everyone was silent for a moment.

"I'd miss her," Shelley said. "I enjoy having her around, and heaven knows Aiden and Emma would be sad not to see so much of her. But I understand why you need to give her this choice."

Diane chose her words carefully. "If Adelaide wasn't a handicapped child, she would probably have moved out already. And gone farther away," she added, thinking of her own two children, usually far-flung. "You've been fortunate enough to have her close for a long time."

"Honestly," Margaret said, "we assumed we always would. When she was small, we never dreamed she would grow to be as capable and independent as she is. When I was a little girl, Downs kids didn't have opportunities to maximize their potential like she has." She sniffed and blotted her nose with a tissue from her jacket pocket. "I'm happy for her, really. I'm just not as happy for me."

"And you need to be able to share that," Shelley said gently, "so you can put a good face on it when you tell her about the opening at the Klings'."

"Exactly." Margaret nodded. "Thanks for understanding."

Diane had been listening to Margaret. She knew that she had missed something very important in her dealings with Justin: her own need for support. But she simply hadn't been able to force out the words. Until now.

"Having an adult child come home to visit can be wonderful," Diane said, "but it also can be a terrible worry."

Instantly, all three of her friends focused their attention on her. "You're speaking of Justin." Margaret made it a statement.

Diane nodded sadly. "I would have told you before, but I just...I just couldn't."

Her friends listened intently, making sympathetic faces and noises as she described Justin's error and the effect it might have on his future.

"And I'm so worried about his mental state," she finished. "He seems depressed to me, and I don't know if it's something normal, or if I should be trying to get him to talk to someone."

"Maybe," Margaret said, "you should wait until he gets this current mess straight in his head. Then, if the depression doesn't lift, you probably should discuss it."

"Or let Jessica," Shelley said wryly. "He might be more receptive to her suggestions."

Diane had to smile, knowing Shelley was thinking of her mother-in-law's never-ending "suggestions."

"On the other hand," Shelley said, "your kids value your opinion, I've noticed. I bet you've given him good advice.

Look at how helpful you've been to all of us when we have a problem."

Diane's smile evaporated and she shook her head, dispirited. "I don't have a clue how to fix this."

"You can't." Margaret spoke up, her eyes perceptive. "And he doesn't expect you to. Don't you see? That's not what he needs. He knows you will be there for him no matter what, and he just needs you to keep him emotionally afloat for a bit. Why else would he have come home?"

"You may be right." Diane thought about her friend's words. "Because Marble Cove has never been a real home to Justin or Jess, as it is for me." Her heart lightened a little at the thought that Justin had come home because he *needed* her.

As they walked, Margaret wrapped an arm around Diane's shoulders, giving her a warm squeeze. "Of course I'm right. That old adage 'Home is where the heart is' was created for a reason."

Shelley nodded. "Home is *you,* Diane."

"Hey, Miss Diane, lookie what I found!" Aiden came tearing up with something clutched tight in his fist. Diane sincerely hoped it wasn't a sand dollar, or he was likely to have nothing but a handful of broken pieces.

But when Aiden opened his fist, something shiny glinted on his palm. "It's a dollar!"

Actually, it was a quarter, as Shelley informed him.

"But that's pretty cool," Diane told the child. "You found some treasure."

Aiden's blue eyes opened wide with renewed excitement. "Maybe there's more!" and off he zoomed to resume his hunt.

"Speaking of treasure," Margaret said, "we need to take the metal detectors down to those rocks below Old First and see what we can find."

"If anything," Beverly added. They could always count on her to keep them firmly grounded.

Diane grinned at her friend, shaking her head. "The voice of reason speaketh."

Beverly punched her lightly on the arm. "I just don't want to get too excited and then have a big letdown."

"It'll have to be after Easter," Margaret said, thinking out loud. "We have Maundy Thursday services tonight."

They all nodded, indicating that they did also.

"And tomorrow's Good Friday and then the weekend."

"How about Tuesday?" Shelley proposed. As the others agreed, she gave a little wriggle that involved every part of her body, and her ponytail bounced. "I can't wait!"

Diane loved her young friend's enthusiasm. "I'm excited too," she said. "Who knows what we might find?"

CHAPTER TWENTY-FIVE

Dan and Shelley attended Good Friday services at their church the following morning. They had invited Dan's sister Annie and her family over for supper, since Annie wouldn't think of letting Shelley pay her for her baking efforts of last week.

In the afternoon, they dyed the two dozen eggs Shelley had hard-boiled on Thursday. Last year, Emma had been too little to do more than watch and coo, but this year she was a toddler and intent on doing everything by herself. If Dan or Shelley tried to help, she would shake her head and say, "No-no!"

After the eggs were dyed, Shelley shooed them all out of the kitchen so she could bake and put together her vegetable lasagna.

Two hours later, Dan finished putting the last flatware on the table just as the doorbell rang. Prize ran barking ahead of Aiden, who opened the door to a flurry of relatives. Annie was first and after she kissed Aiden and tickled him until he shrieked, she advanced on Dan, Shelley, and Emma.

Following Annie were her daughters, Megan and Laurie, almost carbon copies of their mother and just as pretty.

Annie was in her early forties, but she looked as young as Dan. And she had the same sandy hair and blue, blue eyes as those of Shelley's husband and son. Annie's husband, Quentin Eddington, had been her high school sweetheart. Taller even than Dan, Quentin had strawberry blond hair that he regularly buzzed off to hide the fact that his hairline hadn't just receded, it had retreated clear back to the crown of his head. Still, he was a handsome man with an easy, flashing smile.

Shelley hugged Annie enthusiastically. "You have no idea how much I appreciated your help last week! I was so panicked when the other baker called and said she had the flu."

"No problem, it was fun," Annie told her, grinning. "Meg and I felt like the real deal, baking with your recipes here in your kitchen. Shelley, I had no idea your business was going so well. That's awesome!"

Over dinner an hour later, after she and Quentin had pelted Dan with questions about his new job, Annie said, "So Mom confessed what she did when you were away."

Aiden, never one to miss a conversation, chimed in indignantly, "Meemaw cut my hair! An' Mama an' Daddy were really, really mad."

"I bet they were," Annie replied. "I would have been upset too."

"I'm surprised she told anybody," Dan said. "How'd you find out?"

"She told Vera and me on Sunday." She grinned. "Vera tore a strip off her hide that's probably still raw."

"Ah-ha," Dan said. "I wondered why she came over here Wednesday night and apologized."

"I think she was planning to anyway. For once, she really seems to understand why you were so upset."

"It's water under the bridge," Shelley said. "I don't think she'll ever do that again to anyone's child."

"No, but she'll do something equally over the line," Dan predicted.

Quentin laughed. "Of that I have no doubt."

"Enough of this," Shelley said in gentle reproof, rising. She actually felt sorry for Frances. She promised herself she would never be a mother-in-law whose visits her children's spouses dreaded. And why on earth was she thinking about that? It was light-years away!

"Okay, change of topic. This is great," Dan said, waving his fork at his plate. "Not quite as great as meatloaf and mashed potatoes, but great."

Annie laughed. "That's been his favorite meal since he was old enough to talk. I can't believe it still is."

"Better save some room," Shelley said. "I have mini blueberry cheesecakes and truffles made with Ghirardelli dark chocolate for dessert."

Dan and Quentin cleared the dinner dishes while Annie and her girls got the plates out for dessert. Soon everyone sat around the table trying to digest the big meal.

"Hey, I have an idea," Dan said. "Anybody want to play Monopoly?"

"Me, me!" Annie waved her hand. "I used to trounce you all the time when we were kids; I bet I still have the touch."

"I was eleven years younger than you," Dan said in mock outrage.

"*Oooh*, Mom," Laurie said, shaking her finger at her mother. "Shame on you, picking on a little kid like that."

"He was a horrible little kid," Annie informed her. "He used to hide on the stairs and squirt water from water pistols at my dates."

They all laughed, and everyone rose to help clear the dessert dishes. In less than ten minutes, the dishes were in the dishwasher, the extra food was put away, and Dan had brought out the Monopoly board from the shelf of games.

"I don't want to play Mop'ly," Aiden announced. "Laurie, will you come play with me?"

The sixteen-year-old smiled. "Sure. Can Emma come too, Aunt Shelley?"

"Of course."

Once the little ones and Laurie were gone, Meg chose the wheelbarrow token, Shelley the dog, and Dan the horse and rider. Quentin and Annie both grabbed for the top hat, but he was faster, so Annie took the flatiron after some obligatory grumbling.

The game was cutthroat. Shelley had never played board games with any Bauers except Dan, and she quickly saw where he got his competitive streak. It was get bold or get out.

And Shelley did. Very quickly, she got deeply in debt to Dan after he put houses on several of his sets of properties. Finally, she was forced to give him her few pitiful remaining assets. Quentin was Dan's next victim, and then Megan.

Annie survived a while longer, but the hotel on North Carolina Avenue finished her off.

Dan clasped his hands together above his head, mugging like a successful prize fighter. "Thank you, ladies and gentlemen. You may congratulate me."

Megan snorted. "Not likely, Uncle Dan." Then she giggled and danced out of reach when Dan attempted to tweak her nose.

"I demand a rematch!" Annie cried.

Dan laughed. "Anytime, sister, anytime."

Her eyes narrowed. "I'll check my calendar and call you. Dinner's at our house the next time."

⋆　　⋆　　⋆

Margaret and Allan were getting ready for bed when Margaret's cell phone rang. They exchanged a concerned glance.

"I hope there's nothing wrong," she murmured, reaching for the phone. After checking the readout, she gasped. "It's Matt!"

Allan's eyes widened.

Margaret nearly dropped the phone as adrenaline surged through her. Carefully she pushed the button. "Hello?"

"Hi, Margaret, it's Matt Beauregard from Lighting the Way. I'm sorry it's so late, but I wanted to contact you immediately."

"Immediately after what?" She kept her voice calm and cool with an effort.

"My wife and I just returned from a three-week missions trip to Tanzania. I didn't have access to my cell phone, and I was only checking my personal e-mail because I had an auto-reply going out on my business e-mail, which I'm guessing you didn't receive. I have a feeling it must have gone into your spam. So I didn't receive any of your messages until today." He paused.

"Oh," Margaret said in a very small voice.

"I am so sorry you were blindsided by that book cover," Matt went on. "I sent you a letter and copy of the cover design a few months ago. What it said was that you could refuse to give your permission if you didn't like the cover. I gather you didn't receive it?"

"No, I didn't."

"I assumed that since I didn't hear from you, you were okay with it," he said. "I thought they did a fantastic job." Matt sounded genuinely distressed. "I thought you'd be thrilled that your work was going to be the cover art for a national best seller."

"But I wasn't even listed as the illustrator," Margaret added.

"No, it's there, Margaret. The illustrator credit is on the page with the author's bio, and it even lists your Web site address, along with Lighting the Way's, of course."

Now Margaret felt embarrassed all over again. "I'm sorry, Matt. I didn't see that. And in the future, if I don't like something, I can refuse to grant permission for its use?" Margaret asked. She was feeling some relief and even more confusion.

"Yes, if it really bothers you. I don't recommend it, though. Margaret, the point of sublicensing is to make money. I'm not in the office right now, but on Monday, I can e-mail you more information about the specific licensing agreement we made with the publisher. It's a small but reputable publisher based in Massachusetts—"

"Matt, I apologize for my reaction. Please disregard my voice messages. Apparently, I need a course in legalese to help me interpret my contracts, because I didn't understand the sublicensing agreement."

"No apology needed," Matt said, his voice gentle. "I'm sorry I didn't ensure you understood that. I'd probably be upset, too, if I thought someone was using my work without authorization."

After a bit more conversation, Matt reassured her that he would send her information on Monday, wished her a blessed Easter celebration, and hung up. Margaret ended the call and turned to Allan. "I have been a ridiculous fool."

Allan's eyebrows went up. "Oh?"

"He says my contract gives him the right to approve sublicensing." She started out of the room. "Let me get my contract and see if I can find the reference."

She returned a moment later, already paging through the agreement. Grabbing her reading glasses off the bedside table where she had laid them, she searched for the clause Matt had mentioned. "Four-B...Four-B...here it is." She read it silently, then handed it to Allan, pointing to the words. "Oh, do I ever feel stupid! Right here it even mentions 'right of refusal.'"

"Are you unhappy with this agreement?"

"Not at all. Matt really does have my best interests in mind." She dug in the stack of books on her nightstand. She'd buried the book in question in the middle of the pile so she wouldn't see it every time she walked into the room. "I suppose I should read that book, shouldn't I?"

Allan smiled. "You might want to, just to reassure yourself. But we liked Matt, remember, and thought he was trustworthy. I, for one, am glad my impressions of the man were correct."

"Me too," Margaret nodded. "I feel like an absolute idiot." She smoothed a hand over the cover in question. "I guess it's quite a compliment that this publisher chose my painting."

CHAPTER TWENTY-SIX

Beverly watched through the window on Saturday morning as Jeff parked his car in front of the house and strode to her door.

They had made a date to go antiquing and have lunch together today, and she had as many butterflies in her stomach as she had the first time they'd gone out.

"Good morning," he said when she opened the door. He stepped inside and gave her a warm hug. "I've missed you."

"I've missed you too." She hugged him back before picking up her jacket. Having coffee a few weeks ago with Dennis had made her realize how much she appreciated Jeff. "Ready to go?" she asked brightly.

They drove down the coast toward southern Maine, where she had a favorite little shop she occasionally liked to check. Their selection of Depression glass turned over quickly, and she was always looking for a few more pieces for her mother's collection. To her delight, she found a large pink glass ice bucket in her Apple Blossom pattern with a pour lip so that excess water could be removed.

Jeff had brought along his cameras, and they drove out to Quoddy Head State Park near Lubec.

"The West Quoddy Head Light is really picturesque," Jeff told her. "Have you ever seen it before?"

"No," Beverly admitted. "Does it look like ours?" Meaning Orlean Point Light, of course.

Jeff shook his head. "No. The lighthouse itself is painted with thin red and white horizontal stripes from bottom to top. It's still active."

"Really?" She was delighted.

"And," he said, obviously enjoying his role as tour guide, "Quoddy Head is the easternmost lighthouse in the country. You can even see Canada across Quoddy Narrows."

Beverly stopped to read a sign. "Oh, too bad. The boardwalk through the bog doesn't open until May first."

Jeff shrugged. "We can come back again," he told her as they walked on. "Now that you live here, we can do this any weekend."

"True."

He snapped his fingers. "I almost forgot. How was your last day of work? It was Thursday, right?"

"Yes." She told him about her coworkers' little party. "So Monday I start being a consultant full time," she said. She pressed a hand to her stomach. "Yikes. Just thinking about it makes me nervous. I can't believe I quit my job!"

Jeff grinned at her. "You're going to be fine. As soon as the word gets out, you're going to have clients lined up around the block for your services."

"Oh, I hope you're right," she said fervently.

They continued on along the rocky path. "When it opens, I'd love to hike along some of these trails and check out the boardwalk," he told her. "There are some really cool plants blooming in the bog in the summer." He took her hand. "Come this way. I'd like to walk out to the edge of the cliffs."

"Okay, but I'm not going anywhere near the edge," Beverly said.

He laughed. "Afraid of heights?"

"Let's just say I have a healthy respect for them," she said in a wry tone.

They walked around the lighthouse, and Jeff took some photos of Sail Rock, an enormous hunk of rock sticking up from the water in the distance. Not long afterward, they hopped back in the car and drove northeast to a small pull-off above the park.

Jeff wanted to get some photos of the shorebirds that were migrating. "We can get to the shoreline from here and walk to the bog," he told her. "There are gazillions of birds there."

There were indeed a lot of birds: plovers, sandpipers, and many other shorebirds that she didn't recognize. "I've always thought bird-watching would be interesting," she said.

"Me too. It would really help with my work if I could recognize specific species." Jeff glanced at her, his eyes warm and tender. "We could learn together."

Beverly smiled at him. "That might be nice."

Jeff put his arm around her shoulders as they walked toward the bog. "You're not coming to the San Francisco conference with me, are you?"

Beverly smiled gently. "No, I'm not. I would like to meet your colleagues...someday."

They walked in silence for a while, but it was companionable rather than uncomfortable. "That's okay," he said at last, as if she had just finished her last sentence. "Someday."

★   ★   ★

Diane was planning to host Easter dinner after church tomorrow. So today, she was busy baking and making and cleaning all sorts of things. As she worked, she was aware that April was slipping away quickly. Her son soon would be leaving. But for what?

Baseball season had arrived, and they sat down together to watch the Red Sox take on the Yankees. Diane's husband Eric had been a rabid Red Sox fan. Although neither of the kids nor Diane was quite as passionate, they did tend to follow the team—and when it came to the New York Yankees, they really wanted a win.

At the top of the third inning, Diane cleared her throat. "Can we talk a bit?"

"Sure, Mom." Justin didn't take his eyes off the screen; she had figured out that his method of avoiding deep discussion was to pretend he was deeply engrossed in some program.

She reached over and nipped the television remote off the arm of the couch. Hitting the button, she turned off the TV.

"Hey!" Justin sat up, protesting in surprise. "What are you doing?"

"Talking with you." Diane calmly set the remote on the arm of her chair farthest away from him. "You're avoiding me."

"I am not." Justin scowled.

"Okay, you're avoiding thinking about what's going to happen when your leave is up. And that happens very soon."

Justin sighed. "Mom. I'm not avoiding it. I've been thinking about it."

"And?"

His gaze slid away from hers. "I haven't really decided."

"Honey, it's normal to feel discouraged when something you really, really want doesn't work out. But at some point, you have to pull yourself together and go for it again."

"You mean recycle through OCS? Mom, you don't understand. Didn't I tell you I'd have to take the whole course again?"

"No," she said patiently, "I didn't necessarily mean for you to retake your course. I meant, decide what avenue you want to take and get started." She paused. "Do you still want to be an officer?"

Justin hesitated. Finally, he gave a small nod. "It's been my dream for a while. I hate that I fouled it up."

"Okay," she said. "You made a mistake. You've acknowledged it. You've learned from it. So what's stopping you?"

Justin looked squarely at her, his eyes miserable. "What if I fail again?"

"I don't know. If you fail again and wash out of the course, will you die?"

He blinked. "No. Oh, I get it. Could be worse, right?"

She only smiled. "Will you still have a job?"

"Well, yeah. Until my ETS date."

"Speak English," she reminded him.

He laughed. "Estimated Term of Service, I think. Or End Time Served or something like that. I don't know what the acronyms mean, I just use them."

She grinned, suspecting there was more than a grain of truth in there. "Okay, so if by some unlikely chance you fail again, you have a job until you decide to leave the service."

"Sort of. If I want to get out, I'm going to have to let my company know and turn in my leave form as soon as I get back, or I won't make a September separation date. I need to figure out how much leave I've accrued, because it will help if I can continue getting paid by the army for a little while; it'll give me time to get on my feet."

It sounded to her as if he had given this an awful lot of thought.

"If I'm getting out, I also have to go through ACAP—Army Career Alumni Program—first. I think I have to start that a hundred days before ETS, so I'll have to do it soon. It's supposed to help you transition back to civilian life. There's a bunch of other stuff too," he added, "but those are the basics."

"You sound as if you've made a decision already." She kept her voice soft and nonjudgmental.

He shook his head. "I don't know, Mom. I can *see* myself as an officer, you know? I can't see myself in the civilian sector. At least not yet." His eyes appealed to her. "What do you think I should do?"

She shook her head. "I can't answer that, honey. I want you to do whatever's going to make you happy." She held up a finger. "But if you want to be an officer, why don't you retake the course again? I'm pretty certain you won't fail Military History this time." She indicated the book on the coffee table she'd seen him reading from time to time. "You said it was going well until that test."

"It was." His eyes cleared. "You're right. I have no reason in the world not to try again. The worst that can happen is that I stay enlisted and ETS as soon as possible. I have skills that will help get me a civilian post—a job, I mean. I'll have to stop speaking army if I get out." He jumped up and came over to her chair to hug her. "Thanks, Mom. You have a way of helping me clear out the cobwebs and see the heart of things." Then, while she was still savoring his smile and hug, he reached over and snatched back the remote, dancing out of range when she grabbed for it. "I'll take this back, thank you very much. Gotta watch our Sox trounce the Yankees."

★　　★　　★

On Easter Sunday, Beverly awoke before the sun rose. Which wasn't a good idea for two reasons. Obviously, she'd be tired later in the day. But much worse, it gave her far too much time to agonize over the upcoming performance.

Four hours! She had a measly four hours before she had to go play the piano in front of hundreds of people. Oh, why had she ever agreed to do this? She must have been insane. Certifiably insane, without question.

Over breakfast, she attempted to chat casually with her father, but her hands were shaking so much she spilled her coffee.

"Beverly? What's wrong? Are you getting sick?" Her father peered at her. "You're as white as a sheet."

"I'm all right, Father."

"Are you worrying about playing for the choir?"

She tried to smile. "How did you guess?"

He rolled his eyes. "Do you think I don't remember when you were in high school? We went through this every time you ever walked onstage to play piano."

She nodded. "Not much has changed, it seems."

"I used to tell your mother it wasn't worth it, that it upset you too much and we should let you quit."

"You did?" That was startling. She'd had no idea. "What did she say?"

He snorted. "That we all have to learn to deal with things that upset us, that you're a fine piano player, that the fear of failure is all in your head…you name it, she said it." He chuckled, shaking his head. "But the bottom line was no. She was not about to let you quit. She said, 'Do you really want to teach her that every time something is too hard, she can quit?'"

Beverly smiled, remembering her diminutive mother's giant-sized personality. "I can hear her saying it."

He nodded, and his smile was a little wistful. "So can I."

She went to shower and get ready for church then. She hadn't worried too much about an Easter ensemble because she knew she would be wearing a choir robe, but she would be going to Diane's for an Easter meal after church, so she chose a pretty pink suit with a gored skirt. She could remove her paisley silk scarf and her jacket during church and just wear her shell and skirt beneath the heavy choir robe. She'd noticed nearly everyone wore layers, because the robes just got too hot to wear suit jackets and sweaters beneath.

It was time to go long before she was ready. Her father had decided to go with her, although it was early. That way, he said, he could get a good seat at his own speed.

In the choir room, Maddie greeted her with a warm hug and a bouquet of flowers to thank her, while the whole choir clapped and almost brought Beverly to tears. Then they ran through their music with the piano only. As they finished, Estelle, the organist, stuck her head in and winked at Beverly and said, "I'm going to go start the prelude. Don't forget our deal."

Beverly laughed; as if she could! If she hit one single wrong note, she intended to stop for a measure before plunging back in. The butterflies in her stomach grew larger and fluttered more wildly as the choir processed into the sanctuary. She walked with Maddie at the end of the line, peeling off to take a seat on the front pew near the big

Mason & Hamlin grand. They had been lucky to have the pew repaired quickly, but it was another expense that Old First would have a hard time absorbing. As she walked up the aisle, she tried to find her father's silver head, but she had no luck.

She hadn't gone to church at Easter for many years. In fact, she couldn't remember the last time she had. Reverend Locke's assurance of the promise inherent in that tragedy on the Cross brought a lump to her throat, and the joy with which the congregation sang the Easter hymns of resurrection and rebirth in Christ were equally moving.

Twice, she got up and played when the choir offered the first two of the pieces they had prepared.

And then it was time for the last two.

She rose and went to the piano on legs that felt distinctly wobbly. Her hands were shaking as she adjusted her seat, arranged her music, and set her fingers on the keys. Thank goodness they were doing an arrangement of "Crown Him with Many Crowns" first. It would warm up her fingers and maybe even settle her nerves, since she'd made it through "Because He Lives" and "Christ Is Risen" without incident.

Maddie looked at her and smiled before giving her the tempo, and Beverly launched into the music. As the last notes faded away, she braced herself to begin the *Messiah* momentarily.

She was shaking so badly she was certain the congregation could see it.

And then, one person came into focus from the sea of faces before her. It was Diane! And beside her, her son Justin, seated right beside her father. In stunned disbelief, she saw that Jeff was seated on her father's other side; he sent her a wink and a grin when their eyes met. The rest of the pew was filled with her friends too: Margaret, Allan, and Adelaide, Shelley, Dan, and both little ones.

Shelley caught her eye next, smiling. She lifted both hands, fingertips pressed together, in a subtle gesture, but Beverly immediately realized what Shelley was telling her. They had prayed for her. These dear, beloved people whom she'd grown so close to over the past year had missed their own churches' Easter celebrations in order to be here for her today. A sense of peace and calm spread through her, and all the butterflies flew away.

Maddie was already in place with her music stand before her, and the trumpeters she had recruited from the high school orchestra lifted their instruments.

Beverly put her hands on the keys, took a deep breath, and nodded. Maddie gave them the tempo and then brought her hand down for the opening beat.

CHAPTER TWENTY-SEVEN

Diane, with Justin's help, had moved all of her living room furniture back against the walls. Then she'd used every sturdy table she had to set up one long dining table down the center of the room.

She and Justin rushed out of church as quickly as possible when the service ended. She felt bad not staying to talk to Beverly, but she would see her in a very short time.

At home, she shut Rocky in the bedroom. Too many people and too little space was a recipe for a dog's tail or paw to get stepped on. Justin sliced the fragrant ham she removed from the oven while she quickly prepared the raisin sauce for the ham, garlic mashed potatoes, the broccoli and cauliflower casserole, green beans almandine, sweet potato rolls, deviled eggs, a citrus fruit medley, and a strawberry-spinach salad for the first course. The table already was covered with two matching linen cloths, and she'd set vases of daffodils and tulips there and around the room to brighten it up.

She had made a lemon sponge pie and a carrot cake for dessert—Shelley was bringing some chocolate torte for the chocoholics in the crowd—and she sliced those and set them on the sideboard.

"Mom, that is an insane amount of food!" Justin had finished with the ham and was helping her set the salads and fruit at each place.

"I got a little carried away," Diane said sheepishly.

"That's okay. Whatever doesn't get eaten, you can send back with me." Justin was leaving at four to head back to Fort Benning.

"And how are you going to carry food on a plane? In your carry-on?"

He patted his stomach. "Where there's a will, there's a way."

Their guests began to arrive then, the friends who had joined them at Old First earlier that morning, plus Mrs. Peabody from down at the Wheelands' end of the street, and Augie Jackson, whom the Hoskins had been kind enough to pick up. As she was piling coats on her bed, she heard Beverly, her father, and Jeff arrive.

There was an increase in the decibel level in the small living room as everyone rushed to congratulate Beverly. She had played every note in the "Hallelujah Chorus" flawlessly and even looked as though she was enjoying herself.

A moment later, the object of her thoughts appeared in the bedroom doorway, bearing three coats.

"Hello and congratulations!" Diane said. As Beverly dropped the coats on the bed, Diane leaped for her, giving her an enthusiastic hug that Beverly, after one stunned moment, returned wholeheartedly.

"Thank you," she said breathlessly. "I was a train wreck waiting to happen, and then I looked out into the congregation and saw all of you, and my fear just faded away. I can't believe you all attended Old First on Easter Sunday to support me."

Diane grinned. "Believe it. Honestly, I was awed by your playing. That 'Hallelujah Chorus' sounded fantastic! You made it look effortless."

Beverly smiled. "Maddie and the organist Estelle were both really helpful. They were certain I could do it, although I was a lot less certain until I caught sight of my cheering section. Then I felt as though divine inspiration was flowing through my fingertips."

Still laughing, Diane and Beverly rejoined the rest of the guests. In short order, the ham and mashed potatoes joined the rest of the meal on the table, and everyone had taken a seat.

Diane sat at one end of the table, Justin at the other. "Mom," he said, "would you like to offer the prayer?"

She nodded. "Absolutely. Could we all join hands, please?" And as the group bowed their heads, Diane began to pray out loud after swallowing the lump in her throat. "Dear heavenly Father, as I gather with my dear son and my wonderful friends on this day of resurrection, I am reminded anew how incredibly blessed I am..."

★   ★   ★

Later that afternoon, Diane settled into a chair in the living room that Justin, Dan, and Allan had rearranged to its normal condition. Her Easter meal had been a huge success. Justin was taking some ham, potatoes, and dessert back with him in a sealed container, but there had been surprisingly little left over. Diane' friends had helped with the dishes, and they'd been done in no time at all.

Justin was in his room packing. She heard his cell phone ring twice before he said, "Hello?" in such a gruff and forbidding voice that she frowned. Then the door closed, muffling the conversation.

A little. Diane could still hear Justin's responses, if she listened carefully, and she eavesdropped without shame.

"No," he said, "I'm at my mom's...yeah, in Maine."

Another silence. "No, I don't have any plans to come down that way." His responses were surprisingly clipped and curt. "Yeah, I've decided to recycle." There was another long pause.

Finally, he said, "I'm really not interested in pursuing any kind of personal relationship again, Dani. I need— and deserve—someone who will support me through the bad times as well as the good. I'm sorry if you're unhappy. Good luck with that new assignment." A moment later, the distinct beep of his conversation ending sounded.

And Diane leaped to her feet, hopping around in her socks doing a silent cheer.

*　　*　　*

Shelley hurried through the house and opened the front door on Monday morning when the doorbell rang. Her eyes widened in surprise when she saw Liza Cramble, the baker from the Cakery, on her doorstep.

"Liza! Hello, come on in." Shelley scooped up Emma, who was about to make a dash for the great outdoors, and stepped back so Liza could enter.

"Hi, Shelley." Liza carried a white bakery box in her hand. "I brought you something, along with my most sincere apologies for letting you down when you went away." She shook her head. "That flu hit me like a ton of bricks."

"Oh, Liza, you didn't need to do this." Shelley gestured. "Come on back to the kitchen. Would you like a cup of coffee?"

"I'd love one."

In the kitchen, Liza set down the bakery box and draped her coat over the back of a chair. "Honestly, Shelley, I feel absolutely terrible about what happened. If you give me another chance, I promise not to get sick ever again."

Shelley laughed. "You wish! Really, Liza, you don't need to apologize. Illness doesn't give us a lot of options sometimes. As it turned out, my sister-in-law and niece came here, and I walked them through the stuff I needed. They actually had a great time—*they* thanked *me*!"

Liza laughed. "Thank heavens. You have no idea how bad I felt—not flu bad, guilty bad."

"Please don't." Shelley liked this girl tremendously. "If it'll make you feel better, you can open the box and we can treat ourselves. I'm sure it's something delicious. Aiden!" she said sharply. "Is that yours?"

"No, Mama." Her son, who'd been hovering over the box like a honeybee over pollen, stepped back. A short step, she noted.

"I bet you'd like some of this too," Liza said to him. "Mom, has he been good this morning?"

"He's been very good this morning," Shelley said. "I guess he can have a piece of whatever it is."

"Baklava." Liza lifted a piece of the nut-and-syrup-filled Greek pastry. "Turned out pretty well, if I do say so myself."

Each piece was presented in a cupcake paper, Shelley saw. Tasting a bite, she savored the sweetness. "Liza, this is fantastic. I've never tried it. Is it difficult?"

Liza shook her head. "The first time I ever made it, I cheated. Bought phyllo dough at the grocery store. Was really good, but I read that freshly made phyllo is better. So the next time I tried it, I made my own phyllo."

"Isn't that hard?" Shelley eyed the tissue-thin pieces of baked pastry.

"Yes, if you do it by hand. But I cheated again. I used my pasta machine."

"What a great idea!" Another goody to add to her growing repertoire.

Chapter Twenty-Eight

Margaret was feeling blue.

Today was the day they were going to tell Adelaide about the opening at Elsa Kling's house.

They'd had such a lovely Easter day yesterday that it made her feel even worse today. Adelaide loved to hunt eggs. She loved to sing in church. She adored Margaret's neighborhood friends, and getting to eat Easter dinner at Diane's had pretty much been the icing on her cake.

When the shop doorbell rang as the door opened, she looked up without interest. It was Ham Levesque, the postman.

"Good afternoon, Margaret," Ham said. He crossed to where she sat listlessly at the counter. She wasn't even trying to paint today. It would probably be all black and gray. "Got some mail for you. Oh, and I found this outside the door. Heaven knows why they didn't bring it in." He handed her a flat cardboard mailer.

"Thanks, Ham." As the burly postman took his leave, she ripped open the envelope and withdrew a sheaf of folded papers. Legal stuff? She leaned over and looked at the address on the envelope. Oh! It was from Matt Beauregard.

She was going to have to have a talk with him about the courier service he used.

Impatient now, she flipped open the papers. The topmost one was a short letter from Matt, apologizing again for not getting back to her in timely fashion. The second was the page in her contract on which was the information about sublicenses. Matt had highlighted it, as well as her right of refusal clause.

The third was a breakdown of the income that had been made from the painting that had been made into the book cover. She ran a finger down the page, seeing the amounts to be basically what she already knew.

And then she came to the figure next to the book cover licensing. The sum made Margaret smile with relief. A wave of heat flooded her face, and for once, it wasn't a hot flash. She was mortally embarrassed. She had doubted and misjudged Matt badly, and she owed him an apology.

Digging in her drawers, she withdrew a note card. It was printed in black on heavy cream-colored paper, and it featured one of her drawings of the lighthouse. In fact, it was one of the sketches she had created for Diane to use in the historical booklet in January. She'd liked it so much that she'd had these personal note cards made.

Quickly, she jotted Matt a note apologizing for the hasty conclusions to which she'd jumped when she couldn't get hold of him.

Leaving the gallery at five, Margaret trudged homeward. She waved to Mrs. Peabody, but pretended not to notice when the old lady beckoned for Margaret to join her. She was in no mood for chitchat tonight. Besides, she had to get dinner started so they could get this awful conversation over with.

As it turned out, Allan had already started dinner. It was an eggplant casserole from a tried-and-true recipe they all liked. Who would make it for Adelaide when she moved out?

She set the table with the cheerful spring placemats that she'd woven a few years ago when she'd been on a weaving kick. Then she went to change her clothes and wash her hands, and when she returned, Adelaide was already in the kitchen with Allan.

"Hi, Mom." Adelaide came over and gave her a long, sweet hug. Margaret felt tears sting her eyes. How could she live without these hugs? She told herself that other mothers did it all the time. Diane's children had left home, and she saw them a lot less than Margaret would see Adelaide, and yet Diane appeared to accept that it was the nature of things. And in most people's lives, it was.

They all sat down together, and Allan offered a quick blessing.

"Yum!" said Adelaide upon seeing what was on the table. "I love eggplant."

"I know you do." Allan smiled, and Margaret realized he'd made it especially for this evening. He was hurting too, although he hid it better than she. Across the table, their eyes met. *Do you want to tell her?* His gaze asked. Margaret shook her head imperceptibly. *I can't. I just can't. You do it.*

Allan cleared his throat. "Adelaide, honey, your mother and I need to talk to you about something very important."

Adelaide looked up, a sober expression on her face. "I already promised no more cats, Daddy."

Margaret surprised herself by laughing. "That's not it, honey. This is something good."

Adelaide's face changed, the childlike delight returning. "What is it? I love surprises."

"Your mom and I visited Mrs. Kling, Maryann's mother, the other day."

"She's nice," Adelaide said. "She gives good hugs."

"I bet she does. Anyway, Mrs. Kling told us that one of the girls is moving out in a few weeks. She's going to have a new opening."

Adelaide laid down her fork and turned her full attention to her father as if she sensed he was about to say something very important.

"Mrs. Kling would like to know if you would like to move into her house with your friends."

Adelaide pushed her chair back from the table and jumped around, shrieking, "Yay! Yay! Yay!"

"I take it you want to do that?"

The young woman nodded vigorously. "Yeah! That would be so much fun." Then the happiness drained out of her face a little. "But you and Mom won't be moving with me?"

Allan shook his head. "No, honey. Your mom and I would stay right here in this house, and you can come and visit us."

"A lot," Adelaide said. "A whole lot."

"A whole lot." Margaret spoke for the first time. She'd forced herself to push away her tears. If Adelaide saw her cry, that might be enough to stop her from moving. For the merest instant, Margaret considered it. And then she discarded it nearly as fast. No, she could never do that to Adelaide.

"Mom?" Adelaide was looking at her searchingly. "Are you sad?"

"A little," Margaret temporized. "We enjoy having you live here. But we know Mrs. Kling will take really good care of you, and you'll have lots of fun there."

"Yeah." The sparkle returned to Adelaide's eyes. "An' I'll come visit a lot. I'll bring Lizzy. I'll bring Butterscotch." She stopped. "Do you want to keep Oreo so you're not lonely?"

Adelaide was looking at her expectantly. Allan pushed his chair back abruptly and went to the tissue box on the counter, blowing his nose loudly. Margaret suspected it was just an excuse to wipe his eyes. "Honey," she said gently. "Here's the thing. Lizzy, Butterscotch, and Oreo can't come with you. Maryann is allergic to them. Remember her guinea pig you met? Marshmallow? You'll be able to snuggle him. He's very sweet."

A worried frown made a furrow between Adelaide's eyes. "But Mom, I can't leave my kitties. Who would take care of them?"

It was another oh-so-tempting opportunity to influence Adelaide's decision. But Margaret, forcing herself to take the high road, said, "Honey, if you decide you want to move, your dad and I will take very good care of the cats. You'll be able to see them every time you visit."

Adelaide looked stricken. "Can I think about it?"

"Of course," Allan said. He came over and kissed the top of her head before sitting again.

They finished the meal and cleared the table. Adelaide appeared lost in thought, and she wandered up to her room right after dinner.

Margaret showed Allan the paperwork that Matt had sent her. "I sent him a note of apology," she said. "It's so embarrassing."

Allan shrugged. "I read that contract too, and I didn't get it either. I guess this is why people have attorneys or agents look over contracts first. Lucky for you, Matt's a good guy looking out for your interests."

They watched some television. Adelaide came down and watched with them but didn't say a word about moving, so they didn't either.

Later, as they were getting ready for bed, Adelaide knocked on their bedroom door. "May I come in?"

"Sure." Margaret had just climbed into bed. She sat up and smiled at her daughter. "What's up?"

Adelaide climbed up on the bed. "Mom, I don't want to move out."

Allan came out of the bathroom just in time to hear her. "Why not, honey?"

Adelaide shrugged. "I love you guys. I love my kitties. I'd miss you too much."

"Are you sure?" Margaret asked.

Adelaide nodded. "I'm sure."

As their daughter kissed them both good night and left the room, Margaret had to restrain herself from dancing a jig. "We'll wait until tomorrow, let her sleep on it, just in case she has second thoughts."

Allan nodded, miming wiping sweat from his brow. "But I really hope she doesn't."

"Me too. But I'm glad we made the offer. We did the right thing. Now she knows that moving out is a possibility. If the day ever comes that we can't keep her with us, or she chooses to move, she'll be a little better prepared."

CHAPTER TWENTY-NINE

It was another glorious spring day. Margaret, Diane, Shelley, and Beverly had headed in the opposite direction from their usual route. They had walked past the lighthouse and down the beach parallel to the area that had been the first settlement of Marble Cove, if all their research was right.

Beverly had brought string and made them lay out a grid as if they were archeologists on a dig. "That way," she'd said, "we can keep track of where we have and haven't searched."

They chatted as they worked. Margaret had just told her friends about their conversation with Adelaide last night, when Shelley turned to Diane. "So Justin's gone now, hmm?"

Diane nodded. "Yes. He's headed back to his platoon until the next one of these officer classes opens up."

"I knew you'd help him figure it out," Shelley said.

Diane smiled. "I don't think I did much but prod him a little and listen a lot. I'm incredibly proud of him for pursuing his dream after such a disappointment."

"You're a great mother," Shelley told her. "If you were my mom, and I had a major problem, I'd definitely come to you. In fact, I have!"

They all laughed.

"It is a good feeling to know I helped him a little bit," Diane confessed. "I was feeling pretty low there for a while."

"We could tell," Beverly said. "It's nice to have our optimistic, energetic friend back."

They separated then, going back to their respective sections over which they were running the metal detectors.

There were only three little squares not yet filled in on the chart she had made. Diane and Shelley finished their section, and finally Margaret hefted her metal detector and walked back with Beverly across the rocky landscape toward them.

"Nothing," Diane said in disgust.

"Nope." Margaret set down the large tool.

"But the coastlines match and we know the town was south of Old First," Shelley protested. "It has to be here somewhere."

It was warm enough that they had discarded their jackets in a pile on a large boulder, and they all plopped down nearby.

Diane shaded her eyes, looking toward the north, where the steeple and tower of Old First speared into the sky. "I just have a hunch," she said, "that the answer to our quest for treasure is not down here where the first Marble Cove was, but still up there in that old bell tower."

"You did find the letters up there," Margaret commented. "Maybe there are more clues that you missed."

"Well, then," Beverly said, "I guess our next move is to get into that tower again somehow."

"That tower that we're not supposed to enter," Shelley reminded them. "I don't want anyone getting hurt."

Diane chuckled. "Okay, little mother, we'll be careful."

Margaret smiled at her friends. Beverly was perched on a boulder, her efficient little charts in her lap. Diane was already facing the church, where their next challenge lay. And Shelley was . . . "What are you doing?" she asked Shelley, who was bent over examining her pants, socks, and shoes.

"Making sure I don't have any ticks on me," Shelley said. "And I'd suggest you all do the same. They're not likely this time of year, but who wants to take a chance?"

Margaret smiled as they all began examining their own clothing and each other's. It really was a miracle of sorts that she had fallen in with this diverse group. God had pulled them together through the common bond of their miraculous stories, and He continued to work in each of their lives. She winced. She had completely forgotten to trust in God to help Adelaide make a decision about her home, but He had answered anyway.

As Margaret straightened, a faint noise arrested her movement. "Listen!" she said.

Everyone froze.

"What are we—" Diane began. "Oh!"

In the distance, there was the unmistakable *bong* of a deep bell ringing. One, twice, and then a third time they heard it before it fell silent.

Beverly's eyes were rounded in shock, and Shelley had put an awed hand to her mouth.

Diane was smiling. "Do you suppose anyone else heard that?"

Margaret chuckled. "I wouldn't count on it. That bell seems to be tuned to a special frequency only the four of us can hear."

"But what do you suppose it means?" Beverly asked thoughtfully.

"I think," Margaret said, "that our presence is requested back at the old bell tower. I have a feeling we're not done with that place yet."

ABOUT THE AUTHOR

Best-selling author Anne Marie Rodgers has published more than forty novels since 1992, the last eleven for Guideposts Books. She was the launch author for Guideposts' *Stories from Hope Haven* series and has been a finalist for the prestigious RITA Award. Anne Marie has been involved in animal rescue efforts for many years. Currently, she volunteers at Centre Wildlife Care, rehabilitating injured and orphaned wild animals, and serves as the coordinator of the Orphaned Kitten Program in State College, Pennsylvania, where she and her family make their home. She considers irises, beaches and babies of any species some of God's finest creations.

A Conversation with
Anne Marie Rodgers

Q. Which story line in New Horizons *most resonates with you? (Spoiler alert!)*

A. Several of them spoke to me as I was writing this book. Margaret's daughter Adelaide's social growth was exciting because I grew up with a Down syndrome cousin who had none of the advantages available to Downs children today. Diane's concerns for her child seemed familiar because I have young adult children, and although they haven't had experiences like Justin's, it was easy to imagine. I also have a son-in-law in the army. Additionally, Diane's book-signing scenes were great fun and brought back memories of my own career launch, which began with a talk at the local library.

And then there's Beverly. Her panic at the idea of publicly playing piano echoes my own. There was little that unnerved me as a child more than a solo instrumental recital. I even worried when I wasn't the performer. One of my daughters used to accompany the high school choir. To her, it was no big deal. To me, it was an agony of praying: praying she didn't hit the wrong keys, praying she didn't lose her place in the music, praying she didn't miss the conductor's cues. But those things never happened, and I uttered a little heavenward "thank You!" at the conclusion of each performance, as I mopped my brow and stilled my shaking hands.

Q. *What would you like to share with readers about your rescue work with orphaned kittens?*

A. How many pages do I have? I coordinate a nonprofit organization that takes in unweaned orphaned kittens, usually less than four weeks old, referred by local veterinary practices and other rescues. Late spring, summer, and early autumn are our busiest times; the smallest kittens need to be fed every four hours around the clock. During the busiest days, I feel as if I barely get done one feeding before starting the next.

I spend the winter recovering and preparing for the onslaught of the next year's kitten season. This includes inventory, taxes and budgets, updating forms and information, and stocking up on food, formula, medications, and the astonishing amount of stuff it takes to keep an infant kitten alive.

In 2011, we placed fifty-nine kittens in forever homes! It's extraordinarily encouraging to see a healthy kitten snuggling in its new family's arms, while I recall the sickly little "will-he-survive" days the kitten has overcome. It is truly a blessing to be able to give these wee ones a chance at life. Another blessing is my fantastic team of volunteers, foster families, and supportive veterinarians without whom this program could not happen. You can learn more about the Orphaned Kitten Program on our Web site: orphanedkittenprogram.org.

Q. When did you know you wanted to be a writer?

A. I was a voracious reader as a child. When I was ten, I discovered Alfred Payson Terhune's novels and stories about collies. I loved the books, and I believe that is when the seeds of my desire to write my own stories was born. (It was also the seed of my desire to have collies of my own someday, but that's another tale!)

My first "published" effort was a neighborhood newspaper I sold for a nickel when I was nine. I wrote almost constantly after that: stories, poems and essays, composition assignments, and research papers. I couldn't *not* write. I had fantasies of being published, but I never really considered that I could become an author. Real writers were all famous in my mind. It wasn't until I had small children at home that I realized all my years of reading had morphed into a drive to create my own written work, and the determination to keep at it until I succeeded.

Q. Which of our four main characters—Diane, Shelley, Margaret, or Beverly—are you most like?

A. Those who know me would probably call me a "Diane." I am an organizer, and I also enjoy researching all the facets of a given topic and ferreting out the unknowns. Like Diane, I'm a take-charge enthusiastic leader who also is open to other people's ideas. Also like her, as someone who works from home, I have a fair amount of self-discipline. Finally, she rescued Rocky; I have made animal rescue my life's work.

One way, though, in which we differ is our interest in people. Diane is a true "people person." She loves making new friends and revels in groups of people. I fake it well, but underneath, I am easily overwhelmed by groups and rather shy. As one friend of mine describes it, Diane is a person who thrives on "people energy," while someone like me finds social situations an energy drain!

Baking with Shelley

Meemaw Bauer's Pound Cake

1 pound salted butter
4 cups sugar
12 eggs
4 cups all-purpose flour
1-ounce bottle lemon extract

Preheat oven to 350 degrees. Cream butter and sugar together. Add one egg at a time, mixing well. Add flour gradually. Mix in entire bottle of lemon extract.

Pour mixture into large Bundt pan, greased with shortening and floured, to about one to two inches from the top. Bake for one hour or until knife comes out clean. Allow cake to cool thoroughly and then serve. Note: Do not double recipe.

FROM THE
GUIDEPOSTS ARCHIVES

This story, by Leonard E. LeSourd of
Boynton Beach, Florida, originally appeared in
the October 1982 issue of *Guideposts.*

When our sons Chet and Jeff were teenagers, they always celebrated the end of a long trip home to Florida by dashing out of the car and jumping into our swimming pool. It was the finishing touch to a journey—as much a family tradition as the prayers that started a trip. My wife Catherine, our children and I never set out without first asking for God's protection from trip's beginning to trip's end.

One year before leaving Virginia, the family prayed together as usual, asking God to be especially close. We made the trip south without incident. But on arriving home, the boys failed to make their customary dash to the pool. "Too tired," they said.

In checking things around the house, I started to switch on the underwater light that creates a beautiful glow in the pool. But the switch was already in the "on" position. Odd,

I thought. Well, I guess the bulb burned out. But then a prickly feeling crept over me.

Immediately I taped the switch in the "off" position and made sure that no one was to enter the pool.

The next morning, I called an electrician, who checked the pool light carefully. "You've got an old, obsolete fixture here," he said. "Must've been here before you bought the place. Anyhow, water got into the light socket and shorted the circuit. Good thing nobody went swimming—they would have been electrocuted."

More than a good thing. For our family, it was one more example of how God touches our lives in a supernatural way when we seek His help.

Read on for a sneak peek of the next exciting book in
Miracles of Marble Cove!

Setting Course
by Susan Page Davis

B everly Wheeland jogged along the beach, enjoying the sea breeze. Her short ponytail bobbed as she slowed to a walk and mounted the boardwalk that led up to Newport Avenue. Her friend Diane was in her yard with her dog. Beverly waved and kept on, checking her pulse as she walked, until she reached her father's Victorian house at the other end of the short street.

Her father had lingered at the breakfast table, and when she entered the dining room, he was folding the latest edition of the *Marble Cove Courier* in half. The weekly paper had arrived on Saturday, but he liked to keep each issue around for several days and absorb all the town's news at a leisurely pace.

"Back already?" he asked.

"Yes. Would you like more coffee?"

"That would be nice."

Beverly carried her father's breakfast plate and coffee cup to the kitchen, refilled his cup, and took it back to the table.

"Old First is having an anniversary, I see," he said, peering at the bottom half of the front page. "I guess I missed that story on my first read-through."

"Yes, there's been some talk about it." She'd heard a few announcements at church services about the upcoming event and calls for volunteers. "It's the two-hundred-fiftieth anniversary of the church. Not the building, but the founding of the congregation."

"*Mmm.*" He took a sip of coffee. "The old church burned, didn't it?"

"I think so, yes."

"Ha!" He smiled at her over the folded newspaper. "It says here that it burned in 1789."

"There you go." Beverly gathered up his silverware and empty juice glass and turned toward the kitchen again.

"Do you suppose this building should be called 'Old Second'?"

She looked back at him, and he winked, then returned to his paper.

The next time she returned, he had more information. "They're going to celebrate Founder's Day the end of June, and they want people to lend their memorabilia for a display."

"That's nice," Beverly said. "Do you have anything connected to the church?"

"I don't think so. It says Frances Bauer and Madeleine Bancroft are on the committee together." He grinned at Beverly. "Wonder how that will work out."

"Well…" She shrugged. Both women were strong-willed and energetic. If they didn't butt heads, they'd probably do a great job. "Too bad we don't have much material on Jeremiah Thorpe."

"You gals haven't found any more clues about his so-called treasure?"

Beverly shook her head. The money the colonial minister had brought from England to help found the church and community was the object of much speculation in Marble Cove. She and her friends had tried to unearth information about it, and about the colorful Thorpe, but with limited success.

"Maybe you should volunteer for the committee. You might learn something."

"That's not a bad idea." Beverly hadn't considered it, since building her new business was keeping her fairly busy, but Father had a point. Boning up on the history of Old First couldn't hurt their investigation.

Her cell phone rang, and she took it from her pocket. The screen read "Jeff Mackenzie," and she stepped into the kitchen for a measure of privacy.

"Hi," Jeff said. "I wondered if you're free Saturday evening. I'll be on the mainland."

"Uh...sure."

Beverly liked Jeff and enjoyed his company, but she valued her time alone and the flexible schedule that allowed her to spend time with her friends. Dating again still seemed a little odd. But Jeff was like her in some way—he usually called several days in advance, and this was no exception. He was giving her three days to prepare.

"Great," Jeff said. "I'll come by around five and pick you up. I thought maybe we'd drive up to Rockland."

"Sounds good." They signed off, and Beverly tucked her phone away. Their dates were becoming more or less regular, and, while she loved spending time with Jeff and was interested in a relationship with him, that made her a little nervous.

Right now she was still getting used to her new freedom and the slower pace of her life in Marble Cove. Quickly, she outlined her tasks for the day. She always started her workday by making a to-do list. Today she would put in some time on summer promotional materials for the Landmark Inn. The owner, her friend Victoria Manchester, was eager to get some new print-ready ads to the coastal newspapers, and to have new brochures printed for her guests and people who inquired about the inn.

She'd crunched the numbers, and considering the amount of work she was doing for Victoria, she needed at least three more clients with similar needs for her targeted minimal income. Four or five would put her in the comfort zone. Of course, she really hoped to land a couple of larger, corporate accounts.

A shiver of self-doubt crept over her. Could she really make it on her own? She wouldn't have the staff and resources now that she'd had for her job at the statehouse. Of course, she had savings, and if things got tight, she could consider selling her house in Augusta. But she wasn't nearly to the point of giving that a thought.

She could make this business work. All it would take was some concentrated effort. Beverly set her jaw and opened an Excel file.

*   *   *

Margaret Hoskins was about to walk out the door to go and open the Shearwater Gallery for the day when the home phone rang. She answered it, glancing at the kitchen clock. She'd hoped to arrive at the gallery a few minutes early this morning so she could take care of a few things before she opened.

"Mrs. Hoskins, my name is Rosalyn Neely, and I'm in charge of the Port Clyde Art Fair. It's coming up on Memorial Day weekend. Are you familiar with the fair?"

"Oh yes!" Margaret smiled at memories of strolling the rows of art booths with Allan. "I've attended it several times, and I love the way you pull together such an eclectic group of artists."

"Thank you," Mrs. Neely said. "One of our members mentioned your name to me, and she wondered why you weren't on our list of artists yet. I took a peek at your gallery's Web site, and I do think you should be included in our show. Are you interested?"

Margaret clutched the phone cord to her chest. "Yes. Very interested." Was she going to gain some acknowledgment from the local art community at last? Ever since the condescending remarks she'd heard from a critic at her opening last year, she'd doubted whether she would ever be considered a "real" artist by those in the know—in spite of the fact that her work was now selling steadily.

"That's great," Mrs. Neely said. "You'll have space for an eight-foot table, which you have to provide yourself, and four feet on each side for displays. A lot of people use a smaller table and more vertical displays for their work. We ask that you exhibit at least eight pieces throughout the fair. If you sell some during the weekend, you either replace them with others, or else ask the buyers to pick them up after the fair closes."

"All right." Margaret mentally counted the paintings hanging in her gallery. That shouldn't be a problem.

"Oh, and each artist is required to premier a new piece that hasn't been previously exhibited. Are you able to do that?"

"Well, it's short notice, but I think…Yes. Yes, I can." Margaret had a nearly completed painting that was earmarked for Matt Beauregard and Lighting the Way Greeting Cards. Matt would probably let her exhibit it first, along with the others she'd prepared for him this spring. And she could use the best of those for her debut piece if she didn't get a new painting finished in time.

"Wonderful. I'll send you a packet with all the details." Mrs. Neely took Margaret's mailing and e-mail addresses. "There's just one more thing," she said tentatively.

"Yes?" Margaret asked, wondering if there was some other requirement she had to meet. Or perhaps there was a hefty fee for the exhibitors.

"I have an opening for artists' ambassador for this event. I don't suppose you'd be interested in taking that responsibility?"

"I…well, I hardly know what to say." Margaret swallowed hard. "Wouldn't it be better to have someone with more experience?"

"Oh, I think you'd be great at it," Mrs. Neely said. "I know it's your first time, but I've had a good recommendation for you."

Margaret hesitated. She didn't want to get into something that would demand a lot of her time between now and the fair. "What exactly does it entail?"

"Oh, it's mostly helping out when the artists are setting up, and generally making things easier for them. You might need to arrive a little early and get your own exhibit set up, so you'd be free to assist the others. And if anything comes up beforehand, where someone needs a little help, I might call on you."

"Well, I'm not sure . . . . "

"Oh, please," Rosalyn said. "I really need someone who lives in the area, who's dependable. I've held the position myself in the past, and I can tell you, it shouldn't be too demanding. Really."

"All right," Margaret said, still uncertain.

"Fabulous! I can't wait to meet you. Our next meeting is Saturday evening." She gave Margaret the time and address, and they signed off.

As Margaret replaced the receiver, her husband entered the kitchen.

"Not gone yet?" Allan asked.

"I'm running a bit late," Margaret said. "I just got a call from the organizer of the Port Clyde Art Fair. Allan, they want me to exhibit this year!" She turned to study his reaction, hoping he'd be pleased. She felt about to boil over, she was so excited.

His vibrant smile told her that Allan was on board.

"That's fantastic. It's Memorial weekend, though, isn't it?"

Margaret frowned. "Well, yes. That could be a problem."

"We'll make it work." Allan grasped her shoulders. "This is a great opportunity for you, Margaret. I'm all kinds of happy for you."

He bent and kissed her, and Margaret squeezed him for a moment.

"Thanks. You always say the right thing. But I'll have to fix it with Matt to let me show the paintings I'm doing for him before he takes them. And—oh!" She gritted her teeth. "Do you think that we'll have enough stock left in the gallery for the weekend if I take eight paintings to the show?"

"Now, don't you fret," Allan said. "I can frame a few more of those prints, and we can put one up in any spot where you take down an original."

"All right." Margaret still wasn't sure. "They want me to be a helper too. They call it 'artists' ambassador.' I hope it's not a very time-consuming position, but I'll definitely have to be at the show all three days."

"Okay. So we'll need to line up a little help at the shop. Adelaide can help me some, but maybe your friends would give us a hand. Do you think Diane or Beverly could fill in for a few hours?"

"Yes, I'm sure they'd be happy to, if they can. Diane is awfully busy working on her new book."

"Well, we'll work it out," Allan insisted. "Right now, I think you need to get down to the gallery and open the door."

"You're right." Margaret picked up her purse and car keys. She'd have to drive today, to carry one of Allan's inlaid occasional tables to the Shearwater. "Oh, I should have given her my cell phone number. Mrs. Neely was her name. If she calls again—"

"I'll tell her how to reach you. Now, skedaddle."

Margaret smiled at him and scooted out the door. By the time she reached the car, her lips were drooping again. Eight paintings, and at least one had to be brand new. Would she have time to complete the painting she was working on and maybe do one more? The one in progress was a traditional style seascape for Matt. She couldn't help feeling some of the area artists were a bit snobbish about style. The bolder, more abstract technique she'd experimented with might go over better. Her friends hadn't liked it as well as her usual style, but Margaret suspected some people would find it more meaningful. Could she do another of those in the next four weeks?

Whenever she pushed herself and tried to force the creative process, the painting never came out the way she'd hoped. She'd have to see how things went and trust God to give her the inspiration, skill, and energy she needed. That calming thought flew out the window almost immediately. What was she thinking, agreeing to participate in an art fair on what might be the gallery's busiest and most important weekend?

A NOTE FROM THE EDITORS

We hope you enjoy Miracles of Marble Cove, created by the Books and Inspirational Media Division of Guideposts, a nonprofit organization that touches millions of lives every day through products and services that inspire, encourage, help you grow in your faith, and celebrate God's love in every aspect of your daily life.

Thank you for making a difference with your purchase of this book, which helps fund our many outreach programs to military personnel, prisons, hospitals, nursing homes, and educational institutions. To learn more, visit GuidepostsFoundation.org.

We also maintain many useful and uplifting online resources. Visit Guideposts.org to read true stories of hope and inspiration, access OurPrayer network, sign up for free newsletters, download free e-books, join our Facebook community, and follow our stimulating blogs.

To learn about other Guideposts publications, including the best-selling devotional *Daily Guideposts*, go to ShopGuideposts .org, call (800) 932-2145, or write to Guideposts, PO Box 5815, Harlan, Iowa 51593.